AT HAWTHORN TIME

AT HAWTHORN TIME

Melissa Harrison

BLOOMSBURY CIRCUS
LONDON · NEW DELHI · NEW YORK · SYDNEY

First published in Great Britain 2015

Copyright © 2015 by Melissa Harrison

The moral right of the author has been asserted

All artwork © Lucie Murtagh

Bloomsbury Publishing Plc
50 Bedford Square
London
WC1B 3DP

www.bloomsbury.com

Bloomsbury is a trademark of Bloomsbury Publishing Plc

Bloomsbury Publishing, London, New Delhi, New York and Sydney

A CIP catalogue record for this book is available from the British Library

Hardback ISBN 978 1 4088 5904 9
Trade paperback ISBN 978 1 4088 5905 6

Typeset by Hewer Text UK Ltd, Edinburgh
Printed and bound in Great Britain by CPI Group (UK) Ltd, Croydon CR0 4YY

'I feel like a ghost wandering in a world grown alien.'

– Sergei Rachmaninov

PROLOGUE

Here's where it all ends: a long, straight road between fields. Four thirty on a May morning, the black fading to blue, dawn gathering somewhere below the treeline in the east.

Imagine a Roman road. No, go back further: imagine a broad track, in use for centuries by the tribes who lived and fought and died on these islands, and whose blood lives on in us. When the Romans came they paved it, and for a short while it was busy with their armies and trade. After they left it decayed, though it wasn't forgotten; it came to mark the line beyond which the Vikings lived by their intractable Danish creed. Later it became a drovers' road, trodden by sheep and cattle; then a turnpike, taking travellers, and mail, to Wales and beyond. Now, though, it is simply an A-road, known around these parts as the Boundway but marked on maps with letters and numbers alone.

Imagine driving that ancient road. The light is rising behind you, the dim fields, on either side, are asleep. Soon you will pass a sign for the village of Lodeshill, a turn-off you note each time you come this way, but never take. But before you can reach it you see something blocking the carriageway half a mile or so ahead, something you can't yet make out — though part of you already knows, because what else would it be? The straight road points to it like an arrow, and as you draw closer, as you slow and stop, it moves from the realm of the dreamlike to the disbelieved to the real.

You switch off the engine, and as it dies you realise what every day of your life so far has led you to: two cars, spent and ravished, violence gathered about them in the silent air. One wheel, upturned, still spins.

Hands shaking, you make a call. You fight down panic and open your car door, stepping out onto a million tiny fragments of glass. Reluctantly your legs carry you into the scene. Who else will do it, if not you?

I see it all from where I am: the tyre marks, the crumpled metal, the coins and compact discs spilled across the road. The smaller car, with its huge spoiler and brash paint job, rests on its roof, displaying its brutal undercarriage to the sky; the other, a big Audi, has one door half open, and I can see the mundane, private cargo of the door pocket: tissues, a Thermos, a Simon & Garfunkel CD.

I can smell the sharp grass of the churned-up verge, and I can see what it is that awaits you: a young lad in the custom car, upside down and veiled in blood; a slumped figure in the Audi, perfectly still; and beside its open door, a third body, face down, on the road.

Seven slow minutes have passed since the crash. The sky lightens; the spinning wheel slows and halts; birds, one by one, are returning to the hawthorn hedges and shaking down the heavy blossom — although they do not sing. Life struggles and hangs; different futures intrude and unfold. The fact of the accident insists on itself.

I watch as you move from one person to the next, from the injured to the dead. You hold a hand, gently, and it almost pulls me back. I linger as the sirens come, as we are all tended to, even you. At last I become part of the siren's wail, part of the shimmer of air over the ambulance's hood: neither earthbound nor quite free.

Later, you will recall the things you saw only in fragments. And I will recall nothing at all.

I

Cherry blossom over, daffs turning. Hawthorn bud-burst.

It was a mild, damp night in April when he escaped the city, though the forecast predicted fairer weather to come. It had rained a little, earlier in the day, and the moist night air had called out snails in their thousands to dot the grimy London pavements in ill-fated hordes.

He put on his ancient army coat, took his pack from behind the door of his room and filled a plastic bottle of water from the tap in the communal kitchen. The pack contained seventeen tatty notebooks, some cooking things, a pup tent and an old brown sleeping bag. His bedroll was strapped to the outside, and the pack itself was studded with badges and pins; a few bits of cloth hung from the straps like prayer flags.

He left the hostel and pushed the keys back in through the

letter box; then he began to walk north. At least there was no ankle tag this time, and he knew himself to be invisible to the mobile phone masts he passed and unwatched by satellites over-head. The feeling of walking, after three months locked up, was like when a plane's wheels break contact with the tarmac and it lifts up and away from the ground.

You could dig out cuttings on Jack, if you wished. He was there in the very early days of Greenham Common, before the women drove him away; he gave a brief quote to a local radio reporter at Newbury and his grainy image – if you know what you're looking for – can just be discerned in footage of the poll tax riots. The travellers talked of him at Dale Farm, too, though that could have been someone else.

Mostly self-educated, once a haunter of libraries, Jack walked the lost ways from town to town, keeping clear old paths that no one used, avoiding company for the most part and living off the land when he could. Picked up again and again for breaching bail conditions, or vagrancy, or selling pot, he had done short stretches inside everywhere from Brixton to Northumberland, acquiring prison tattoos and learning the advantages of a Bic-shaved skull and a cocksure posture. When at liberty he mostly worked on farms, picking fruit and helping with the harvest; he avoided towns, slept rough, and slowly, over time, forgot that he had once been a protester – or, perhaps, came to embody his protest more absolutely. Born, so he said, in Canterbury, his life before he took to the road was obscure.

Growing ever more unloosed from what seems to sustain the

rest of us, more stubborn with every arrest and stranger and more elliptical in his thinking, Jack became, with the passing of decades, less like a modern man and more like the fugitive spirit of English rural rebellion. Or – to some, at least – mad.

Not long after the turn of the millennium a sympathetic journalist tracked him down to a wood near Otmoor; but Jack, by then, had little he wanted to say – certainly not the grand narrative of protest and exclusion that the writer had in mind. He spent two days with Jack, broken by a night at a Premier Inn where he was much disturbed by drunken wedding guests, but his piece, when it came out, barely mentioned Jack at all.

Away from the main arteries the night-time streets were quiet: the odd dog walker, a few revellers, foxes, cabs. Here and there flowers nodded dimly to Jack from front gardens as he passed, blanched by the sodium lights to a uniform paleness: irises, tulips, early peonies dropping their petals over the walls.

He crossed Vauxhall Bridge on foot, stopping for a moment to look down at the black water below, full of ship's nails and clay pipes and broken bottles and bones. Briefly, he wished for the keys back so he could cast them in, a kind of offering or parting gift – though they would have been swallowed up by darkness long before he could have seen the river take them, and he was far too high up to hear them fall. Where these arcane impulses came from it was impossible to say.

Finding his way through the centre of town was easy enough. Pimlico was quiet; he skirted busy Victoria before pushing on,

Green Park invisible behind a high wall to his right. How was it that the names seemed so much more than mere streets, or confluences of streets? Belgravia, Park Lane, Marble Arch, Marylebone: you would not think that such places could be so easily abandoned, yet one by one they fell behind him.

He stopped at a petrol station in Hendon in the small hours, walking across the floodlit forecourt to the little window and handing up coins to a Bangladeshi man who seemed all the more vulnerable for the bulletproof glass between them. Two boys and a girl were hunched on the kerb at the edge of the forecourt, pupils dilated, talking quickly and disjointedly among themselves. The girl had glitter on her temples; one of the boys kept clenching his jaw.

Jack ate the crisps and chocolate he had bought and walked on. For a long while there was hardly anyone around: shift workers, cabbies, bin men. He kept to the same road northbound, crossing side street after side street, all untaken.

By the time it began to be light he knew he was leaving the city behind. Later, inured, almost, to the rush-hour traffic, he passed superstores, car plants, playing fields, a golf course, wasteland; then, with the roar of the M1 somewhere ahead, the straight road broke north-west between fields.

It was enough. He pushed his way off the tarmac through a belt of trees and tangled undergrowth where years of sun-faded litter had blown and caught: beer cans, dog shit in bags, crisp packets, hubcaps. Twenty-odd paces through the wood he emerged into a tussocky field from which two rabbits fled, their white scuts bobbing away into some trees on the far side. He let his pack fall from his shoulder and sat down with his back to an oak.

Listening to the traffic behind him he felt the breeze play on the hairs on his arms and watched the sun rise slowly from a distant reef of cloud. Looking at it made a bluish bruise on his field of vision that jumped and twitched, and he shook his head like a horse trying to shake off a fly, finally squeezing his eyes shut and waiting for the insult to his retina to subside. When he opened his eyes again the horizon swam briefly and the light seemed very bright.

Just to be able to go where I like, he thought. *Just to live how I see fit. I don't do any harm, God knows; and there are plenty out there that do. So let me go now, please; just leave me be.*

After a while a blackcap sang from the scrubby field margin and the morning sun began to dry the dew from the grass. Jack picked up his pack and began to look around him for somewhere to sleep.

The field itself was almost entirely without distinction, a nondescript trapezium bordered by overgrown hedges. It had not been grazed or mowed for a long time, and pioneer saplings – scrub oak, sycamore, ash – were stealing a slow march on the grass. There were no paths through it, unless you counted those made by rabbits and foxes, and it harboured no species of special distinction, no orchids or rare butterflies. Yet in summer its edges foamed with meadowsweet, and in autumn it bore clutches of mushrooms like pale golden eggs.

Jack chose a spot in the shade of the far hedge and rolled out his mat. He took a sandwich and a can of Coke from his rucksack, the last of his shop-bought food, and with his back to the city he sat down to eat.

It was still possible to find work on the land almost all year round: picking daffs began in February, and farms often wanted help with lambing; in summer there was hay to mow and soft fruit to pick – although he hated the polytunnels with their close, stale air. You could usually get work picking apples in September and, later, felling Christmas trees; he had once spent much of December making holly wreaths. But fieldwork was what he loved best, and it was spring: nearly asparagus season. He thought back over the farms he knew, and that knew him: he wanted to keep his head down, didn't want to sign any papers this time, and that narrowed the options a little.

He'd set out from Devon in January to walk vaguely northeast. He'd never meant to come to London, but the arrest and the sentence – for breaching an order not to trespass, although all he'd wanted to do was walk an old cart track between villages – had blown him off course.

Now he decided to keep to the old Roman road north out of the city. Eventually it would take him to a little village called Lodeshill which had four farms with asparagus beds clustered around it. There was one he'd promised himself never to set foot on again, but he felt sure that one of the others would take him on for a few weeks with no questions asked. There was some lovely countryside up that way, quiet and slow and unvisited, and not too busy with day trippers – not like Cumbria or Cornwall. It was an in-between, unpretentious place.

Apart from the road, the quiet concatenation of the drink inside its can, when he opened it, was the loudest thing Jack could hear. When he had finished he lay back, thankful for having eaten, thankful for the weather, wondering when sleep would come. And then he slept.

As the sun rose slowly over Jack's head a hawthorn in the hedge behind him felt the light on its new green leaves and thought with its green mind about blossom.

2

Horse chestnuts, swallows, blackthorn (sloe).

As soon as his wife had left the house Howard went about shutting all the windows. It was a warm day, but not so warm they all needed to be open, and anyway, he couldn't bear the sound of the road. Flies were getting in, too; he'd swatted one in the kitchen earlier. Kitty would only complain at bedtime, when there were insects in her room.

It wasn't the road through Lodeshill he minded; there wasn't much traffic on that. Why would there be – there was no shop any more, and the Green Man was hardly the type of pub people sought out. Even the church only got a few of the faithful, and those on foot. Kitty one of them now, of course.

It was the Boundway that bothered him. Straight as a ruler it ran, passing the village less than half a mile away, and the local louts all gunned their muscle cars along it – especially at week-ends. You could hear them changing up from miles off, the whine of it; you'd think they'd find a better way to spend their time, but no. Still, he reflected, putting an old Kinks CD on the hi-fi in the living room, it could have been worse: he'd heard that there'd once been quad-bike racing somewhere nearby, though the track had closed down long before they arrived in the village. *Et in arcadia arseholes*, he thought, and went to the pantry for a drink.

He knew there was a six-pack of lager left over from the last time their son Chris had visited, but it was a brown ale he was after. He'd need to get plenty of booze in for next month, when their daughter Jenny was flying back from Hong Kong and both kids would be with them for the first time in ages. Vodka for Jenny, he thought. Probably.

There was no brown ale. Sighing, he turned and climbed the stairs to the radio room; there was a Marconi 264 that wanted a new valve. Downstairs, a bumblebee knocked twice against the kitchen window before lurching away into the warm spring air.

Most of the time Kitty had the master bedroom to herself; Howard usually slept downstairs, in what had previously been the study. Before they moved to Lodeshill from north London, a year ago, it had only been an occasional thing; now, apart from when the kids visited, he was down on the sofa bed every night. It was something they did not discuss.

There were three bedrooms upstairs; one was Kitty's, one had briefly been Jenny's until she left university, and still was when she visited. The light was good in the third, so when they moved in Howard had taken the old pink carpet up and built a counter around two sides, set his tool chests underneath. Then he bought a craft light and a stool, carried the radios up from the garage – he had just four, then, and one in bits – and got to work. He had thirteen vintage wireless sets now, all pre-war; good working examples, not boot sale stuff. Five more he'd sold or traded. Where do you stop? There were people who had two hundred.

You could find them easily enough on the Internet, of course, but he felt – obscurely, though with some certainty – that it wasn't the right way. He went to swap meets and the odd show, but preferred local auctions and private sales to buying from other enthusiasts, despite the extra legwork it entailed. Admittedly, most of what came up that way was rubbish – either cheap to begin with, bodged about or beyond repair, good only for parts – but not always.

Word of mouth had got him more than one tidy example: 'I know a bloke who'll take that off your hands.' He had a Ferguson 366 Superhet that was found by a local family in the attic of a house they had just bought; it came to him covered in dust for five quid. The Marconi he was working on now turned up in a barn near Deal, and had barely been touched the cabinet full of mouse shit, the dial clogged with cobwebs and chaff.

As well as finding them, doing the work himself was what he loved: replacing the knobs, restoring cracked Bakelite, a new valve here and there. He wasn't an expert, not yet, but he did

OK, and his experience with guitars and amps helped. There was something almost magical about taking an old wireless and bringing it back to life: the way they could be woken, no matter what state they were in, to pull living sounds from the air. The lovely old cabinets hiding such comprehensible innards; the simple heft of them in his hands.

It was gone four when the letter box banged; he was trying to get at the capacitors, deep under a block of resistors, and was working carefully and with minute concentration. He considered ignoring it but it rattled again, followed by the slap of something landing on the mat. After a moment he carefully set down his tools and went downstairs. For God's sake, a telephone directory. As if anyone used those any more.

Back upstairs he peered again through the magnifier at the circuit, but found he couldn't narrow his focus properly, failed to feel again the thread of the stubbornly absent current and its likely pathway and hindrances. He replaced a capacitor, but even as he did so he was remembering knocking on doors after school when he was a child and running away; and he thought, too, of the time he picked May blossom from the churchyard, with its ripe and heady scent, and brought it home to his mother, who had chased him, cursing, from the door. Half a century ago, but still like yesterday. That such moments could remain latent somewhere in the intricate cortices of the brain; that he, not far off sixty years of age now, should still detect their resonance. It was a mystery.

He swung the craft light away and stretched his back. A beer before Kitty came home; why not? Not the Green Man, though, with its unfriendly farmers and local doleys; the Bricklayer's Arms, in Crowmere. It was only ten minutes away, and it was a nice day for a walk. He fetched the paper from the sitting room, switched off the Kinks and set out.

Lodeshill was barely a village; more a hamlet, really. As well as Manor Lodge there was a grand Elizabethan house with mullioned windows and a box maze at the end of a long private drive; a pretty church, largely overlooked by the ecclesiastical gazetteers; a Georgian vicarage (the vicar himself served several churches, and lived elsewhere); the Green Man; a dozen modern houses of varying quality, and a cul-de-sac of ugly bungalows inhabited mostly by the elderly. What had once been the shop and post office was now a private house, though it still had a red letter box set into one of its stone walls.

Past the church the houses gave way to fields and the road began to climb gently as it passed the outbuildings of one of the four farms that surrounded Lodeshill. In places the centre of the road was faintly mossy, and here and there was dung, for the most part dry and pressed into the road's surface by tyres. Bluebells and celandines starred the verges, and the leaves on the blackthorn hedges were very green.

After a couple of hundred yards Howard turned left onto a footpath that ran through Ocket Wood. The path followed the line of a ditch and bank which had once marked the wood's boundary, but which the wood itself had at some point in its long history overspilled. It was mostly oak, with some ash, alder and holly, and had been coppiced and felled on a regular cycle since the Dark Ages – though not for a long time now. In medieval times it had supplied the manor house with timber and the villagers with kindling for their fires; their pigs had been turned out in it each year to eat the acorns and mast. Later still it became a gamekeepers' preserve, the public kept firmly out. Now it was mainly visited by dog walkers, and the understorey had not been cut for years.

Jenny was always telling them to get a dog; she said the exercise would be good for them. But what his daughter hadn't yet learned was that there was an age beyond which you stopped really caring about what was good for you – especially if, as in Howard's case, you'd fucked yourself up pretty comprehensively when you were younger and were just waiting for the damage to become apparent. Now, every year that passed without cancer – or something worse – was a bonus, he told himself. Anyway, here he was, out for a walk. And he did it a couple of times a week. You couldn't argue with that.

The Bricklayer's Arms had been extensively refitted and the inside was all blond wood and chalk boards. Howard leaned on the bar and nodded at the barman, who brought over a bottle of Newcastle Brown Ale and a half-pint glass.

'Wife not with you?' he asked in his cheerful Australian accent. Kitty hated the Bricklayer's, had only set foot in it once or twice, but it pleased both the barman and Howard to pretend that he was there more often with his wife than without her.

'She's at the shops,' Howard replied, the merest hint of an eyebrow standing in for the hackneyed observations about women and shopping which had long since been exhausted between them. In fact, Kitty was not a woman who shopped for pleasure, and Howard had no idea where she had gone. She may well have taken her easel with her; he hadn't checked.

With a brief feeling of bleakness, quickly pushed away, he surveyed the available tables before making his way to a seat near the window and opening the newspaper.

He left just before eight, as the sky outside started to grow dim. If Kitty had been painting she'd not outstay the light, and there was no harm in getting back before her.

Ocket Wood was a shadowy mass on either side of the footpath, and although he'd only had three bottles of Brown the fact that he couldn't see much around him made Howard feel drunker than he was. It was association, too, he thought, groping towards the insight; you were *supposed* to weave home from a pub in the dark, it was ingrained. Not that it was quite dark yet, but still.

He found, to his surprise, that he still had his empty bottle with him, and with a growing awareness of a need to pee he struck off the path and made for a huge ash stool nearly six feet across, a ring-shaped remnant of a single tree that had been coppiced repeatedly many years before. The new trunks it had sprouted, now ancient themselves, leaned outwards as the crowns competed for light.

When he got back to the path the image of his piss puddling hotly on the dead leaves between the trunks remained in his mind all the way home, as if spotlit somehow in the otherwise black and secret spinney.

Kitty's car was reversed in next to the Audi when he got back, and inside he found her in the sitting room, ironing. 'Good day?' he asked, edging past the board and switching the TV on. 'Gin and tonic?'

'No thanks,' she replied. 'Have you been to the pub?'

'I popped in,' Howard said. 'Did you paint?'

'No, I went to see Claire. I did tell you.'

Claire was an artist Kitty had met not long after they'd moved to the area. She exhibited at local galleries and craft shows across the county, pictures of dogs, mostly, and the odd group of cows. She wore copper bracelets on both arms and thick-soled flip-flops that she claimed were the same as going to the gym. Howard disliked her.

'So you did,' he said neutrally. 'Are you sure you won't have a drink?'

'Perfectly sure. There's a pork pie in the fridge if you want it, and some potato salad. I went to the good butcher's.'

'Thanks.' Howard had poured himself a whisky and subsided into a chair, from where he sat flicking irritably through the channels. 'Christ, there's never anything on.'

'Switch it off, then,' Kitty said.

'It's all bloody repeats,' he said, before slyly assuming his wife's long-standing position: 'I don't know why we even have one.'

Kitty didn't reply.

Howard was at the fridge door eating the pork pie when Kitty called out to tell him that Jenny had phoned. 'She asked to speak to you. I told her I thought you were at the pub,' she said.

Jenny had a year's internship at an investment bank in Hong Kong, and although she would be back for a visit in less than three weeks' time Howard missed her terribly. That Kitty had delayed telling him was, he knew, a kind of subtle revenge for him having gone for a drink. Why it should bother her what he did with his days was beyond him; it wasn't as though he ever drank to excess. Not any more.

'So how is she?' he called back carefully from the kitchen.

'She sounded fine.'

'Anything else?' Despite himself, Howard had drifted through.

Kitty appeared to relent, and looked round at him where he hovered in the doorway of the sitting room. 'She said to give you her love.'

'Right.' Howard looked down. 'And . . . she's still coming?'

'As far as I know.' She turned back to the ironing. 'I'm doing your shirts, by the way.'

The pork pie finished, he wiped his hands surreptitiously on his trousers and passed Kitty to reclaim the armchair. 'Thanks. What are your plans for tomorrow?'

'Oh, I thought I might do a walk. I don't suppose you'll want to come.'

'Are you taking your painting things?'

'Just the camera for now. I've finished the one of the bluebells, so I'm looking for something new. I want something with a bit more history to it this time. A bit more meaning.'

Howard grunted, changed the channel on the TV. Since they'd arrived Kitty had thrown herself into local history, and now she was full of facts about local churches and pollard oaks and ruined castles. It was she who had wanted them to retire here; she had spent the last two decades dreaming of a life in the country, and Howard had always known that their life in Finchley wouldn't be for ever.

The kids and the business were what had kept them in London. Howard had run a small haulage firm, and for a long time he'd needed to be at the depot every day: managing the drivers and mechanics, purchasing fuel, doing the books and dealing with the day-to-day running of a fleet of lorries, a ware-house and a yard. Once he took on a general manager he could have reduced his hours, true; but he enjoyed it, and by that time the kids were doing their exams, so there was no danger of them moving anyway. Nevertheless, Howard had always known that he was keeping Kitty from what she really wanted, which was something obscure, a connection with place that he found hard to understand. 'But you were born in Hemel Hempstead,' he'd said, more than once, as she leafed through the property pages of *The Times*. 'You're not even *from* the countryside. You're just picking somewhere pretty out of a hat; you won't belong there, not properly. You're a townie, you know, like it or not.' But she'd just shake her head and look away.

Chris had taken over the business a year or so before they moved to Lodeshill. He'd worked there for five years at that point, he knew the ropes; it wasn't complicated, though Howard didn't tell Kitty that. She'd got serious about house-hunting once Jenny had finally gone to university after her gap year, the family home strange and silent with just the two of them knocking about in it; and when she found Manor Lodge Howard had known, deep down, that he owed her: that despite his affection for their scruffy, gobby corner of north London, their time there was coming to a close. And would it be so bad, a fresh start somewhere new? Without the business to run he could really get into the radios, give it some proper time. And it wasn't as though he went out much in London any more. He was practically a pensioner, for God's sake. Not that he felt it.

The Lodge was very handsome; even he could see that. The previous owner, a Mr Grainger, had sold it to pay for his care fees but prior to that it had formed part of the Manor House's estate, although these days a conifer belt stood between its back garden and the Manor House's remaining two acres. It wasn't as old as the big house, and dated from the time when it was being remodelled; it had probably been intended for guests or, perhaps, the gamekeeper. It was built of warm red brick, with three pointed gables and two sets of ornate chimneys; Virginia creeper covered a third of the facade up to the gable, green in spring but deepening to crimson every autumn before falling away to leave a ghostly tracery on the bricks. Their surveyor had advised them to get it stripped, but Kitty wouldn't hear of it.

She had gone to a series of local auctions when they'd first arrived, buying old furniture she wouldn't have looked twice at in London but which, Howard had to admit, seemed to work here: a Welsh dresser, two battered oak chests, a semicircular hall table with spindly legs. She'd also picked up half a dozen pictures in old-fashioned frames to fill the extra wall space they now had: botanical prints, a county map and an oil painting of someone else's ancestor who looked down disapprovingly at Howard while they ate. 'It fits with the house,' Kitty had said, shrugging. 'It's got history.'

She was right. There was a proper scullery with a chipped butler's sink, a coal hole with a lead chute cover by the back door and, until they'd had it repainted, a series of marks on the kitchen door showing the heights of what looked like generations of little Graingers – probably including the old man they'd bought the house from. But now it was theirs, and it was clear that Kitty loved it fiercely, and the countryside around it. She was happy now; anyone could see it. It was what she had always wanted.

Now Howard stood on the drive in the dark, an empty tumbler in one hand, a cigarette in the other, as the parallelogram of yellow light cast on the gravel by her bedroom window disappeared and made the darkness press closer around him. He didn't smoke any more, not really, but every so often he had one outside, after Kitty had gone to bed; and even without one he liked to come out for a moment in the fresh air before sleep. Now and again as he smoked he could hear the distant whine of a car changing gear far away.

Did he love it here? He wasn't sure. Manor Lodge was an achievement, certainly; something to show for all those years building the business up. It was proof that he'd made something of himself: he, Howard Talling, who'd left school with four O levels and had started his career as a jobbing roadie for bands nobody now had even heard of. He thought about the invisible village around him: the old people in their beds; the half-dozen families; the rich people who lived at the Manor House, who nobody ever saw; the unguessable farms. Did they all have a proper reason to be here, more reason than him?

A breeze drew a sigh from the massed leaves of Ocket Wood, and two hunting bats rode a breath of wind over the house into Lodeshill. Howard saw them flit across the flung stars of the Milky Way above him, their tiny calls, like a wet finger on glass, inaudible to him as he slipped the cigarette butt back into the box and went inside.

3

Wild garlic, dog violets, sycamore bud-burst. A cuckoo calling.

Jack could cover twenty miles in a day when he wanted to, but once he'd left London behind his pace had slowed. He walked the old Roman road north as thousands had before him: Diddakoi, tinkers, prophets, fools; the footsore army of men who once tramped England's byways looking for work.

Usually he navigated by a kind of telluric instinct, an obscure knowledge he had learned to call on even when the land he walked through was unfamiliar: the wind on his face; the pull of the water table deep beneath the ground; the change from chalk to greensand to lias under his feet. Yet in the land just north of the capital it was hard to feel those things, though he couldn't have said why. There were towns in which he could still sense the soil beneath the streets and feel the land's scars and sly take-backs and reburgeonings; here, though, it was as though the green acres were half mute, and it made him uneasy.

The road ran like a ruler through paddocks, arable fields and golf courses; from a car it probably looked bucolic, accessible, but in fact every acre was fenced off, divided up, used; it did not welcome walkers, and almost everywhere, apart from the busy road's wind-thrashed and perilous verges, was private.

It was trespass that had landed him inside the last time. He'd set out in late January from the farm on the edge of Dartmoor where he'd spent the winter dry stone walling, heading roughly north-east at a slow couple of miles an hour and hoping to bring spring weather with him. The first arrest happened in Somerset as he was crossing what turned out to be some rock star's estate; the second was in Wiltshire, for damaging a crop – or so they said – and after that it was over and over. He was pretty sure the police in one area had warned the next to look out for him, or maybe word had just spread among the locals – who could say? They cooked up some kind of order in the end, telling him to stay off private property, but it had just made him more deter-mined. Eventually he'd ended up in a magistrates' court in Berkshire and had been given a four-month sentence, which had been a shock – though he'd only served two.

He could have made it easy on himself, cooperated with the police, pleaded guilty; he could have agreed to get some of those maps that showed rights of way in green and stuck to them. But there was a principle involved. All he wanted to do was walk the land in which he'd been born, peacefully and subject to no one else, and if you compromised that idea, he thought, you might as well give up.

Years back he'd lived for a few months in a van belonging to a Marxist called Tommo. The van had been parked up, with a few others, on the derelict forecourt of an old Elf petrol station. Tommo did evening shifts as a pot-washer in the titty bar across the road where the lorries stopped, and Jack had always wondered how he managed to square the cash he took from the bar with the ideals of freedom and equality he'd espoused. He'd talked a lot about land ownership and private property and the Inclosures, and about The Man who kept the English proletariat — by which he mostly meant Jack — down. Passive resistance was what it was all about, he'd said. Eventually Jack had moved on because he couldn't stand to see the girls come and go; but he still thought of Tommo now and then, and about some of the things he'd said.

Jack felt the spring sunshine warm on the back of his neck, felt the beginning of a poem flicker tantalisingly somewhere, just beyond the place where he could think about it. But that was OK, he could wait. Perhaps he would get his notebook out later, if it had shown itself by then.

Although the Roman road ran, in one form or another, nearly all the way to Lodeshill and its farms, after a couple of miles walking he struck off it, preferring to take his chances on private land again than suffer the lorries' constant roar at his back. He wasn't in a rush, and there was more to see that way, anyway: a fugitive stand of wild hops; a thrush's nest in a hedge with four blue eggs; spoil from a rabbit scrape rich with little shells from deep in the soil. He'd found an arrowhead like that a long time ago, vicious and beautiful; where it was today, though, was anyone's guess. Perhaps it had found its way into the hands of some policeman's child after one of his many arrests.

Jack found it hard to keep track of all the things he owned, although in fact they were very few: his notebooks, two biros, his cooking things, some stones and feathers and a few coins. In prison he'd had nothing, not even the sad, private little collections of matches and sweets and oddments that the other men guarded so jealously, or the curling photographs they stuck to the cell walls with smears of toothpaste. And when he left he hadn't wanted to keep anything from there, nothing that might bring with it that shut-in, musty smell.

In one field the young oilseed rape had been decimated by pigeons and slugs, a victim of the wet winter and late spring. In the next, the rows of beans were small for the season, despite the pellets of fertiliser like hailstones in the furrows. A row of pylons strode away from him, their cables slack in the sunshine, and the shadows of hobby aircraft raced across the soil, their whine drowning out the wrens and great tits singing in the thickets and raising Jack's hackles as he walked.

As he passed under, and then away from, the big jets' flight paths far overhead he filed his knowledge of them somewhere beyond explaining, along with the invisible lines of lost causeways or underground streams. Once, there had been none at all for more than three days, and it had troubled him so much that he had taken refuge in a derelict lock-keeper's hut by a canal as still as glass until the aeroplanes had appeared again.

Now he tried to prospect his way ahead for a path he knew had once been there. To walk its lost route would be to slog across a vast ploughed field in which a distant tractor dragged a disc harrow back and forth, its clanking roar borne to him intermittently as the breeze shifted. He would be exposed; but not to honour it felt to him a betrayal, even here.

Deep down the earth was still heavy with moisture, but a few days' sun had dried the surface to a friable crust so that it gave softly underfoot like half-baked sponge. Jack set out, crossing the shallow ridges at an angle that made stepping from one to another something he had to concentrate on, the gap between them not quite long enough for his loping stride. In the warm soil around him flints gleamed dully or glowed like bone. He knew of field edges, elsewhere, that were piled high with them, the necessary harvest of generations of children and women. And yet still the earth sent them up.

Above Jack red kites wheeled and tumbled into sudden dogfights, and somewhere to his right the sun flashed off the windscreens of the traffic on the Roman road. A cuckoo called, and Jack froze, scalp prickling, until the soft note came again, settling lazily over the field like a pair of falling feathers. *Summer's coming in*, he thought, turning a coin over in his pocket and grinning to himself. It felt like a good omen. He would write it in his notebook later on.

In a small copse stinking of ramsons he stopped to eat. He'd netted a rabbit the night before and there was a late cabbage in his pack he'd filched from a back garden in one of the dormitory towns he'd passed through; it was a shame he had no onion, but with the wild garlic it was enough for a simple stew.

Rabbits were easy to catch, mostly because of their curiosity: if he sat very still at dusk, downwind of a warren, and made the sound of a crying kit he could often make the does take notice. If he kept it up they'd creep closer, eyes wide, ears twitching. His net was made from knotted string; years back he'd been taught how to make them by an old poacher with pockets full of wriggling ferrets. Now he was never without one. Flung fast enough, with a flick of the wrist, he could entangle a coney into a knot of kicking feet and cord. He felt no compunction about taking what he needed to survive, though when he came across an animal in a snare he'd always free it, if he thought it might live; and he'd bend the snare into uselessness and leave it where he'd found it, a lesson to whoever might come.

Coneys were easy, and he could take squirrels, too. But he wouldn't touch hares. They were wise and unearthly, and he felt sure that they knew something about him, something that he didn't even know himself.

Early one morning in a meadow somewhere – Stinsford, was it, or Selborne? It was hard to remember now – he'd been sitting quietly with his legs stretched out as the world slowly grew light, watching an orange sliver of sun needle, then dazzle, through a silhouette of far trees. Next, the sound of thundering feet – and before he'd had a chance even to look round a brown hare had cleared him in one leap and disappeared. A half-second later another hare appeared in pursuit, but this one braked hard and came to a stop just short of him. Jack flinched, froze; and for a long moment they regarded one another, the hare's tall ears swivelling, its beautiful, gold-flecked eye taking his measure. And then, quite calmly, it seemed, it had left, and Jack had let out the breath he hadn't known he was holding.

After he had eaten the stew he took his clothes off and dunked them in a metal cattle trough fed by a hose and ball tap. He dunked his head, too, opening his eyes underwater to see the mosquito larva twisting in the bubbles and shafts of sun. The water was icy cold and smelled faintly of iron, and reminded him, for some reason, of the milking shed at Culverkeys Farm in Lodeshill: the patient cows in the clanging stalls, the plastic teat cups tight on the udders, the warm, white milk filling up the steel tank.

Perhaps, if he got to Lodeshill and the asparagus wasn't ready, one of the farms would need a relief milker. Fieldwork was what he wanted, but dairy work was OK – just as long as he could keep moving around, as long as he didn't have to stay in one place for too long.

He wrapped himself in his sleeping bag and spread his clothes out to dry in the afternoon sun. Then he took a plastic razor from his pack and began to drag it roughly over his scalp, feeling it catch here and there on old nicks and scars. Just before he began on his beard, he stopped and rinsed the razor out in the trough. Perhaps he'd let it grow a while this time.

4

Ribwort plantain, common bugle, bird's foot trefoil.

This was Jamie's earliest memory: a magnet drawn dripping from black water on a rope. His grandfather's strong hand prising a bright blade from it; the red drops hanging from his fingertips. And then, as he shook it off, the old man's blood landing warm on Jamie's lips and streaking the back of his hand when he tried to wipe it away.

They had called it dipping, and looking back it seemed as though they had done it every weekend – although of course he knew it couldn't have been so. The magnet was huge, like a drum; God only knew where his grandfather had got it from. They'd lower it into the water together, see what it brought up: coins, keys, rusty sections of iron wheels, and once a broken knife, what was left of the blade notched and vicious still.

Sometimes the magnet would catch on something really big – too big to be recovered. Then, his grandfather would let him hold the rope, let him feel the weight at its end as it shifted, sending bubbles up to the surface: the only sign of something long lost that they would ever see.

The old man, of course, had thrown everything back. 'She'd go spare,' he'd say, shaking his head ruefully; but even as a very small boy Jamie had known that his nanna Edith had died giving birth to his mum.

They did all the rivers around Lodeshill and Ardleton, and a couple of canals; they did the lake that had at one time been part of the grounds of the Manor House, and the old tin workings on the slopes of Babb Hill. He fell in there, once; he could still remember the shock of the icy water and how his flung arm made desperate contact with the rough, wet rope that held the magnet, how his grandfather hauled him from the pond like a fish onto the muddy bank. It hadn't put him off; in fact, there was something about how little it had mattered, how uncon-cerned his grandfather had been about his skinned knee and wet clothes, that had comforted him. It felt as though, when the old man was there, nothing could go wrong; not really.

Jamie never asked his granddad why he did it, why he dredged the water for finds and then threw them back. He just liked going out with him, and it was enough. The little boy holding tight to the crossbar; his grandfather behind him, pedalling. His strong arms around him on either side.

★   ★   ★

Jamie was a Lodeshill boy; he'd been born nineteen years before in the overheated bedroom of a 1950s bungalow whose scrappy garden bordered Culverkeys Farm. He had begun to arrive at the Queen Elizabeth one still and bone-cold November day, then had seemed to change his mind; his parents were sent home, told to come back once the contractions were more regular. He waited, so the family story went, to be born in Lodeshill, like his grandfather before him, and back at the bungalow had slipped out quickly and silently onto the duvet cover as his mother wept and next door's cows sympathised in the byre.

His father worked at a landfill site a few miles out of the village; his mother was a dinner lady at the local primary and also cleaned at the Green Man, and at the village hall and sometimes the Bricklayer's Arms in Crowmere. But a lot of the time she didn't work at all, because she didn't want to see anyone; then she just sat on the settee ordering things off QVC that she would return a few days later, or going on eBay for her doll collection.

Five of the dolls sat on the windowsill in the lounge, while two – his mum's favourites – sat on a pouffe in the corner of his parents' bedroom; there were more in a box in the loft. Jamie had more or less stopped seeing them, though when he was younger it had been part of why he didn't ask any kids from school over to play. 'It's just a hobby, son,' his dad said.

Even when she was OK, which she mostly was at the minute, she wasn't like other people's mothers. It wasn't just her weight; you had to be careful not to upset her, you had to think about what to say so you didn't set her off. It had got easier as he got older, it was more or less second nature now; he could tell how she was feeling by a million different things: what she put on in the morning, the way she spoke, how long it took before she replied. But it was hard to explain to people outside the family, and even he and his dad didn't really mention it. When things were OK he preferred not to think about it, and when they weren't he didn't want to bring it up.

For a long while, though, he'd felt part of another family as well as his own. Until they were both thirteen Alex Harland had lived next door, on Culverkeys, and they had been inseparable. The farmhouse was so different to home: always bright, busy, and full of voices. Alex had a little sister, Laura, whom he would alternately tease and ignore; Mr and Mrs Harland talked about things loudly while they were having their tea, like what was on the news and the price of cattle feed, and during the day a string of farmhands came and went. To Jamie their family life seemed loud and exciting and uncareful; he never stopped feeling wary of its unpredictable ebb and flow, but at the same time, it was as though something in him loosened when he was there. For instance, once he'd dropped a mug in their kitchen and the handle had broken off, and he'd turned and held up the pieces to Alex and his mum and said, 'I can't get a handle on it,' just like that, and everyone had laughed. He could never have done that at home.

Culverkeys Farm itself – the fields and woods, the stream, the barns and tracks and dew pond – had been a shared territory, something he and Alex had possessed completely and with all the thoughtless complacency of childhood. And then, when Jamie was thirteen, Alex and Laura had been taken away, and everything – *everything* – had changed.

He had always struggled a bit at school, but without Alex to keep up with things went downhill. It bored him, it was stupid; there was no point to half the stuff they made you do. The teachers just said he just wasn't very academic, whatever that meant, and when he left, at sixteen, it wasn't with many qualifications to his name.

By that time he had a Saturday job in a bakery but no real idea of what came next. He'd spent that first summer kicking about the bungalow, playing computer games in his room while flies buzzed against the window, and watching TV with his mum. The meadows around the village were mown and the hay baled or wrapped for silage; other families went away on holiday and came back tanned; a new school term began. The gap in the hawthorn hedge he'd once used as a short cut to the farmhouse filled in and grew over; meanwhile Jamie felt stranded, becalmed, as though his limbs were weakening or the air around him growing clotted and slow. When he locked himself in the bungalow's tiny bathroom and made himself come into the handbasin there was no excitement in it, or even desire. He put work into not catching sight of himself in the mirror.

His dad just wanted him to get work, any work, but although he made a CV and looked at the job websites every morning there wasn't much to be had. Eventually someone had tipped him off about Mytton Park, a huge distribution centre just off the motorway. The next day Jamie had put on his school trousers and a shirt and rode his 125cc trail bike there, puttering in amid the fumes from articulated lorries and following what felt like several miles of signs to the site office where a sour-faced personnel woman had him fill out several forms before telling him, to his absolute and lasting surprise, that his first shift would be in two days.

The scale of Mytton Park had been a shock. All his life he'd lived less than a dozen miles away, yet in the seven years since it had been built he had never known it was there. Its blank, windowless sheds covered, so the site map said, nearly four hundred acres, yet its low, grey mass was hidden from the motorway by trees, and while lorries may have served it like worker ants, at ground level – at deer and boy and village level – the countryside in which it squatted seemed almost to have absorbed the affront, to have agreed not to speak of it. Almost.

But two years on Mytton Park was so much a part of Jamie's daily life that it was hard to remember a time when his world hadn't included it. His official job title was Warehouse Operative, though at work he was called a picker and packer; he moved goods around from two in the afternoon to ten at night, five days a week, shifting boxes on and off wire-guided forklifts and conveyors, directed by recondite stock-control systems that made of him a minor component in a vast logistics superorganism that supplied goods to stores almost as they were being bought and fulfilled online orders overnight. Sometimes he tried to imagine the places the lorries took the stock away to, the shops and flats all over the country: people with different accents, different houses, different lives.

He'd bought his first car when he was still at school; what else was there to do? His dad put in a couple of hundred quid and made Jamie earn the rest; he'd used the money he got from the bakery, staying on there after he started at Mytton Park so as to save up for insurance and petrol. His mum had been against it, had said the bike was bad enough and that he'd get himself killed; but for once his dad had overruled her. He'd passed his test first time.

He'd kept the Clio on the drive next to his father's old Ford Focus and tinkered with it with a boyish obsession everyone said he'd grow out of. But then, when he was just a few weeks' past his seventeenth birthday, he'd surprised everyone by selling it at a profit to a boy who'd been in the year above and trading up to a Corsa he'd seen in the local paper. It didn't look like much – in fact, his dad thought it was a bit of a wreck – but Jamie had been adamant that he wanted it. It was why he took every shift he could at Mytton Park – the tyres he wanted cost £500, and after that there were the alloys, the exhaust, the turbo, the audio system; the money he could spend on it, really, was limitless.

'Are you putting something by?' his dad had asked him once. 'Course,' he'd replied; but he wasn't. What he didn't give to his mum for housekeeping or spend on going out went on the Corsa. There was no use in saving up; it wasn't as though he'd ever be able to afford his own place or anything – not that there was any affordable housing around there anyway, as his mum often pointed out. So it just seemed futile.

Underneath the tarp the car had been undergoing a slow transformation. He could see now that he'd come at it all wrong, of course, sending away for a cheap body kit that turned out to be all but useless bar the sills and bumpers, and spending too much time on a flashy instrument panel. He'd known to leave the custom stencils until last, but it was obvious now that he should have tackled the engine before anything else: one of the new sills was already cracked where he'd knocked the block and tackle onto it a few weeks back. But he was learning.

There were places you could go to show off a car like his. Not just shows and rallies, but service stations and car parks on certain nights. The cars would have the bonnets up, showing off the engine work; some might have their sound systems turned up loud, the whole car bouncing, engine revving, all the lights on and a police car parked up nearby in case of trouble. He'd never been to anything like that – not yet – but he'd heard about such things locally. He wanted to be part of it, though of course it seemed a bit intimidating from the outside. But once he was there the car would speak for him: people would come over and ask if it was his, if he'd done all the work himself, and he'd be able to say yes. He pictured it sometimes: an appreciative nod, a casual question about the exhausts, or the spoiler. 'I'm James,' he might say, offering his hand. 'And what do you drive?'

On Saturdays he still rode the trail bike into nearby Connorville, leaving the village by deep lanes more familiar to him than his own body, and sold doughnuts and leek slices from nine to two. One day, though, he would live somewhere different – 'somewhere real' was how he described it to himself. Though how that would come about he couldn't have said.

'Dicko! Oi, Dicko!' – that was Jamie's line manager Dave, in the glass office in the corner of the vast hangar, swinging around fatly on his chair with a look on his face that usually meant he'd found some choice piece of Internet grot to shock him with – 'Dicko! Get your arse over 'ere!'

He had been named after his grandfather, James Albert Hirons, yet Jamie Dixon had been Dicko all the way through school and was Dicko again now – although when he left school he had hoped to leave it behind.

'Here, Dicko,' said Dave again as Jamie stuck his head round the office door. 'Look at this –' and he gestured towards the desk where the local freesheet was spread out over the keyboard. Dave had been a forklift driver until a slipped disc had made of him, in his late forties, a transport clerk. Now he was growing fat, though to Jamie, still as scrawny as a calf, he seemed like a pow-erhouse of a man.

Jamie stood behind his swivel chair and looked down at the paper, glad at least to see that it wasn't porn this time. At home, by himself, was one thing, but at work – around other people – it just made him uncomfortable.

'Lodeshill, it says – ain't that where you live?'

'Yeah.' Jamie reached down to the thin paper, smoothed it so the light from the computer screen hit it more directly:

'Is that the farm where ...?' Dave turned to look up at him, one eyebrow raised.

'Yeah.'

'P Harland, it says here. Did you know him?'

'I – I was friends with their son. Our house is right next to the farm.'

'Poor kid. He OK?'

'I don't know. Him and his sister moved away with his mum six years ago. Nearly seven.'

'So they're selling off the farm. What about the land? That going to auction?'

Jamie shrugged. 'Two months since he died and we've still not heard.'

'Probably go to a developer: new houses and that. Or they might look for coal, or shale gas – you thought of that? Going on all over.'

'Maybe Mrs Harland will come back and live there, maybe it's hers now.'

'Well, you don't know, these days,' said Dave, sitting back in the creaking chair. 'Could be a lot of money in it. You'll have to wait until the lawyers have finished with it all, I suppose.'

Riding home after his shift that night through the dark lanes, Babb Hill black and invisible to the east, Jamie thought about Culverkeys, about what might happen to it and what it would mean. The cows – seventy or so Holstein-Friesians, mostly milkers plus some calves and in-calf heifers and a Hereford stock bull – had been taken to market a few days after Philip Harland had died, and now the dispersal sale suggested that the farm would not be sold as a going concern; what wasn't clear yet was what would happen to the land.

When he thought about Culverkeys he pictured the aerial photograph that hung in the hallway at home; a man had knocked on the door one day and told his mother there'd been a plane over, and it had come in the post a few weeks later. In it the village looked like a jumble of grey squares surrounded by green; you could see the main road through it, and the turn-off to Crowmere, and a bit of the Boundway in one corner. And you could see his house at the end of the little cul-de-sac, with its tiny rectangle of garden behind; and beyond that, Culverkeys stretching north and west as far as the big field called the Batch with the oak in it: the green squares with their ghostly crop marks, the clumps of dark trees and the dew pond reflecting the sun like a drop of mercury. It looked, from that height, as though the back gardens on the west side of the cul-de-sac had been carved out of Culverkeys land; and perhaps they had. Perhaps the earth in Jamie's back garden had once belonged to it.

And he thought about Alex's father, and the terrible way that he'd died. Jamie had come home after his shift one Friday night back in February to find all the lights on in the bungalow and both his parents in the lounge. The telly wasn't on and they both stood up when he let himself in; he'd believed, for one heart-stopping second, that his grandfather had passed away.

What he first felt, when his dad told him, was that it was in some way his fault – as if the long, slow process of the Harland family's unravelling, now concluded with Philip's death, had been set in motion by Jamie many years ago, tracked to the happy farmhouse from the bungalow somehow like a virus in the treads of his shoes.

It was stupid, he knew. But the feeling had persisted. This wasn't how things were supposed to have turned out; he and Alex were supposed to have been friends for ever, and the landscape into which they had both been born was something that should never have had to change.

And yet Jamie had never quite had Alex's optimism, never quite trusted the future in the way that Alex, back then, had seemed to. 'What will you do when you grow up?' he'd asked Alex once, back in primary school. Alex had answered for them both: 'That's easy. We'll live here, on Culverkeys. I'll be the farmer, and you can be the herdsman.'

He'd wanted to believe it, but even then Jamie had known that life was more complicated than that.

5

Nettles, yellow archangel. Rabbits.

It took Jack a long time to cross the motorway. The Roman road met it at a big junction up ahead but it frightened him, so he went back and tried a narrow turning signposted to a garden centre. Half a mile past the garden centre it became a lane leading to a white water tower of some kind, fenced off and monolithic behind a square yellow sign reading simply 'A'. The structure bristled with aerials and masts; a Portakabin squatted beside it. Jack's heart thumped irrationally as he passed.

Then, after a short rise up into the light, the lane leaped over the sudden, roaring river of the motorway. As he crossed it Jack was a brief silhouette to the cars beneath him, a glimpsed figure that left nothing behind but a single white petal blown from his coat that was caught briefly by a windscreen wiper far below him and then given up to the slipstream and the infinity of the wind.

On the other side of the motorway the lane ran alongside a ditch that looked as though it had recently held water, before rejoining the old road north. Behind a derelict pub, once clearly a drover's inn, two old paddocks were now given over to a machinery and plant hire firm, and a makeshift footbridge made from plastic trench covers crossed the ditch to where an Alsatian barked repetitively at Jack through a steel gate. A brown rat darted to the shadows under the bridge, watched both by Jack and by a buzzard wheeling easily over the old Roman road, its primaries spread like fingers in the late-afternoon sun.

That evening Jack decided to walk on into the night. It wasn't just about staying unseen, it was a way to immerse himself in a world that most people didn't know existed. At dusk the countryside came alive, and it was then that Jack felt most at home, as though his true peers were the blunt-nosed badgers in their centuries-old setts, the owls hunting the field margins and the otters slipping quietly upstream. When he died, he sometimes thought, it would be at night. The sky would slowly lighten to dawn, the morning sun would creep up to touch his beard and the still, green folds of his coat, but he would be gone.

But not yet – never quite yet. Spring was advancing, warming the soil, and somewhere up ahead there would soon be asparagus to pick. He was probably a third of the way to Lodeshill at least, and he'd not been stopped so far; as he cut invisibly through the darkened car park of a Travelodge, he allowed himself to imagine, for the first time since leaving the hostel, that he was free.

Later that night, deep in a pine plantation, Jack found a forest ranger's high seat and climbed up to sit a while. The wind was coming from the south-west and the branches moved around him, whispering, sighing. On the far horizon an electrical storm flickered silently, although the sky above was clearing.

He thought about the ranger he'd known, what, twenty years ago now? He must have been about the age that Jack was now, taciturn but with a feeling for wild places that had rivalled Jack's own. He had understood the woods he managed like nobody else Jack had ever met, and when he shot deer, or magpies, or trapped grey squirrels, he had done it with a deep and absolute respect.

He'd found Jack's camp one night while he slept, had woken him gently with the toe of his boot; but then, as he watched Jack gingerly putting on his boots he'd crouched down quietly to look, pushing Jack's hands away. Then, brooking no argument, he'd put Jack in the back of his truck with his two curious pointers, driven him to his cottage and cleaned and dressed the blisters himself.

Jack had slept on his sagging, dog-smelling couch for a week, spending the days working with him in the forest; at the end of it he had offered to teach Jack to shoot, perhaps to train him up to work alongside him. It was the one time, since he'd taken to the road, that Jack had considered putting down roots. It was the idea of having a territory and how well the man knew it:

every rabbit warren, every woodpecker's nest, every drey. To belong in that way, to have such a close focus, felt right: a home parish. But ultimately, Jack knew that he needed to be on the move. Something impelled him, though he couldn't have given it a name.

Now, back on the ground, he moved quietly into the wind into an area of clear fell and then to the dense cover of new pines. After a little while he left the wood behind and took to open country, the stars impossibly bright overhead. For the first time since leaving London he felt at peace.

As he followed the curve of an old hedgeline he spotted a shape trotting towards him and froze: a dog fox, something big and dark in its jaws. It passed close enough to Jack for him to hear fox-breath whistle through feathers.

Approaching some farm buildings in the small hours Jack woke a collie, its barks lofting out from its kennel to echo flatly off the corrugated-iron byres, the commotion reminding Jack for a moment of prison.

He crouched behind a quickthorn hedge until the dog was quiet. Then, unhooking the frayed orange twine that held the metal gate shut, he lifted it carefully over the rough concrete and swung it to behind him.

There had been a dwelling of some kind on this spot since Domesday; in fact, for many centuries before. Now it was just a modern set of farm buildings, but in the stand of nettles that still marked the long-gone midden, in the patch of soil near the farmhouse stained black by walnuts from the lost tree in whose shade horses had once been tied, the land remembered.

In the moonlit yard it didn't take Jack long to find what he wanted: a plastic bucket, which he rinsed carefully using the tap in the milking shed. He took his pack from his back and set it by the wall, then skirted the barns slowly, passing through another gate into the pasture beyond.

Many of the cows were lying down, but several stood close together in the near corner of the field. They stamped and twitched their tails as he approached, and he spoke to them softly, telling them his name and why he was there: *Jan Toy, Jan Toy, it's Jack, your green boy . . .*

It was important that the first beast didn't startle, and Jack laid a hand on its warm flank. It blew air from its nostrils and twitched its hide, but it tolerated him. Slowly, he moved into the herd until he was surrounded by their warm, shifting bodies. He closed his eyes and tried to sense which was the calmest animal, but in the dark it was mostly luck.

He ran his hand down the flank of a cow near the edge of the group. It stepped sideways, delicately, but at last it allowed Jack to kneel in the wet grass and press his cheek to its belly. In the dark he heard, rather than saw, the milk jet and froth from the teats as he pulled; he had to listen to its note to tell whether he was directing it into the bucket or onto the ground. As he milked he looked past the breathing herd to the dark horizon where a bright iridium flare announced the slow passage of a satellite overhead.

Afterwards he carried the bucket back to the yard where the collie watched him from the gate with its ears pricked.

'Hello,' he whispered, pouring the warm milk carefully into a plastic bottle he took from his pack. 'It's me, Jack.' The collie regarded him. After a moment he returned a little to the bucket and tilted it for the dog. It slunk forward, belly low, and drank. Jack gave it his hand to sniff before he left, and hoped for a welcome if he came that way again.

6

Arum (cuckoo pint, lords and ladies, bobbin joan) –
spadix first formation. Ash trees in flower. Sunshine.

Kitty took a seat in the back pew of the church and clasped her
hands in her lap. As the echo of the heavy door closing behind
her faded away, the air seemed to refold itself in perfect stillness.
It wasn't totally silent – she could hear rooks cawing outside, and
the distant sound of a mower – but it had a pellucid, listening
quality that she believed could be found nowhere else. Briefly,
she shut her eyes. Over the faint reek of damp and the odour of
wool kneelers she could smell the flowers brought in for the
Easter service several days before, now wilting slightly in their
blocks of green Oasis.

Hundreds of years of prayer had filled the space around her,
bounded by the building's cool walls and tall windows: hundreds

of years of village breath. Lodeshill's faithful surrounded her, all loved in their time and their passing mourned; remembered for a few lifetimes, then lost. A name scratched into the back of a pew. A stone slab from which the legend had been worn away by centuries of feet.

She had only meant to pin a notice up in the porch, but had found herself coming in. It was a moment of stillness, that was all. Just a way to step outside your life for a few minutes. Who was it who talked about places where prayer had been valid? This was surely one of them. The vicar had once told her that the whitewashed walls would at one time have been lurid with pictures of heaven and hell, an incentive for people to confess their sins – as she perhaps should one day. It was hard to imagine now, though the leering face, wreathed in oak leaves, on one of the roof bosses spoke of a more vital and mysterious past.

Why did these places persist? she wondered. What hold did they still have over people? The ancient fear of damnation was no more; the approval of the local community hardly mattered to most. And what was that, anyway – community? The faltering congregation, the parish council, the clique of diehard regulars at the Green Man? A year in and she still only really knew a few people in Lodeshill, although the sense remained that there was a core of village life somewhere to which she, an outsider, did not have access. Where this might be if not at church was beyond her; but still.

The door groaned and clanged again behind her, and the dust motes danced in the draught. 'Oh, Katherine, hello,' the vicar called out, in less than reverential tones. Still, this was his work-place, she supposed; he couldn't always be treating it like some kind of monument. 'A moment with God?'

'Something like that,' she replied, getting up. 'I just popped in to put a notice in the porch,' she said. 'My friend Claire – she's an artist. She's got an exhibition in Connorville. Is it all right?'

'Of course, of course. And how is your painting? The weath-er's been lovely – perfect for you, I'd have thought.'

'Oh – yes.'

'You'll be exhibiting them soon, no doubt. You must let us have a preview!'

'Oh, I'm not sure about that,' Kitty said. The truth was, she seemed to have hit something of a wall. All those years spent dreaming of moving to the countryside, all those years of still lifes and art classes and day trips to beauty spots – yet now she had it all at her fingertips the landscapes she was producing looked nothing like the shining visions she had carried around in her head for so long. Technically they were passable, she felt, but there was some-thing missing, something she couldn't quite identify or describe. When she thought about it, which was often, the word 'imma-nence' kept springing unhelpfully to mind; but it wasn't anything religious that her paintings were lacking, it wasn't that at all.

That afternoon she took the camera and went out looking for possible locations. Nowhere too obvious, but she did want it to be beautiful. She wanted it to sum up her feelings about the area, somehow; to communicate what it was really like.

How she had yearned for green places when she lived in Finchley; for somewhere ancient and unchanging, somewhere where the past lived on in the woods and fields, where you could imagine its previous generations and feel connected with the things that were there now. When Chris and Jenny were young she had insisted on holidays in the Lake District or Cornwall; there, out in the landscape, she had felt herself expand, felt something in her quieten – if only momentarily. When the kids got older it had not been so easy; they had wanted to go somewhere hot, like their friends, and Howard had been only too happy to agree. So it was Italy, Morocco, the odd skiing trip in between; meanwhile, she had the walls of the house hung with images of the countryside: watercolours, etchings, prints, it didn't matter. And eventually, as the kids grew up, the long campaign to escape London had begun.

Now she drove to Babb Hill and parked in a little car park formed from an old quarry. The route to the summit was busy at weekends, and with joggers and dog walkers in the mornings, but it was a Thursday afternoon and there were only a couple of other cars there. She slung the camera over her shoulder, locked the car and set out.

The path was wide and for the most part shaded by the trees that clothed the hill's flanks. The beeches were almost fully out but the ash leaves were still locked in their black buds and plenty of light filtered down. Here and there were pools of bluebells, luminously ultraviolet where the sun hit them, but Kitty had already painted bluebells, and moved on.

Apart from the TV mast, trig point and toposcope, the hill's broad spine was undulating and bare, its ancient hill fort now no more than two massy humps bisected by the path. The views were breathtaking: on clear days like today it was easy to believe you could see nine counties. Kitty set the camera's zoom to infinity and fired off some pictures, but she already knew that what she had captured was both too distant and somehow too general.

The climb had taken it out of her somewhat, but she didn't want the day to be wasted. Back at the car she got an Ordnance Survey map out from the glove compartment and spread it out on the bonnet. Just north of Babb Hill was a little village she'd seen signposts for, but hadn't yet explored. She decided to go and have a look.

It turned out to be bigger than Lodeshill, with a listed church and some fine old almshouses. She parked near the war memorial and took the lane north out of the village past fields where fat lambs butted their mothers, the camera banging against her hip. Although it was still warm the afternoon was beginning to draw in a little: her shadow was long on the road beside her, and the hedges on either side were filling up with birds.

Years ago, before Jenny had been born, she had taken a photography course. The group had gone out on field trips designed to teach them how to look, how to notice the things that spoke to them, so they could learn to capture them in a way that other people might enjoy.

'That's what art's all about,' the teacher had told them. 'The philosophers say there's no way of really knowing that other people even exist. But art proves them wrong.'

Kitty hadn't really understood, and it had been another student, weeks later, who had explained it to her. They had been in a hotel at the time, his hand warm on her breast, the damp sheet tangled around them.

'I wish I could capture this,' he'd said, gazing at her.

She'd laughed. 'You could take a photo.'

'No, more than that. I mean how you are, how I feel. The light. All of it. That's what art's for, isn't it? And poetry, all that. A way of capturing a moment of reality and transmitting it to someone else, maybe years in the future.'

'You want people to know our secret?'

'No, I mean – this is real, you know? *Us. Now.* But soon it'll be over – gone. As if it had never happened.'

Kitty had reached for him and they had made love again, and later she had gone home to Finchley, and to Howard. But since then she'd felt it, sometimes, looking at paintings, and even, once or twice, reading a poem: the shiver, the magic, of another consciousness revealing itself to hers. *I existed, I felt this, I thought this: you can feel it too.*

Not that she thought she could emulate proper artists: of course not. But everyone could try, everyone had a chance to leave their mark. Tucking the camera securely under her arm, she pushed her way awkwardly through the hedge to her left. There was a broad ditch on the other side choked with oily orange water, and glad of her walking boots, grimacing slightly at the stretch, she took a long step over it into the ploughed field beyond.

In its centre was a single oak, stag-headed but dressed on its lower branches with young, bronze leaves. In a couple of weeks it would perfect, she thought: iconic, but somehow melancholy, too, its dead top section, white as bone, contrasting perfectly with the rich earth below. She picked her way towards it along a set of tramlines, stopping every few minutes to take a photo, trying to remember the rule of thirds as she framed each shot. Already she could feel the painting she might make forming in her mind.

It happened just as she was about to recross the field drain by the road. She felt briefly dizzy, like floating; then it was as though her legs failed and she found herself half sitting in the ditch, her boots deep in the mud and her hands and trouser legs coated in oily slime.

Again, she thought, with a sudden wash of fear that made her gorge rise; the last time she'd been in the bedroom, drying her hair, when her vision had blurred and a sudden weakness in her arm had made her put the hairdryer down.

She sat very still on the ditch bank with her eyes closed for a few moments, taking deep breaths; then she groped around for the camera with a shaking hand – but it was nowhere to be seen.

7

Ground ivy, purslane. Beeches in full leaf. Hornbeams first flower.

At sunrise Jack was walking a lost green lane behind the gardens of a nursing home. Seamed into the land like a crease in a palm, it was impossibly ancient, its silence the accumulated silence of history. Thick with nettles and Queen Anne's lace, its centuries-old wheel ruts were lost in dead leaves from the trees that formed a nave overhead; midges danced in columns in its still air. Part of its length marked the border between badger territories and at intervals along the bank were their latrines, the bare soil clawed over and pungent with scat. Jack grinned approvingly to himself as he passed, and batted a leggy black fly from his cheek.

The last two times he'd slept he'd felt the peturbation of a large town not too far ahead running like static through his dreams. He didn't want to walk through its precincts or shopping streets, didn't want to negotiate its roundabouts or estates or business parks. It was a new town, still more like a wound than a scar, and Jack knew it held nothing for him – nothing that wouldn't cost. He had decided to take the long way round it; it was probably safer that way, too.

It had felt like they were waiting for him, that time in Berkshire. Why? What good did it do anyone to lock him up; what harm to let him be? Walking the old cart track then he'd pictured it as it once might have been, the trees hung with wisps of hay for weeks after the last of the wagons had come in from the fields each year. Its ghost bisected a fragment of hazel coppice between farms, a little wood it would have taken him a few minutes to pass through had he been let alone.

How could a wood be private, anyway? What did that even mean? But by that time he was breaking an order. 'You've run out of chances, mate,' the arresting officer had said, pushing him roughly into the waiting van; 'it's not like you wasn't warned.' But he wasn't Jack's mate; in fact, it felt as though he really hated him, and that, after thirty years on the road, was new. 'Fucking homeless,' he'd called to the other copper over the roof of the van. 'I can't stand 'em, you know?'

They'd taken his notebooks from him in prison, which was almost the worst part. It wasn't until he'd got out that he'd had a chance to write it all down. That was one of the first things he'd wanted to do when he got to the hostel, but by then his memory of events had become hazy; either that, or his mind just didn't want to go there any more.

Where are the primroses that used to carpet that wood? he'd written, in the end. *Why don't you coppice it if you say it is yours? You think it doesn't matter, that it is just a wood. You think things will always be the same. You think you have dominion – that you're not part of things. Like in that book. But if there is no light the primroses can't come. Is it spring you are afraid of or something else? Life finds a way but not like you think. I am still here.*

He'd known it didn't make sense even as he wrote it. He hadn't been well then; London had disordered him somehow.

He was much better now.

After half a mile a blaze of yellow rape opened up on Jack's left and sunbeams lanced down here and there into the green lane's gloom. For a while it was bordered by a fragment of laid hedge so ancient it was merely a line of trees with strange angles in their trunks. As he put a hand on one he saw the men who had laid it two hundred years before: the billhooks glinting in the pale winter sun, the earth thick on their boots, their hands white with cold. He saw the brutal wounds to the young stems, cut nearly through, thrust sideways and secured with stakes hammered into the reluctant ground. The skill of it, and the pride in the neatness of the pleaching. Later, the green buds bursting into life on the shattered stems as spring came; the hedge filling out, a living stockade of thorns. Years of useful life, and then left uncut for one winter; two. Eventually, the base thinning, holes appearing. Finally the branches disentangling from one another, the trees growing taller and assuming separate lives.

The lane was heavy going underfoot, and Jack scrambled up the bank and burst through into the sunlit field beyond. A stile at the far end took him onto a roughly surfaced farm track edged with giant hogweed, the thick, purple-spotted stems obscenely virile at the base. Caught amid them was a scrap of red and white: a chocolate wrapper dropped by a careless walker or blown there from one of the litter bins by the school fields not far away. Jack bent to pick it up; it smelled almost overpowering of sugar. He tucked it into his pack with a few other bits of rubbish he'd collected.

The closer he got to Lodeshill and its farms the more he found himself thinking about Culverkeys. He'd had work there twice, both times for only a few weeks – though it had been hard to believe, when he'd arrived the second time, that it was the same place. The farm kitchen – which was as much as he ever saw of the house – was dirty, Philip Harland sallow and unshaven; he'd not dared ask what had happened to the wife and kids. Philip was clearly drinking, though he seemed for the most part to have it under control; until the last day, when Jack had had to quit, he hardly spoke beyond what was necessary – but Jack hadn't minded that.

The first time he'd worked there had been very different. The Harlands had three children, if he remembered rightly: two teenage boys, one tall and quiet, one more high-spirited, and a little girl. Though he'd never had much to do with the family, something about the eldest boy had troubled him; the sense, perhaps, of a self held at a remove, shut away beyond reach – as he himself must have been at that age, before he found his true path. He'd wondered then why one child should be so affected and not the others, and when he'd arrived at the farm a second time and had seen the way things were he'd been glad, in a way, to think of that boy – and the other two kids – elsewhere.

Jack walked on, thinking about the other farms near Lodeshill where he might find work. After a little while a tune came to him unbidden, attaching itself to him with instant and unarguable authority and driving the past from his mind. Where was it from? It had the simple, lilting melody of a nursery rhyme, but it wasn't one he could think of. 'Uncle Tom Cobley', he realised after a few bars, and smiled to himself, feeling the tune furl out behind him as his whistle got louder; and then, 'It's like a ribbon,' he said out loud in a sudden West Country burr, 'a girt green one!'

He let the whistle die away and closed his eyes for a few paces, feeling the nettles swishing against his boots and being crushed juicily underfoot. Briefly, he felt sorry for their bruised leaves, but he knew that it evened out: his passage across country left seeds and spores swirling in his wake, and everywhere was better for his having come through.

Eventually the green lane gave out onto a B-road, but long before it did he stopped and thought his way ahead, feeling the pull of the town's quiet margins, the untrodden ways past its centre that would keep him safe. When he did cross the road it was in tree-shadows, a mere flicker at the edge of the windscreen to a passing car changing down for the bend. In the rear-view mirror: nothing. He had melted into the sun-dappled trees on the other side.

8

Celandine, cuckoo flower, meadow buttercup.

Jamie slept badly and woke on Friday morning from a dream in which he was in the back garden of his grandfather's house, except that it was also Ocket Wood and the old man wanted him to cut down all the trees. He didn't have an axe or a saw, and he'd tried to explain, but his grandfather just got angrier, urging him again and again to fell the trees. Eventually the old man turned and, his familiar face disfigured by fury, snarled at him: 'You always were a waste of space.'

'You look awful,' his mum said when he came downstairs in his tracksuit bottoms and T-shirt. 'I hope you're not coming down with something.'

'Thanks,' Jamie yawned. 'Is there any bread?'

'In the bread bin. What's the matter, you're not poorly?'

Once, when he was very small, a bout of strep throat had turned into a raging fever that nearly saw Jamie taken into A&E; all he remembered about it now was his mum's impatience, and how his dad had stayed at home to comfort him until the banana medicine began to work. Now Jamie was an adult he could see she couldn't help it, so there was no point being upset about it. Being upset didn't do anyone any good.

'I'm fine, Mum,' he reassured her now. 'Just didn't sleep well.'

'Why, they not working you hard enough?'

'Plenty,' he said, turning away. Her hair was lank and she wasn't dressed yet, her loose breasts and belly distorting her pink pyjama top with its cheerful cartoon.

'I get paid today,' he offered her, in a deliberately upbeat voice.

'That's good, you can give me some housekeeping.'

'OK. I thought I might go and see Granddad before I go in.'

'I've got a couple of meals you can take him. Pick him up a copy of the paper on the way, too, will you?' She drew her dressing gown around her and turned away, her slippers whispering on the lino.

'I'll go on the way to work, Mum. Got some stuff to do on the car first.'

There was no sense in showering until after he'd finished, so when he'd had his toast Jamie put his trainers on, went out to the front drive and took the tarp off the Corsa. A robin sang in the forsythia by the driveway as he lifted up the car's bonnet and began to work.

★   ★   ★

Jamie's grandfather had been born in Lodeshill just after World War I, the eldest son of an infantryman who'd lost one eye and his hearing to a stick grenade near Pas-de-Calais in 1917. Now he lived in the pebble-dashed post-war semi in Ardleton of which his wife had been so proud, and in which Jamie's mother, and his three uncles, had grown up.

Ardleton had once been a thriving market town, but in the 1960s the new town of Connorville had increased in mass and pulled in everything around it. Its road signs were taken down or altered; even the football team was renamed. Nowadays its streets were merely part of Connorville's general sprawl – although Connorville wasn't even a proper city, as the old man often said. It was just a collection of retail parks and roundabouts, when all was said and done.

It had been that way for two decades now, but Jamie's grandfather still lived as though the old landmarks remained valid, and continued to navigate by them: the cattle market; the handsome Edwardian library, now a job centre; the derelict site of the once-busy foundry; the old abbey fishponds, long silted up. He'd caught bream there as a child, probable descendants of the monks' own fish – or so he had told his grandson, on more than one occasion. There was no one left any more to contradict him.

'Did you bring the *Post*?' he asked now, opening the door.

'I forgot. Sorry. I've got a couple of dinners for you, though: beef casserole and a tuna pasta bake.' Jamie went through to the kitchen and put the Tupperware containers in the fridge. In the front room the old man sank back into his armchair.

'Bloody dinners,' he muttered. 'She thinks I can't look after myself.'

Jamie wandered through. His grandfather was trying to tune a little battery-operated radio, his liver-spotted hands turning it testily in his lap.

'You got something on, Granddad?'

'Not yet. Three o'clock at Kempton Park.'

'I could look it up on my phone if you like.'

'Phone, lad? That's no good to me.'

Jamie sighed. 'I'll pop out and get the *Post* for you now. It'll only take a second. Is there anything else you want?'

'Take an apple with you, on the hall table. And don't be long.'

The land his grandfather's street stood on had been an orchard before the second war, and the washing line in his garden stretched from the back of the house to a rogue Worcester Pearmain that had grown slowly from a windfall after the trees themselves had been grubbed up. Every autumn the old man stored the apples carefully in newspaper in the shed, where they would sweeten through winter and fill the air with their fragrance; he'd always put a couple of boxes at the gate, too, but hardly anyone ever took them – or, at least, not that Jamie could remember. He looked for one on the hall table, but there were none there. April, nearly May: it was far too late in the year.

'Your granddad send you out?' said the man at the shop.

Jamie nodded.

'How is he?

'OK,' said Jamie, fishing in his pocket for some money. 'Bit on the grumpy side.'

'No change there, then.'

But it was a change. Jamie had always loved spending time with his grandfather, had taken to riding his bicycle all the way to Ardleton when he was only seven or eight. He saw more of the old man now than even his mum did, something he'd never really noticed until Alex had pointed it out one day. 'Does she not ever visit him at his house?' he'd asked, and Jamie had realised, belatedly, that although his grandfather often came over for Sunday dinner, it was usually only he and his dad who dropped in on him at home.

He'd never been too sure why he spent so much time there. It wasn't as though they never argued, because they did – like when Villa were playing City, for instance. But it never made any difference, and when he next visited things would be just the same. It helped that his granddad spoke his mind, too: he just said what he thought, and you didn't have to try and work out what he really meant, didn't have to worry that things were any different than they seemed.

But over the course of the last year or so the old man had turned inward. Often he was irritable; sometimes he didn't answer when Jamie spoke but sat with his hands on his knees, his face towards the window. It was as though he was listening to something else, something Jamie couldn't hear.

'Is he going senile?' he'd asked his mum a few weeks back.

'Don't be stupid,' she'd replied.

'He seems different.'

'He's ninety-three,' his mother said, and it was true – he was far older than any of his friends' grandparents, after all.Yet he still went to the corner shop every day, still kept the house tidy. But something was changing, and Jamie could feel it.

Once, years before, his mother had told him about the nightmares he'd had when she was a little girl.'Screaming and shouting, every night, sometimes,' she'd said. It was upsetting for Jamie to even think about.'He'd never admit to it the next day, of course. It was like it never happened.'

'Why, though?'

'Too proud. He didn't like anyone knowing.'

'No – why did he have nightmares?' he'd asked.

'The war, Jamie,' she'd said, folding her arms and looking at him. He'd nodded, but hadn't been sure what she meant; he felt as though he should already know somehow – yet the one time he'd asked to see his granddad's medals he'd told him he didn't know where they were. It had been Harry Maddock, the gamekeeper, who had eventually filled Jamie in about the prisoner-of-war camps, and how lucky James Hirons, who had served his country as a coder in the navy, was to have come back from Singapore alive.

Jamie used to help Mr Maddock out now and again; Harry would let him drive the shooting brake sometimes, which was probably where his love of cars had begun. He remembered the keeper's imprecations about not flattening the crops; remembered, too, the smell of blood on the night air from the warm, stiffening rabbits slung into the cage on the back. That smell was tied up, now, with what had happened to his granddad: the mysterious thing that had branded him invisibly and that Jamie – lucky, soft, with his indoor job and his computer games – would never understand. He had wondered then how it was that Harry knew, and not him; and whether his grandfather would ever speak to him about it.

Back at the house he dropped the paper in his grandfather's lap and sat down in the other armchair. The old man leafed through it, listlessly, then turned to the classifieds at the back.

'I see Culverkeys is being broken up.'

'You've seen the ad?'

'Someone's set to make a mint. It's wrong, I say.'

His grandfather had spent his married life working for a firm that made household appliances, first on the line and then in the office, but before the war he'd been a farmhand. He'd once shown Jamie an old black-and-white photograph in which two huge Suffolk Punches strained towards the camera, the single-furrow plough behind them guided by a boy no more than fourteen. 'Recognise it?' he'd asked, tapping the photograph. A huge oak was just visible in the field behind the plough. 'That's the Batch, on Culverkeys. I first learned to plough there, with my old man. Always thought I'd go back, you know? After the war. But it was a different world by then: women doing men's work, tractors all over. And I had the TB to get over, of course.'

'So d'you think they'll build on Culverkeys?' Jamie asked his grandfather now.

'Build on it, dig it up. There's no money in farming any more.'

'Is that why he killed himself – Mr Harland? He couldn't make it pay?'

'Who knows, boy. Who knows. But I saw a farm sale once, when I was a lad. There was terrible shame in it for the farmer to lose his land, terrible shame. And Philip was never the same after the wife left – or so I heard. I was surprised he carried on for as long as he did – it can't have been easy, just with hired hands. And they say it was always her as did the books.'

'Maybe he thought she'd come back.'

'Maybe. But I'll tell you something, lad: that place goes back a long way – they're one of the oldest families around here, the Harlands. You'll find them in the churchyard, dozens of the buggers, and the war memorial, too, of course. That's why I was surprised about the crematorium. They should've buried him in his parish church, where he was baptised. God forgives all, or so they say.'

'The farm'll go to Alex's mum now, won't it – to his wife?'

'I doubt it – she's not a Harland any more, not if they got a divorce. But we'll see. We'll see what the bloody lawyers do now, eh?'

'I have to go now, anyway, Granddad,' said Jamie. 'See you next week.'

'Take an apple with you,' called the old man as the door swung shut.

★　　★　　★

That evening, after he got back from his shift, Jamie slipped his jacket on and went out. 'I'm just going for a quick pint,' he called from the hallway. His father, watching TV with his mum, held up a hand in acknowledgement. But instead of turning up Hill View towards the Green Man Jamie forced his way through the grown-over gap in the hedge at the end of the cul-de-sac. It was the first time he'd set foot on Culverkeys since Alex had left.

Jamie could remember when the field in which he stood had been two fields, Hope's Piece and Lower Hope, both designated set-aside and so left unmown. The grass in June had grown chest-high — although of course he had been smaller then — and was purple with wild marjoram and pyramid orchids and alive with butterflies. There was no set-aside any more, though, and looking at the huge field now you couldn't tell where the old hedgeline had even been.

At the top of the field was a copse, planted generations ago as cover for foxes and to improve the country for the hunt. Not long before Alex had left, the two of them had discovered a pair of goshawks nesting there. Jamie had made Alex swear to protect the chicks, when they hatched out, and they had taken turns to check on the nest using a heavy old pair of binoculars Alex had found in the farmhouse. It had been their secret, the last they would ever have together, and Jamie had tried not to think about it since.

He wondered when the last time was that anyone had come this way. The farm had felt like forbidden territory after Alex had gone; he'd been cast out by Mr Harland, and by fear. But being there again was bringing it all back, as he'd known it would: the landscape of his childhood, its grassy uplands and shadowy thickets. He had believed it lost to him somehow, but of course it had been there all this while.

The air was cooling, the stars bright above, and Jamie hunched his shoulders and jammed his fists into his pockets as he walked. Far away to his right he could just about make out the farmhouse, crouched within the dark huddle of its outbuildings, and beyond that, Great Reave and Five Acres, where the heifers had been until a few weeks ago.

Slowly, he crossed the field's gentle flank to where a silvery disc spoke of the wet winter they'd had. It was the last place on the farm to hold the snow, a slab of white that remained long after the other fields had warmed up. He wondered if the new owners would know this; whether they'd care. Whether the fields would even be fields any more.

9

Avens, dog's mercury, harebells, vetch. Otter spoor by the river.

It wasn't the first time Jack had woken up covered in birds. He gave a start and was surrounded by the whirr of pinions, the breeze from their wings fanning his face as a dozen or so birds exploded from his body up into the branches of the little wood in which he lay.

For a moment he froze, willing them to return; but as his eyes adjusted to the low evening sun he saw that there was someone standing over him, their shadow reaching across his sleeping bag. He leaned up on one elbow, shading his eyes, his heart lurching in his chest. But only the trees' long shadows lay black on the ground.

The birds seemed to have melted away, too, like a dream that disappears before you can snatch at it. Corn buntings, he thought for some reason; not that you saw them in numbers any more – or ever would again, probably. He lay back down for a moment, unseeing eyes fixed somewhere beyond the branches. In the police cells they woke you every hour to check you weren't dead.

The wood he had camped in was young, having sprung up in the 1960s in the no-man's-land between a power station and a golf course on Connorville's scrappy outskirts. Myxomatosis had devastated the local rabbit population in '53, '54, and without their nibbling teeth far more saplings had survived their first few years than usual; on the golf course the greenkeeper kept them down, and the land around the cooling towers was managed, but in the area between the two a few hundred trees had quietly set down roots. Now the wood was almost established, though it had yet to be marked on maps or given a name. Jack liked it for its opportunism, and for the stray golf balls that dotted the ground. They worked on him like conkers, and he couldn't help but pick them up and walk with them for a while.

And there was something else, too: in places like this he felt invisible in a way that he rarely did in the proper countryside with its signposted walks and intelligible views. Places like this, in the shadow of a power station, were far from picturesque, and they were somehow wilder for it. Hardly anyone went there except for lovers and local children, who sensed that these ungovernable scraps of land were somehow outside the law. Jack had lost count of the tepee-like dens, stained mattresses and secret camps he had stumbled on in such places over the years. He always left them untouched.

His own childhood was almost entirely lost to him now. It had lingered on in his memory for a little while like a contrail in a clear sky, growing fainter and fainter, until now, when he thought about the past, he thought less of his own and more of the line of men who had gone before him, a dim procession out of some dark history, their future uncertain.

Nearly dusk. Jack sat up slowly, working the knots out of his neck and shoulders. Was he actually being looked for? Maybe, maybe not. He was supposed to be on a doorstep curfew, required to sleep every night at the hostel in London for the next two months. But he could no more survive in a city than a swallow could live underwater.

He'd spent much of the day trying to find a lane marked by a line of oaks with double trunks that he'd heard about from a gypsy family he'd travelled with years back. They'd told him their forefathers buried children with an acorn in each hand, and that this lane marked a succession of stillbirths born to one woman many years before. Now he was in the area he'd wanted to see the twinned trees and pay his respects, but although he knew it was somewhere nearby he couldn't find it. When he'd heard a distant siren he'd decided to slip away and find somewhere to rest for a few hours.

Now he took a notebook out of his pack, unwound the rubber band that clasped a biro to it and tried to write down some of the things he'd seen that day in case they might make a ballad or a poem, but the rhythms wouldn't come. Instead, he flicked back through its pages: scribbled observations, metaphors, flights of near-visionary fancy. 'Half mad,' he muttered to himself. 'More'n half.'

Before putting his boots on he checked his socks and trouser turn-ups for ticks, rolled up his sleeping bag and stashed it away. Then he shouldered his pack and made his way out of the wood towards the cooling towers. There was a river on the other side of the golf course where mayflies would probably be emerging; if there weren't too many fishermen around he had a good chance of a couple of brown trout.

Behind him, bats began to hunt the clearing where he had slept as the red sun slipped slowly behind the trees.

Not far away, in Ardleton, the television's cold light was flickering across the seamed landscape of James Albert Hirons' face. He sat looking past it, unseeing; thinking instead of the lurcher puppy that Edith had taken in rather than see drowned in a bucket. Tess, Edith had called her; she had such soft ears, that dog, and he smiled now to remember them. She'd had a kennel in the garden, but when she got old and her back legs began to go he'd relented and folded up a blanket for her by the range. One clear, ice-bound winter night not long after Gillian had started school Tess had kept asking and asking to go outside, but every time he opened the back door she just dragged herself to the flower bed, out of the way, and lay down. Three times he'd carried her back in, knowing but refusing to know what was happening; she'd died in the kitchen the next day.

And he thought about when he and Gillian's boy used to go

dipping in the ponds and canals for old iron. How the lad had loved it; it was funny the things that fascinated you as a child. He probably didn't even remember it now, great lanky beanpole that he was. Still, it had done the child good to get him out of that house from time to time. Not that his father wasn't a good man, but Gillian had them all wrapped around her little finger with those nerves of hers.

She'd always been needy, though, all the way through her childhood: always crying or poorly, something wrong with her every day, it had seemed. It wasn't him she'd got it from – after all, you couldn't have behaved like that in Changi, you wouldn't have lasted five minutes.

He'd had a friend in the camp, Stan, a Lincolnshire lad a few years younger than he was. One day they were all moved, without warning, from their attap huts to the prison itself. The stone cells were tiny and crawling with rats and lice, and when the guard locked the door behind them Stan had broken down and sobbed. He'd never forgotten how the other two men in the cell had turned away, pretending not to see, as though Stan's distress was contemptible – or even worse, contagious.

After a while the old man slept and dreamed he was a little boy again, stumbling behind his father who was sowing, his right hand, brown from the sun, broadcasting seeds from a hopper at his chest evenly onto Culverkeys' warm soil. He craned to see past his legs to the big tree ahead – and when he did he saw that the sun would soon go down behind its branches. 'We must go home,' he said, suddenly afraid; 'Dadda, night's coming.' But his father, deaf and half blinded by the Great War, strode on; and James saw that he was sowing mung beans, not barley, and that above him shone not the Plough but the Southern Cross. And then he heard the clanking sound of the harrow coming up fast behind, and he woke up in his chair, his father long gone, Edith and Tess too, the television stark and loud in the corner and his old heart frightened in his chest.

I O

Herb Robert. Bracken unfurling. Snakeshead fritillaries.

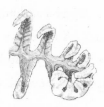

Chris arrived just before lunch on Saturday, announced by the crunch of his Mini's wheels on the gravel drive. It was a blustery, rainy May morning, the sunshine, when it came, blindingly bright on the wet roads before the sky darkened and another shower blew in.

'No thanks,' said Howard, as he always did, pretending to shut the door on his son where he stood on the mat, only to open it again and usher him in with a grin and a mock bow.

'Where's Mum?'

'Oh, she'll be down in a minute, I'm sure. She's got a bit of a headache. Said she was going to have a nap.'

While Chris took his coat off and hung it on the newel post, Howard took his son's bag to the study, where he would sleep.

As always when the kids visited he would be back in the master bedroom, with Kitty, something he had mixed feelings about.

'This for us?' he said, returning from the study with a bottle of Malbec in one hand. 'Shall we?'

'Oh, just a beer for me, Dad,' said Chris.

'Right you are. How's everything?'

While Howard poured the drinks, Chris began to tell him about the last month: a driver had left, problems with the IT system, and his continuing efforts to woo a new client, an electrical retailer with stores all over the south-west. It wasn't a move Howard would have made, but then, he wasn't running the firm any more.

'There's no money in the south-west, son,' he'd said when Chris first told him of the plan. 'It's all poverty down there, they're on EU grants, they're not buying bloody flatscreens. By all means go ahead, but don't bank on them surviving long.'

'Most of it's web-based, though, Dad,' Chris had said. 'Doesn't matter where the actual stores are any more. People know the laptop they want, they read the reviews online; if this lot can do it at the best price people order it. Doesn't matter where they are, or how well established, as long as it's mainland UK.'

Maybe he was right. It seemed a saturated market to Howard, electrical; but then what did he know? And it had been part of Chris's business plan when he took over: twenty new UK clients to fund the container warehouse in Felixstowe he'd leased. The risk of it still made Howard's heart lurch sometimes, especially the way the country was going; but it wasn't his business any more.

'We need to offer proper freight handling if we don't want to be crowded out,' Chris had said; and he was probably right. 'If we can hold goods off the ship and get them out direct we can pull in bigger clients. We need to be scaling up, Dad. People aren't just going to stop wanting stuff all of a sudden. Someone has to get it to them; it might as well be us.'

'What about fuel – have you found another supplier?' Howard asked now. There was a diesel tank in the yard that was topped up by a tanker every week, but the cost had been climbing steadily.

'One or two are coming in a bit under, but there's no guarantee they won't go up too,' Chris said. 'I'm not sure it's worth changing. Plus we get good credit right now; it could take ages to build up a relationship with someone new.'

Howard nodded, held his peace. He would have changed supplier, more than once if necessary, kept the cost down month on month. But then, he hadn't been looking so far ahead; he'd been content for the firm to earn him a good income and pay the wages of his office staff and drivers. Old-fashioned, he knew. But still.

After lunch the three of them put on outdoor shoes and went out for a stroll. He and Kitty had gone for quite a few walks when they'd first moved to the village, but after a couple of months the habit had fallen away. Yet when the children visited it was a way to offer them something, a last remnant of family as well as a look at the countryside neither of them had on their own doorsteps.

Chris walked in the middle; Howard put his hands in his

pockets and thought about how they used to take him to the park when he was a toddler and swing him between them. It was as though his muscles still retained the memory of the little boy's weight, as though his hands could still feel the terrifying delicacy of his son's hand and wrist as between them they lofted him over puddles to his squeals of delight.

They passed the church with its massive yew, jumbled gravestones and simple war memorial marked with eleven names, and took the lane that led off past the vicarage onto the fields. Stiles from one field to the next were marked by yellow arrows; Howard thought of what Kitty had said the week before and wondered if perhaps this was one of her ancient paths, centuries old. If it was it didn't look like much.

In the distance the grey hulk of Babb Hill dominated the skyline; moving dots beneath the summit were either kites or hang-gliders, it was hard to tell. 'Blue remembered hills,' said Howard. It was one of the only lines of poetry he knew.

The fields were mostly just grass, still wet and heavy with the morning's dew. Every so often a tiny, pale moth would flutter uselessly before their approaching feet, and from one paddock a pair of horses regarded the three of them briefly before dipping their heads again as they crossed the top of the pasture and took the stile into the next field.

'I've been reading about one of the local legends,' said Kitty. She walked with her head down, almost shyly offering the topic to the two men. She had been quiet over lunch, Howard thought, but she seemed fine now.

'Oh yes?' said Chris. 'What's that?'

'Puck – a sort of hobgoblin, you know, or a fairy. Very ancient. Anyway, I thought I might use it for a painting one day.'

Howard looked quizzically at her profile as they walked, a glance he intended, at some level, for her to see. So far her paintings had all been of landscapes or flowers, and not particularly interesting ones to boot – so how a hobgoblin was supposed to come into it was a mystery.

'What's it all about, then?' asked Chris.

'Well, this goes back hundreds of years, of course. He lived on a farm near here – although I think there are lots of Puck stories from all over the country, actually. Anyway, this one goes that in return for a tenth of everything the farmer harvested Puck made sure that everything grew: the crops never failed, the well didn't dry up, the animals didn't get sick. He wouldn't cross the threshold into the farmhouse, or do any of his magic on people, but he brought fertility to the land and the animals so the farm prospered, even in bad years.'

'Sounds like a witch, more like,' said Howard. 'Or he made a pact with the Devil.'

'No, he wasn't evil, not at all – though he wasn't exactly good, either. Anyway, after a while the farmer got greedy; he started to wonder why he should have to give a tenth of his harvest away. So he began keeping back some of the sheaves. Puck found out, of course, and when he did he turned into a hare and ran away. But before he went he cursed the farmer and the land, and since then all sorts of misfortunes have been blamed on him.'

'Like what?' asked Chris.

'Oh, you know. Cows' milk drying up, haystacks burning down. And there's an old track where he's said to appear from time to time, demanding that the farmer honour their bargain. Anyway, I thought I might go and have a look at it later this week. I don't know, I like these old stories. They're part of what makes one place different to another.'

'Even if all the stories are the same?' Howard chipped in. 'I mean, if you collected together all the mischievous fairies, black dogs and, I don't know, haunted houses from all over the country, you'd soon see they're all of a type – just ways of explaining what was unexplainable back then. Fortunately,' he continued, turning to Chris with a grin, 'we have science now.'

'Oh, I don't know, Dad. It must have been amazing growing up in those times: there'd be a story attached to every cave, every rock, every tree. It wouldn't be, you know, *there are some trees* –' Chris waved an arm at the general view – 'and we know everything there is to know about them, though hardly anyone actually bothers to learn their names. It would be a case of, this tree, this *oak* tree, has a wicked witch in it, this willow tree is magic –'

'Rowan,' said Kitty, taking her son's arm. 'Rowan trees are magic. You wouldn't dare to cut one down. Elder trees some-times had witches in them. And hollies were planted in the hedges to show you where to turn the plough. It wasn't all magic, you see, but everything meant something. It still does, we just don't know how to see it any more. I think it's a shame.'

Howard looked out across the workaday landscape of fields

and roads. It was hard to imagine it all being suffused with magic and meaning.

'So how are you going to paint him?' he asked. 'This Puck?'

'I'm not going to paint Puck himself,' she replied. 'I just want to go and see the path the legend talks about. I don't know, I feel as though I've been wanting to paint the countryside for years. And now we're actually in it I want it to mean something, not just . . . look pretty. Do you know what I mean?'

'But you have been painting it,' said Howard. 'You're out there twice, three times a week.'

'I know. I just . . . it's complicated,' she said.

It had been a miserable, wet winter, and there were still signs of it all around: many of the farm tracks were thick with mud, though it had dried now to a hard crust, and some of the old holloways that doubled as watercourses off the higher ground were still blocked with stones and branches.

The soil had quickly become waterlogged and the dairymen had taken the herds in early; some of the arable farmers with low-lying land hadn't been able to drill for winter wheat, the fields were so wet. Those on higher ground had gone ahead, but just before Christmas a day of battering rain had flooded the newly sown crop out of the fields and leached the fertiliser from the soil. Much of the wheat around Lodeshill and Crowmere had had to be resown.

Normally Philip Harland's herd would have been grazing the pasture Howard, Kitty and Chris were walking through; without them the grass had grown tall and lush. Trails through it were evidence of the secret lives of badgers and foxes, and here and there lay the clustered droppings of deer. The route they were following took them onto a narrow road green with moss in the centre and flanked by a bright rivulet of water for a hundred yards; then they would turn left through a farm gate, cross another field diagonally and pass a farm on the right. From there it was possible to pick up the road again into Lodeshill.

But once Howard had secured the gate behind them he turned to find that Kitty and Chris had stopped. The field ahead was full of farming equipment: two tractors, one of them huge, one smaller and older, two quad bikes, a trailer and some other huge machines and attachments that they didn't recognise. There were several very old, rusty contraptions that looked as though they had recently been torn from the undergrowth, a pile of what looked like car and tractor parts and another of tools, a set of startlingly white uPVC windows, a couple of dozen blue sacks of something, coils of fencing wire and mesh, a stack of ladders and more, filling the field and marching away from them towards the farm buildings.

'Oh – I wonder what's going on,' Kitty said, surveying the field.

'Spring-cleaning the barn?' said Chris.

'It'll be a farm sale,' said Howard. 'He must be selling up. They'll be getting rid of all this – if some bugger doesn't nick it first.'

'I'm sure there's a twelve-bore trained on it from the

farmhouse, you know what these farmers are like. Is it all just farm stuff, though, d'you think? Anything good?'

'Don't know. Maybe. Sometimes they do the house contents too; depends if they're taking it with them somewhere else, or it's an old boy who's hung up his boots.'

'You should stop in,' said Chris. 'See if there's anything worth having.'

'I was thinking just the same thing. Long shot, but you never know. Old wirelesses often get binned when people move house, but these farmers, you see, they don't move. They stay put for donkey's years, you know? Could well be one in there, hiding away.'

'It'll be in the parish newsletter,' said Kitty, turning her back on it all. 'The auction. We can look it up when we get back.'

'Do you hear much from your sister?' Howard asked Chris as they skirted the last field and made for the road.

'Not a lot. She called a couple of weeks ago, but that's it. Mum said she's still complaining about her flatmates.'

'Yes, coming in at all hours, apparently. She has to get up early for work.'

'Out having fun, are they? Can't have that.'

'I know, I know, and you're right: she's still young, perhaps she should be having more fun herself. But she's *driven*, you know. Not like I was at that age. Anyway,' he continued, fixing Chris with a sly grin, 'speaking of fun, when do we get to meet her?'

'I'm not seeing anyone right now, Dad, you know that.'

'Oh come on. Course you are.'

'Nope.'

'No more Internet dates?'

'Not right now. What is this – are you after grandchildren all of a sudden?'

'Not me, your mum,' he said. 'She'd make a terrific grandma.' He felt, rather than saw, Kitty wince at the word. It was true, though; she'd love it. Give her a bit of purpose again, even if she didn't like the terminology.

'God, I hope Jen gets this kind of treatment when she comes back,' Chris grumbled, but good-humouredly.

They took the lane back three abreast as the sky above them cleared to blue and a breeze shook the last raindrops from the sycamores at the side of the road.

When they got back to the house Howard and Chris went up to the radio room. When Chris was ten or eleven Howard had bought him a crystal and a cat's whisker detector and showed him how to build a simple receiver. He still remembered fitting his old piezo earpieces gently to his son's ears and watching his face as the hissing turned to whines, undersea mutters and, finally, speech. Chris hadn't been able to believe that something with no batteries, no slick plastic housing and no fancy logo could let him listen to the radio, even if it was only AM.

As he got older he had preferred listening to dance music in his bedroom, but whenever Howard got hold of a new wireless he'd always found a reason to drift out to the garage and stand at his dad's elbow as he got into the cabinet and had a look at the circuit – although, had he been asked, he would doubtless have said it was boring.

Now, Howard switched on the craft light and swung it out over the Marconi he was working on. Chris pulled the spare stool out from under the counter and sat down. They sat in silence for a while, the only sound the faint rasp of Howard's screwdriver as he tried to remove the front of the cabinet – and, after a while, the distant sound of church bells. Carefully, Howard put the cabinet down, gave Chris a tiny screw to hold and closed the window.

'Dad, you know when Jenny comes back in a couple of weeks?'

Howard was trying not to damage the 'M' on the speaker grille. It was rare to find one with the M intact, so it would be irritating to chip it now. He flicked a glance at his son, then peered through the ring of the craft light again.

'Don't tell me you can't make it. Your mother's got a big welcome-home dinner planned. She'll hit the roof.'

'I know, I know. It's just – remember Glen, from school?'

'Glen, Glen, never again?'

'It's his stag do.'

'Is it! Little Glen, getting married. Well I never.'

'I'm not the best man, I don't have to go.'

'But you want to.'

'Which day are you having the meal for Jenny?'

'We're picking her up on the Friday night – well, Saturday morning, really. So your mum wanted us all together on the Saturday night. And – I do, too. I want it to be nice. Family, you know?' As Howard said it he could feel his throat unexpectedly

88

tighten. Bloody fool, he thought; what the hell was there to get upset about?

'Don't you think Jenny'll be tired?'

'Look, I'll speak to your mother,' Howard said. 'Maybe we could do it on the Sunday instead. It would mean you staying Sunday night, though, and I don't want you getting in trouble with the boss.'

Chris grinned. 'Shouldn't be a problem.'

'She'll doubtless want to go to church, but we can always help to peel the veg.'

'She's still going, then?' asked Chris.

'Oh yes.'

'Have you been at all?'

'Nope.'

'No interest?'

'Course not. I can't understand it, you know. To find God, now. She was always such a rational woman. It just seems so . . . out of character. Anyway, I'll speak to her. Perhaps the vicar won't mind her missing one service.'

'Thanks, Dad.'

'Now, what do you think to this?' he said, holding up the speaker cloth, thick with three-quarters of a century of dust, cigarette smoke and God only knew what else. 'Clean it up? Or replace?'

I I

Ground ivy (hedge banks). Ash flowers.
Warm and sunny; breeze from the south-west shifting east.

There was sickness and sickness, Jack thought, pausing by the roadside and looking up at an ash. Always the heart-rot and bracket fungus and gall wasps and wood-boring beetles, the old to-and-fro. But now there was something else: a hand on the trunk and he could feel it, like sadness in an embrace. The ash trees were steeling themselves.

He remembered the graceful elms. So did the rooks; you could hear the loss of them in their chatter still. Things didn't always turn out as you feared, though; the countryside was still full of saplings, but fugitive, sheltered in hedgerows and abetted by taller trees. One day they might come back. It was something Jack tried to believe.

The ash was hung here and there with lilac and green frills: some flowers male, some female, and perhaps different again next year – and it was that indiscrimination that would save it, if anything could. Above Jack great tits picked caterpillars from its leaves, and a slate-blue nuthatch decanted itself like a shot cork from a hole.

Oak before ash, around here at least. This year, and for another few years to come, he thought, the lovely pinnate leaves would burst bud and cast the road surface in shifting, moving shade. For now, though, the noon sun drew the bare branches starkly on the ground.

On the other side of Connorville Jack briefly regained the old Roman road; it was a warm May morning and the tarmac ahead shimmered with mirages, pools of water forming and re-forming far away. *Not far to go now*, he thought, *not far to go*.

A speed-limit sign had two bunches of rotting flowers secured with cable ties to its grey post. Jack tried to read the card which hung from one bouquet by a twist of lilac ribbon, but it was wrinkled and faded, and although he could see there were some faint letters remaining he could not get the sense from them. He tried instead to picture what had happened, but it wouldn't come.

The road sign itself wasn't damaged, and was probably just a convenient place to make a shrine rather than the site of the accident itself – which was, in fact, fifty yards further on, not far from the place where, in less than two weeks, another collision would leave two cars spent and ravished, violence gathered about them in the dawn light, coins and CDs spilled across the road where Jack now stood. He felt briefly cold, as when a chill current finds you in the warmer sea, and walked on.

The cars seemed to speed past him in groups with long pauses in between, so that when a piebald cob trotted by pulling a sulky with a bare-chested boy in the seat, Jack could believe for a moment that he was in another time. But although he had often camped with them, he knew that with travellers often came police, and he decided to get off the road.

He vaulted a gate on which a home-made sign read 'Ardleton Allotments' in defiance of Connorville's acquisitive town planners. He liked allotments, always had. There was something a little anarchic about them: strawberries growing in a pile of car tyres, a shed made from pallets, a greenhouse full of tidy rows of cannabis plants. He thought about the old home fields these allotments could well be built on, and the long-dead villagers, each with their strip to subsist from: carrots, onions, broad beans, lettuces. Some things endured, didn't they? Although the context changed.

There were too many people about for Jack to risk taking anything to eat, and he wondered if it was a weekend. A woman weeding some raised beds gave him a hard stare, and he guessed he'd been talking aloud. He still couldn't afford to be noticed, and he frowned and shook his head as he walked on: *stupid, stupid*. He had to concentrate, sometimes, to remember how normal people were supposed to behave.

There was a railway track on the other side of the allotments:

he could feel it like a ley line, a change in the way the light and the wind were organised. Jack hadn't been on a train since he was a child, and he wondered if he would again one day – if he'd ever need to get somewhere faster than he could walk. It seemed unlikely. Even so, he liked railways: the desecration their coming had once threatened was for the most part long healed, and like many motorways, their margins buzzed with life and formed corridors along which that life could travel. Abandoned lines quickly returned to nature, or formed their own layer in the palimpsest of paths and routes that crossed the country, joining places whose significance was passing out of common memory.

He threaded his way through the allotment plots to find only a line of scrub and a chain-link fence between himself and the track. Throwing his pack over, he swung himself down onto the ballast, the pale stones radiating heat so that walking on them was warmer than walking beside the track. The line wouldn't take him all the way to Lodeshill, he knew, but he'd walk it a little way. There wasn't that much further to go.

His mind, having always had a lyrical bent and being ready again find its voice, gave him rough iambs that matched his footfall on the stones, a song that might later find its way into one of his notebooks or might simply vanish, the evanescent narrative we each trail behind us like the faint disturbance of air from a sparrow's wing as it flies: barely felt, touching little, and soon lost:

O see the crow there as he unseats him
from the railway bank and hoists himself up
by the sheer incredulous power of
his ratcheting wings and then flap, flap, flap,
a caw for me as he cranks overhead
and lugs himself to the ash where he sits
and hunches and brags to himself in beady silhouette.
I used to know him —

Why do I think now of how a struck flame
feels in the hand, how the massed black feathers
in the roost shield the flock there from the wind?
O but a winter night is long for every living creature
to withstand . . .

The air had become heavy, distances appearing flat, and he could
smell on the wind that the weather was changing.

12

Milkwort, cranesbill. Pedunculate oaks –
first flower tassels. Spring weather: sunshine and showers.

Chris left after lunch on Sunday, and as soon as he had gone
Howard got on the road and headed west along the Boundway.
He'd had word a few days before, through a fellow enthusiast, of
an old electrical shop in Wales that had closed; the grandson had
discovered the stockroom stacked with returns and unclaimed
repairs going back three generations. The chap who'd put
Howard on to it collected gramophones, not radios, so had been
happy to pass on the tip. Howard was hoping for some lead
solder, at least; you couldn't buy it any more, so places like this
were useful sources. He wondered who else would turn up.

Many of the other collectors he knew were real nostalgia
buffs; some were into all things wartime, some still considered

the 1950s a kind of golden age. One chap had been in the army, Royal Signals; he'd got into radios that way. Another – a big-time collector who'd turned his house into a virtual museum – had worked for the BBC all his life. Howard was the only one he knew of whose route into vintage wirelesses had been via the music industry. Not that he'd ever been an actual musician, but working for bands was how he'd first learned about audio. Not long after his O levels a lad called Len who he'd known a bit at school had asked him to drive a van for him for a week. He was in a band: some crap name Howard couldn't even remember any more. Howard had spent six months with them: Harlow, Oxford, Windsor, Basingstoke. He would set up the speakers, ensure the amps and the guitar pedals were working. There wasn't any money in it, not really, but it was easy, and more than that he enjoyed it, liked walking into a venue carrying the stuff, liked being able to see what went on behind the scenes. Something about belonging: about having a backstage pass, going through a door where others couldn't. Pathetic, really.

The band split, predictably enough; they owed him money, so Howard had taken the old Morris as payment and gone to work for another lot. By late '73 he had a decent van and was roadying for a band called Burning Rubber, who had an actual album out and a single that was getting some serious airtime. He could set up in under half an hour if he had to, he knew his way around a lighting rig and he'd learned how to tune guitars, too. He'd loved being on the road, travelling from place to place like some kind of vagabond; but even then he could see that you couldn't spend your entire life like that. The older roadies he knew were pretty sad, on the whole, with their tics and scars, and the stupid sobriquets they insisted on. Sometimes he'd found himself looking at them and wondering why they hadn't just ... you know, got a life.

One night he met Kitty at a gig in Luton, or was it Bedford? It was hard to remember now. She'd been dragged there by a couple of friends; they were giggly, excited about meeting the band. She kept herself apart a bit, seemed to be taking everything in. He'd admired that, for some reason.

They started to go out together; he was proud to have her with him, she was different from the other girls he'd been with. It bothered him a bit that she wasn't into music; not just the music he liked, but any music at all. But it wasn't the most important thing in the world – in fact, it was something he'd probably grow out of himself one day, he'd thought, and anyway, no relationship was perfect. The important thing was that she told him there was more to him than roadying, that there were things he could achieve. He was still only twenty-two, and he knew she was right.

Before long he'd chucked the roadying in, found a semi in Wood Green with a big parking apron and Talling's Vans – later Talent Haulage – was born. Settling down felt right; it was what people did – although for a while he'd considered having a go at lighting, or even sound engineering. He missed having a stake in that world, being a bit different to everyone else. Why it should have mattered he couldn't really have said.

They got married in 1980, and Chris had come along a year later; once Jenny was born they'd moved to Finchley, where they'd stayed. It was a suburban existence, full of the ordinary pressures and triumphs, but it was a long time before he had stopped following Burning Rubber in the music papers and admitted to himself he was a man who owned a fleet of vans and nothing more.

Then one day, when Chris was still a toddler, he'd bought his first vintage wireless – more by accident than design. He was passing an antiques shop on Essex Road on the way to a pub, and outside on the pavement was a hatstand hung with gas masks, a mannequin in a 1940s dress and, on a chair, an Ekco SH25 with its iconic fretwork grille showing the silhouette of a tree on a riverbank. Incongruously, it was playing 'Sunshine of Your Love', and he'd been stopped in his tracks by the contrast between the wartime set and the sixties anthem coming out of it, and the vast gulf – far more than twenty-five years, it seemed – that separated them. He'd paid way over the odds for the radio, he knew now, but it hadn't seemed like much at the time for a fully functioning slice of history.

When he got it home he'd taken it apart straight away to have a look at how it was wired. It was so simple, so intelligible. He went back to the shop the next day and asked the owner where she had got it. She put him in touch with a restorer in Kentish Town, and not long afterwards he went to his first swap meet. It was a small world, but that just helped make it navigable. He had seen immediately that it was something he could belong to.

★   ★   ★

Howard made good time, beating the satnav's estimation by nearly twenty minutes. When he got out of the car jackdaws jinked and quacked above the narrow streets, and the Welsh air, washed by showers, smelled sweet.

He found the old electrical shop with some difficulty; he hadn't realised that the premises had already been sold, its signage and facade replaced with a new plate-glass window framed in red. Howard wondered what it was going to be: a pizza place? a mobile phone shop? There was no way to tell. Kitty often talked about how towns all looked the same these days, the same shops everywhere. But you couldn't hold back progress, and anyway, it was what people wanted.

Tinny music filtered out though the door, which had been propped open. The floor had been taken back to bare screed and a man in overalls was replastering one of the walls. Howard knocked on the glass frontage and stepped inside.

Grubby marks on the walls spoke of shelves packed closely together, and without the new plate-glass front it had probably been very dim. Without acknowledging him, the workman yelled 'Gary! *Gaaaaary!*' towards the back of the empty shop. Howard glanced again at his sheet of notepaper before folding it up and returning it to his pocket.

A big man bustled in through a doorway from which the door had been removed and left leaning against a wall. 'Mr Williams?' said Howard, taking the initiative and holding out his hand. 'I'm Howard Talling. I've come to take a look at your old radios.'

The man shook his hand warmly. 'Call me Gary,' he said. 'Oh, we've got a treat for you here. Follow me.'

Howard rather doubted it, and in any case it didn't do to look too keen. 'Let's hope so,' he said, following him towards the back of the shop. 'I don't want to get your hopes up, though. Many of these old sets are quite common.'

'Oh yes, well, you take a look and tell me what you think.'

Howard had expected a dim stockroom somewhere behind the counter, so when they had gone through the door at the back of the shop he was surprised to be directed upstairs. 'I'll leave you to it, then,' Gary said. 'I'll be down here, in the kitchen. I've got a brew on if you want.'

'Oh – very kind, but I won't,' said Howard, starting up the wooden stairs. 'It's all . . . safe up here, I suppose?'

'Oh yes, quite safe. You'll be fine.'

The stairs were narrow and dusty and marked here and there with paint. Each tread had a tidemark of old varnish worn away by feet to leave a rough half-moon. At the top was a landing of bare boards with a small lavatory leading off it, and three doors with iron doorknobs. He chose one at random.

The room had free-standing wooden shelves against three walls, one set in front of a sash window which had been painted out. The other wall, still hung with faded floral paper peeling gently from the top, had a chimney breast and a small fireplace with an iron grate. Howard looked around and found the old-fashioned light switch; a bare bulb illuminated the room.

One of the sets of shelves was almost empty, although the

pattern of dust showed where objects had been removed. Howard guessed it was where the gramophones and radiograms had been stored. The other two sets were neatly stacked: there were small cardboard boxes of the type once used to hold screws, a wooden crate full of batteries and coils of wire, a cardboard box full of components and perhaps two dozen old radios, a couple still in their original, flyblown boxes. Already Howard could see a post-war Little Maestro, a blue Dansette Gem and a couple of early-sixties transistors; they were no good to him, but if he could pick them up at a decent price he could probably sell or trade them. And on the next shelf up was the familiar rounded back of what was surely a Philco People's Set. He got his pocket camera out, switched on the flash and began photographing the shelves. It was important to have a record before he started moving everything around.

He came downstairs an hour later to find Gary watching TV on a laptop in the shop's kitchen. He closed the lid down when Howard came in.

'Want to wash up?'

'Please.' Howard smiled and made for the sink with its two tin taps and sliver of cracked soap. The water was icy cold.

He dried his hands on his handkerchief and got out his notebook.

'Well, I told you it was worth the trip, eh?' said Gary, nodding eagerly at him. Howard consulted his notes more thoroughly than was strictly required. He'd sorted the wirelesses into two groups and made a third pile of parts and other bits and pieces that he could make use of. Most of the sets were so obscure that only a collector would know their market value; three, though, were well known enough that Gary could have an idea of what they were worth. Trying to stiff him on them could be a mistake; he might as well give him a good price and hope to get away with the rest.

'There are three really good sets up there, as you know,' he said – this was flattery, plain and simple – 'the Hastings, the Bush and the Philco. The Hastings isn't really my period – it's post-war, of course, but it's a nice example, so I'll make an exception. I'll give you forty for it. The Bush – you see them a fair bit, but the Bakelite's in good nick so again, I'll give you forty. The Philco, well, I'm sure you've done your homework. I'll give you a hundred for it.'

Gary looked briefly surprised. 'So that's . . . let's say two hundred, shall we? Now, what about the rest?'

Howard raised an eyebrow, but conceded. 'The rest, well, not so good. A lot of them are what I call "car boot" wirelesses; you might get a quid or two each for them at a boot sale. And a lot of them are fifties and sixties, which isn't my period. I was hoping for some solder, but I suppose that's gone.'

'Your mate took that,' said Gary. 'What about all the parts and the equipment?'

'I can probably put you on to someone.'

Gary considered for a moment. Work on the shop was clearly moving on apace, something Howard had taken very much into consideration. 'So you only want the three?'

'You should take the rest to a boot sale. On a good day, with a following wind, you might get rid of them that way.'

'Tell you what. Give me three hundred and you can take the lot.'

'Like I say, Gary, the post-war stuff isn't really my thing.'

'Two fifty.'

'Got a couple of cardboard boxes?'

Driving back Howard could barely believe what he'd pulled off. In the boot of the Audi were eight pre-war wirelesses – all models he'd be happy to have in his collection – plus two slightly damaged cabinets and a box of valves, knobs, capacitors, batteries and other components. There were sixteen more modern radios that he could probably sell or trade – three in their original boxes – two signal generators, an oscilloscope worth a hundred quid on its own, an avometer and a valve tester. On the seat next to him was a cardboard wavelength calculator, some ancient editions of the *Radio Times* and a couple of old receiving licences. Things like that were worth nothing, of course, but it might be fun to frame them and put them up on the wall of the radio room.

The showers had cleared to leave a warm evening in their wake, and through the windscreen Howard could see a hot-air balloon making the most of the thermals over Babb Hill. Rumour had it that due to some quirk of geography the locals up there sometimes got Radio Moscow coming out of their TVs and radios when the weather was right – although like all such things it was probably a myth.

I'll get a battery in that Dansette, he thought, and I'll take it up there one fine, dry night and find out.

Jack was toiling slowly up a path beside the young wheat when he saw Howard's headlights flash out once as he turned off the Boundway towards the village. The field margins were coming alive around him, and it was the time of day Jack liked best. As the air cooled it was as though the young wheat exhaled, and he could smell the day's sunshine on its breath.

It made him realise he was hungry: perhaps someone in Lodeshill grew vegetables, he thought, or perhaps the pub left their bin store unlocked. He would sleep in the little wood by the village tonight, he decided, and tomorrow he would visit the farms and find out if the asparagus was ready to pick.

As he reached the top of the rise a church bell began to toll, the old notes rolling out slowly over the darkening landscape. Jack crossed a stile onto a narrow lane that ran between the rectory's garden and a paddock in which two horses stood as still as statues in the dusk. Ahead, the church spire marked Lodeshill's position against the sky.

A second note joined the first, increasing in urgency, tolling the living and long-gone villagers in from the fields and farms as it had done for century upon century, gathering them in as night fell. Jack did not want anyone to see him and so he slipped into a quiet garden where he stood bell-struck, eyes closed, feeling the pull of the little church with its porch light and thinking about what it would mean to go in.

After a while the notes became again a single toll, like a passing bell, and then slowed, and stopped. The little village was folded again in silence, and the paths and roads seemed darker than before. Jack lingered until a blackbird scolded him from a magnolia, and when he moved on his face was wet with tears.

St James's drew a regular congregation of about fifteen, though it swelled quite a lot at Christmas, and a little at Easter, too. But the monthly evensong was a different matter – which seemed a shame to Kitty, as it was by far her favourite service.

That night there were only four other worshippers: the churchwardens Bill Drew and George Jefferies, who rang the bell together; Bill's wife Jean, who always had some morsel of village gossip for Kitty and would not be dissuaded; and one of the village farmers, a bent man now in his seventies who looked as though he could very well have tied his plough horse to the lychgate outside. They sat together at the front of the darkened church, except the farmer, who always took the rear pew no matter which service he attended.

When the bell's last note had died away Bill switched the sidelights on and walked up the aisle, turned to them and said, 'Alleluia. Christ is risen.' 'The Lord is risen indeed,' they replied.

The service was short but had a simplicity that moved Kitty in ways some of the grander church occasions never did. It was a coming together of neighbours as darkness fell, and carried with it a flavour of a time when prayer was much more necessary, life's dangers being so very great. She looked at the familiar heads around her, bowed in prayer, and wondered what these ordinary village people confided to their God in the silence of their hearts, and what answer they received. Once or twice she had peeked at the folded notes tucked into the prayer board at the back of the church; they were never anything but heartbreaking. 'Pray for Gladys who has cancer'; 'Please pray that my son will come home safely'; or, simply, 'Pray for John'.

Now she thought about her fall in the field – the momentary numbness, the frightening sense that her legs had for a moment actually become absent – and tried to imagine writing such a note herself.

Although she did not believe in God, neither could she remain silent when the Creed was spoken. The lovely words had a resonance far beyond their literal meaning, and if the calm that she received from them was not the peace of Christ, it was enough.

The old farmer could recite each service without reference to a prayer book, and she could hear him now, calmly intoning the third collect from the dim pew behind her in his cracked country burr:

'Lighten our darkness, we beseech thee, O Lord; and by thy great mercy defend us from all perils and dangers of this night; for the love of thy only son, our saviour, Jesus Christ. Amen.'

At the close of the service they sang the *Te Deum*, Bill's wife giving the first note before their five untrained voices wavered through Britten's lovely setting. At first Kitty had wondered why they bothered with hymns when the congregation for evensong was so small, but as time went one she'd come to respect the awkward honesty of the few hesitant yet brave voices setting off to do justice to the well-loved tunes, and the way that by the final line they had woven together to carry it to its close in something like triumph.

George Jefferies was in his late seventies and growing too confused and forgetful to lead the services at church. In fact, his duties beyond distributing and collecting up the prayer books were now few; but it was unlikely that he would be relieved of his role of churchwarden, which was not just a duty of his faith but a cornerstone of his life since his wife had passed away. The vicar's wife called in on him once a week, and it was she and Jean who had arranged his meals on wheels and home help; Christine Hawton had found a local lad to mow his lawn and weed the beds, too.

Like many elderly people, George retained the persona he had presented to the world for his entire adult life – in his case, one of affable jocularity – though the animus that sustained it had shrunk slowly away, so that beyond his habitual friendly greeting he usually had very little to say. Kitty had learned not to push him beyond his capabilities or try to engage him too much in conversation; it was clear, some days, that he wasn't sure who she was, and on others that, while he was happy enough to greet her by name, his interest in small talk or village happenings had long since receded. So she was surprised when he touched her arm as the little group filed out of the porch and into the soft evening air.

'You, er . . .' he began.

'Hello, George. How are you?'

'Very well, thank you. Yes.'

'Would you like me to walk you home?'

'Oh no, quite all right. Quite all right. I just wanted to mention – that chap, you know, the one who Jean saw at the allotments . . .'

Kitty was momentarily confused. She had had a brief chat with Bill's wife before the service, mostly about the farm that was up for sale, but hadn't realised that George had overheard. More importantly, she'd dismissed Jean's mention of a suspicious man as idle gossip, something Jean always loved to impart.

'Jean thought someone might be sleeping rough nearby, George, that's all.'

'Yes. Now, is it a vagrant of some kind? Homeless?'

'I'm not sure, George. Why, are you worried?'

'I saw him as well. Or at least . . . I think I did. In my garden.'

'In your garden? Are you sure?'

'Oh yes, it gave me quite a start. For a moment I thought it was Margaret, you know; she had a lovely voice. Did you know my wife, or . . .?'

'When was this?' Kitty was trying hard to keep an uncharitable note of scepticism out of her voice.

'Oh, she passed away . . . some time ago now.'

'I'm sorry, George. I meant, when did you see the man? The one in your garden?'

'Earlier on. Or perhaps – no, it was definitely today. Yes, just before the service.'

'And you're sure?'

'Oh yes. Quite sure. And I was wondering, is he dangerous?'

'Why – what was he doing?'

'Well, this is it, you see; that's just it. He was singing.'

Howard was watching the motor racing when Kitty got back from church. She looked, as she came in, almost guilty, he thought; and for a moment he felt guilty himself, that he had caused his wife to feel ashamed of something so harmless as going to evensong. Perhaps if she didn't give him a hard time about going to the pub now and then, though. Perhaps then he wouldn't be on the back bloody foot all the time.

'How was church?' he asked, and then, 'I'll set the table,' without waiting for her to answer. 'I'm having a beer. Glass of wine?'

'Just a spritzer, please. And let's have the television off,' Kitty called through from the kitchen. Howard pretended not to hear.

'That farm sale's on Tuesday,' he said, making for the pantry. 'I had a look in the parish newsletter. They're doing the house contents too. Culverkeys, it's called.'

'Oh yes, I meant to say,' said Kitty, something in her voice giving him pause. 'He – it was a suicide. The farmer. Jean Drew told me.'

Howard turned at the pantry door, came back. 'He *killed* himself? Jesus. How old was he?'

'Fifty-seven.'

'How –'

'I didn't ask.'

'No. Of course.' Howard tried, and failed, to stop himself picturing it: a noose in the barn, a shotgun in the kitchen; one of those things they used to stun cattle. 'Christ. Same age as me.'

'I know.'

'Kids?'

'Two. And an ex-wife.'

'Why? I mean – why'd he do it?'

'It's a tough life, being a farmer. No money in it.'

'Oh come on, they're raking in the subsidies, all of them. Must be more to it than that.'

Kitty sighed. 'Maybe he missed his wife and kids, Howard. Maybe he had depression – who knows. Anyway, Jean's worried they'll put up a lot of houses there – she said that a while back this whole area got earmarked for development.'

Kitty's default position was to oppose any new building in the countryside, something Howard often needled her about. 'The population is expanding,' he'd say. 'Where are people supposed to live?' But the news about the farmer's suicide had left him shaken, and he felt, childishly, that he wanted people to be kind to him, and that he must be kind in turn.

'Let's hope they don't. This is a lovely village,' he said, drawing a look of almost grateful surprise from Kitty.

'Are you still going to go to the sale?' she asked. Howard could tell she didn't want him to, but he realised, now, that they were in accord.

'No. I – it doesn't seem right.'

'No, I can see that,' she replied with a nod.

Howard disappeared into the pantry and returned with a bottle of wine. 'I hope not everyone feels the same, though,' he said, rummaging in a drawer for the corkscrew; 'I mean, the family will need people to bid on all that stuff.'

'Yes, but – we're incomers,' said Kitty, articulating the thought with some difficulty. 'It would be like – like souvenir-hunting, to go over there and carry things off. It's one thing the other farmers buying things they need, and even strangers coming, people who have no idea at all about what happened. But for us – I don't know. It's just – it's not our place.'

I 3

Garlic mustard. Brimstone butterflies. Crab apples in bud.

The swallows that nested in the eaves of Manor Lodge bore the same genes as the ones who had built the first mud cups there nearly 150 years before; the swallows at the rectory went back even further. Every April they arrived in the village from Africa, lining up like musical notes on the telephone wires and swooping for beakfuls of mud from the banks of the dew pond on Culverkeys Farm to repair their nests. When they had first moved in Howard had complained about them shitting on the Audi, but Kitty said they brought happiness to a home. Now they just parked the cars a little further from the side wall.

Jamie stood on the drive and watched them circling the church spire and flickering over the rooftops. The swallows were part of the village; more so, even, than he was. What if the new owners of Culverkeys had the dew pond filled in?

He'd spent the morning at the farm sale, skulking at the back where nobody could see him. The turnout hadn't been that good, and he heard the auctioneers conferring about whether to delay the start a little; there was something, too, about a potential telephone bidder who couldn't be contacted. But at around half eleven they had gone ahead, one of the auctioneers getting up on the case tractor to take the bids. Both tractors made their reserves, as did the quads and the milking parlour; all the feed and some of the machinery went, including an antique winnowing machine and a chaff-cutter, both bought by a specialist dealer. The bids made by the taciturn farmers were barely discernable – or not to Jamie, anyway. Much remained unsold.

When the sale moved on to the house contents, arranged on the drive, the farmers drifted away; the twenty or so people who remained ranged from curious locals to car booters to a few bored-looking dealers. The oval dining table was sold separately to the chairs. The pictures went for a few pounds each.

After the sale Jamie couldn't wait to get away from the village, so he raced the bike around the lanes and along the Boundway for a while before his shift. He kept picturing the farmhouse's once-familiar rooms, silent and pillaged now, and wondering which one Alex's father had killed himself in.

That night, after work, he stopped in at the Green Man before going home. He wanted to know if there was any news about the farm.

When he was a little boy the Green Man had been much busier. He used to go there with his dad of an evening and they always sat at the same table; he'd have a Coke and some Skips and listen to the grown-ups talk. There used to be a dog there, a mangy Alsatian; it often lay under one of the bench seats and he'd crawl under there and give it crisps. He could still remember the feel of its fur under his hand: rough and soft at the same time. He'd liked the smell it left on his skin.

There was nobody in the pub back then that they didn't know. Everyone was either from Lodeshill or Crowmere, or had come with someone who was. It had its own characters and hierarchies: those whose opinion carried the most weight, those who were usually shouted down. Those who were always, whatever they said, mocked.

The Green Man's codes of behaviour were arcane and out of date, and although they were implicitly understood within the protected ecosystem of the pub they bore little relation to the shifting mores of the world outside. Women were tolerated as long as they didn't offer too many opinions, or try to join in with the banter. A slightly aggressive heterosexuality was the dominant note, and just as in school the aim of much of the conversation was simply to confirm and reconfirm the rightness, the normality of the regulars' opinions. It was a closed, inward-looking group, suspicious of change and suspicious of any kind of difference, and although it was utterly stifling Jamie had always believed that one day he'd be part of it.

Yet by the time he bought his first legal pint the Green Man was struggling. It wasn't just that the Bricklayer's in Crowmere had been done up, although that hadn't helped. His parents drank in front of the telly most evenings now, because it was cheaper – and they weren't the only ones. Some people said the pub should start doing proper food, that that was what customers wanted these days. Get a good chef in, build up a reputation, pull in people from the rest of the county – maybe further, even. But Jamie knew what his grandfather would have said to that, and he was probably right.

He took a deep breath and pushed open the door to the public bar. There were perhaps a dozen people there; more than he had expected, although it was far from full. Perhaps it was to do with the sale; maybe people wanted to discuss it, wanted to find out, like him, what was coming for the village.

For a few weeks after Philip Harland had killed himself the talk had all been of his death – whether something could or should have been done differently, and what exactly he had meant by the act – but two months on it was rarely spoken of directly, although it would be many more until it was fully absorbed into the fabric of their communal life.

'Pint please,' Jamie told Jim the landlord, digging in his jeans pocket for a fiver. Jim lived over the pub with a girl who had been a couple of years above Jamie at school; she'd been the local catch for a while, in the pub most nights all made up and with her hair bleached and straightened, but now she just looked like anyone. Jim's wife – better at business than him by far – had left long ago.

Jim put the pint down on a beer towel and rang up the sale without speaking. Jamie took a sip and looked around. 'Few people in,' he said.

'Yep.'

'Farm sale today, I suppose.'

'You go, did you?'

'No, I . . . Have you heard how it went?'

Jim shook his head. 'Could have been better. Though whatever's left'll get taken away soon enough, I suppose.'

'And then what?'

'Who knows, lad. Why don't you ask Harry? You know what gamekeepers are like. Ears to the ground. Speaking of which, I don't know if you want to make a few extra bob this year, but Nigel Gaster over there says he's about to start on his asparagus.'

'Thanks, Jim.' Jamie picked up his pint and took it carefully to a table. Harry, roaring with laughter at a table with Bill Drew and a couple of farmers, looked too far into his Scotch to be easily approachable. Jamie took a swallow of his pint and waited.

It had been an OK shift at work. Not too busy, which was good – although the day didn't go as fast if you were idle. And the blonde girl in the site office had smiled at him; Megan, she was called. He'd heard Lee say it.

'Me and Megan and a few of the others are going to the Vault on Friday night,' he'd said. They were on a fag break; Jamie didn't smoke, but he sometimes went outside with the smokers anyway. 'You in, Dicko?' Jamie had grinned and nodded, and Megan, shoulders up against the breeze, had smiled and blown out smoke. He'd been out for drinks with Lee a few times; he was a couple of years older, but he seemed sound enough. And he'd had a beer with Dave, the transport clerk, once; although Dave was older, more of a grown-up really. He probably wouldn't be coming out on Friday.

Now Jamie sipped his pint and thought about the Corsa. He'd talked about it once or twice at work; they knew he was working on a car, and that it was a bit special. What if he were to take it out on Friday? It wasn't finished yet, not really, but it was taxed and insured. An image came to him, dog-eared with use: the Corsa, full of friends and laughter, roaring away from the village down the Boundway, himself in the driving seat: James Dixon – not Dicko, or even Jamie any more. He held on to the picture for a moment before letting it go, like a coin touched for luck in a pocket. It would happen, it would be like that one day.

It wasn't long until last orders were called. When Harry Maddock got up and went to the bar Jamie drained the last of his pint and went to stand beside him.

'Harry.'

'Evening, lad.' Harry signalled to Jim for the same again, his elbow on the bar, a note between his fingers. 'Drink?'

'Oh, no thanks. Work tomorrow.'

'Work? You don't know you're born. I'm out rabbiting after this. Want to come?'

Jamie shook his head. 'Where's your assistant?'

'Don't know where the bugger is – his phone's switched off. Hold on there a sec.'

'OK.'

Jamie perched on a bar stool and watched as Harry took two halves of bitter back to his table. Bill Drew had left some time before, but the two farmers sat on.

He hadn't been out with Harry for a long time. After Alex had gone he hadn't wanted to set foot on Culverkeys any more; he'd got into *Grand Theft Auto* and *SimCity* instead, stopped helping Harry out, let it drift – so when he had taken on a trainee keeper, a lad in the year above Jamie at school, he hadn't even cared all that much. Messing about in the woods and stuff was for kids, he'd realised; and he'd had the Clio by then anyway.

And yet, when he'd heard that Culverkeys might be built over, he had felt utterly desolate; he still did. It was stupid, but he wanted it to be there, always: untouched and unchanging. The place he had loved as a kid.

Harry came back and leaned on the bar beside him. 'Culverkeys auction today.'

Jamie nodded. 'Heard it didn't go that well.'

'Could've been worse. Some of the old machinery did OK. You know what they use it for these days? Bloody town sculptures, that kind of thing. Stand it outside visitor centres. See that iron turntable they had? From a horse gin, that was. You'd rig a horse to it, have it go round and round and drive machinery off it. My dad can remember being set to throw stones at the horse's backside to stop it going to sleep. Your granddad too, no doubt. How is he, anyway?'

'Oh, you know. I'll bring him in sometime.'

'You should do that. Sure you won't give me a hand with the rabbits?'

'I can't, Harry. Sorry.'

'Ah well.'

'So − is it sold, then?'

'Not that I know. But the lawyers are playing their cards close to their chests.'

'Someone said about mining. That's not right, is it?'

'Depends who's got the mineral rights. I doubt it. Though the Coal Board does come sniffing around from time to time. Whatever it's called now.'

'The Coal Board? You serious?'

'Surface mining, lad. What do you think the landfill is, where your dad works? They were still getting coal out of that when I was a boy.'

Jamie pictured it: a big hole scooped out of the earth, then filled in again with people's rubbish. 'I never realised.'

'Surely your father must've said.'

'But *mining*: I thought all that was ages ago.'

'It's not all wind farms, lad. Not yet. Anyway, I've not heard anything about coal. I reckon the land'll be sold off piecemeal and someone'll buy the house, make it into a family home. That's where the money is these days.'

★   ★   ★

When Jamie got in his dad was still up, watching telly.

'Not seen much of you today,' he said as Jamie hung his jacket up in the hall. 'Did you stop in at your grandfather's after work?'

'I've been at the Green Man. Why?'

'Oh, nothing. Just your mother's worried about him.'

Jamie came into the lounge and stood by his dad's chair. 'Worried? How come?'

'She thinks something's not right with him.'

'Well, I've been saying that for a while. I think he's depressed.'

'His type don't get depressed, he was in the war.'

'Why does she think there's something wrong?'

'She gave him a ring today, see how he was. He kept calling her Edith.'

'So? He got his names mixed up.'

'He never calls her Edith. Never. Anyway, it was more than that, she says. She had to explain, and then he – he started asking after Tess.'

'His dog? The one that died?' Jamie knew his voice sounded incredulous, and he was glad it was his dad telling him and not his mum. It just seemed impossible somehow.

His dad got up and headed into the kitchen. 'Your mum thinks so. Anyway, she's going to make him an appointment with his doctor. She thinks they can give him some tablets or some-thing – though I'm not so sure.'

'She didn't tell him that, did she?'

'About the GP? Why?'

'He won't go. He hates it, having things decided for him.'

'Well, we're going to have to try and make him. Being independent is one thing, and he's done well for his age, but it's not fair on your mother having to worry about him by herself. Your uncles all had the good sense not to live nearby, but if your granddad gets poorly, or – well. It can't all be on her shoulders.'

Jamie's throat was suddenly tight. 'And is Mum – is she OK?'

'Oh, she's – she's not too bad.' He sighed. 'It's not easy for her, son. He's your granddad, and you see a different side to him, but he was always hard on her. He might have put food on the table, but it wasn't easy for your mum having to deal with all that.'

'Deal with all what?'

'Well, she came along a lot later than your uncles, you know that. She was – an accident. Unplanned. And then what with Edith dying in labour – well, your granddad never got over it.'

Jamie's hands felt slick; he wiped them on his jeans and looked down at his trainers. 'Poor Mum.'

'Course the neighbours helped out, and he got in a local woman to cook and clean. But he wasn't . . . he wasn't always kind to her, son. He didn't like her crying or making a fuss, you know? Even when she was poorly. And he never let any of them make mistakes. Things had to be a certain way – he's still like that now, but it's not fair when you've got kids. Some of it was the war, but not all of it; some of it was just how his life turned out, the choices he made.'

'Is that why she's –'

'It affected her, growing up without a mother like that, and him the way he was. And – other things.'

Jamie wanted to ask what things, but he found that he couldn't. Even so, it was the most anyone had ever told him about the buried structures of his family, and he stored it away, feeling both the weight and the privilege of it – though when he came to examine it later, lying in bed, he found it already so familiar, so obvious, that it was as though it had been assimilated instantly and was gone.

In the kitchen his father had put two mugs out on the countertop.

'Oh – not for me, Dad,' he said.

'Righto. So how's the car?'

'OK, yeah. Bit still to do.'

'Work?'

'All right. Quiet.'

'Not too quiet, I hope.'

'Why?'

'I heard they lost another contract, that's all. Big one.'

'Yeah, it's not my section, though. Anyway, you seen how big the place is? It's not about to go under.'

'I hope not. Long as people keep buying stuff, eh?'

'Speaking of work, Dad, I never knew the landfill used to be a coal mine.'

'Didn't you? Good use for it, I say. Once it's full you'll hardly know it was ever there.'

'What d'you mean?'

'They cover it over, son. After a bit you can farm it again.'

'Really?'

'Yeah, good as new, or nearly. You know that empty field by the road between Crowmere and Ardleton? The bumpy one? Ex-landfill, that.'

'No way.'

'They go and test it every so often, check it's all rotting down OK. One day I expect they'll start farming it again.'

'So under that field ...' Jamie tried to imagine it: all the broken toys and nappies and plastic bags.

'Yep. Two hundred years' time they'll be digging it all up again, like on *Time Team*. Unless there's been a – I don't know – a shopping centre built on it by then.'

I 4

Lady's bedstraw, sorrel, bee orchid. Ash bud-burst.
Warm start; heavy showers later.

On weekday mornings Lodeshill came briefly to life between six and eight. A half-dozen or so cars would back out of their drives, some heading towards the Boundway and from there to work, some to drop off the village's few children at the comp in Connorville or at the local grammar. Usually the morning was only broken after that by the postman's van or the meals on wheels, until just after lunch when Jamie would kick the trail bike into life and gun it towards the Boundway for his shift at Mytton Park. Afternoons could be entirely silent until the kids returned from school – unless one of the supermarket delivery vans arrived.

That morning Kitty had only just pulled out of the drive

when she saw the man. He was walking in the very centre of the road, and he looked every bit the old-fashioned tinker; his pack was hung with bits and bobs and decorated with badges, and she thought of the man who used to come to the house when she was a little girl to grind the knives.

She kept the Audi at a crawl and rolled the nearside window down, ready to thank him as she passed. But he didn't move to the side.

The car crept slowly behind him. Did he have headphones on? It seemed unlikely, and Kitty wondered if he might be deaf – or just stubborn. She checked her rear-view mirror; Christine Hawton's car was coming up behind.

He kept walking, his loping gait unhurried, the sun glinting off a little copper pot that banged at the side of his pack. There was a big CND badge on it, Kitty saw now, and, incongruously, one with the Virgin logo; she recognised another, too, with a guitar and the words 'Burning Rubber' arranged in ornate cursive around it. Howard would like that, she thought, and made a mental note to tell him later.

She leaned her head out of the window, considered a friendly greeting; but he must have known she was behind him, and so it would surely come across as an attempt to make him move out of the way. Though she did actually want him to get out of the way, when all was said and done: she had a doctor's appointment to get to. But what if he was a bit ... unbalanced? She rolled the window up again and sighed.

Eventually there was a passing place, and, without him having quite ceded his position, Kitty found there was enough room to manoeuvre the car past, on her face a carefully friendly smile. But when she looked back at him in the rear-view mirror he was gazing past her, somewhere invisible, far ahead.

My grassroots constituency dances as they pass ... Jack thought, watching a cabbage white flutter helplessly against the back-draught from the car. *There are deep truths too deep for them to grasp.*

Was that right? Or did he just think it was because it rhymed? There had been something there, he was sure of it, but as he snatched at the thought it evaporated. He wasn't as sharp these days; he used to know things, he used to know about *deep truths*. Didn't he?

The first farm he asked at had nothing for him; nobody there seemed to remember him, either, and he wondered if maybe he should have shaved his beard off after all, wondered if perhaps it had just been too long since he'd last been up this way. They had a team of Eastern European kids out on the beds; good workers, the farm manager told him: keen. He'd been hearing that a lot in the last few years, and it was true. Sometimes he felt as though he was the last itinerant Englishman still willing to work the land. He wondered if it was true.

He had ruled out going to Culverkeys, and the other three farms had begun to blend into one in his mind, but as he approached the one called Woodwater it began to come back to him. It looked, from the road, like a child's drawing, with a pretty brick farmhouse, a tidy barn and even geese in the yard. The milking shed, dairy and asparagus pack house were tucked away beyond a line of sycamores.

Jack skirted the farmhouse to the ugly bungalow behind it where the Gasters lived, and rang the bell.

'Well, if it isn't Jack,' said Joanne Gaster, opening the door. 'I always look out for you this time of year! Where've you been?'

Such kindness; Jack wasn't used to it, and for a moment he found himself struggling to know how to reply.

'Oh – you know. I travel about.'

'And how are you, anyway? I see you've brought the good weather with you.' She leaned against the door jamb, shading her eyes against the sun, but didn't invite him in.

'Oh, I manage. Place looks tidy.'

'It has to these days, for the B&B. And you know we do cheese now, and ice cream?'

Jack nodded. 'I saw the sign.'

'Had no choice, really. Milk's cheaper than water these days.'

'Asparagus going well for you?'

'It's been a lifesaver, I'll be honest – especially since Culverkeys ploughed theirs under. We put in more beds soon as we heard, and they're going great guns now. We've more or less picked up their order.'

'Culverkeys – that the Harlands?'

'Philip, yes, God rest his soul. Anyway, you couldn't have timed it better – we've just started on ours. We've got six in the bunk-house already though, I'm afraid.'

'That's OK, I – I have somewhere to stay.'

'Shall we see you tomorrow, then? About six?'

Walking back up the lane Jack wondered what Philip Harland had died of, and when. Perhaps it had been drink. He tried to think how old the children would be now, whether one of them would come back to take over the running of the farm. The eldest boy, the quiet one, perhaps, with his clear love for the land: yes, he could picture that. It fitted.

Tonight he would sleep in the sliver of old copse he'd found; not the wood by the village, with its dog walkers and Neighbourhood Watch signs, but another one, further out towards Crowmere, trackless and unvisited. Rain was on its way, but there was a yew there, shadowy and dense; the ground beneath its low branches was bone dry. It had four ancient pennies driven into its trunk, though they were so blackened now and almost grown over that, apart from the squirrels and treecreepers, nobody but Jack even knew that they were there.

Tomorrow he would be back in the fields, and everything would be behind him. He knew that Mrs Gaster wouldn't make him sign anything; she never did.

After her doctor's appointment Kitty decided to go and buy a new camera. Sitting by the drainage ditch after her fall she'd known hers must be submerged in the muck somewhere, but shaken as she was, the thought of groping blindly for it in the cold water with its rusty, polluted sheen made her feel dizzy

– and in any case, it would probably have been beyond repair. She had thought briefly of the photos she had taken, locked away inside it, but when she finally stood up, gingerly testing her balance, she looked round to find that the oak she had wanted to paint looked nothing like as iconic as she had thought; that it was, in fact, just a tree in a field. And so she had let the water claim the camera and had gone back to the car; and, when she felt ready, she had driven home and had a long bath.

It had been easy to conceal the loss of the camera from Howard; he took little notice of any of her art things, most of which she kept in the studio she shared with Claire. More than that, though, it felt natural: photography had always had a frisson of secrecy about it.

She'd met Richard at the evening class she'd begun taking when Chris started at nursery school, and she'd known almost straight away that she was going to have an affair with him. He had an easy grace to his movements, slow and unselfconscious, but more than that there was something self-contained about him, as though he didn't really need others' good opinion, as though he was sufficient unto himself. It was unusual, and it gave him a sense of quiet assurance that she found fascinating.

Kitty had gone into the affair calmly and, it seemed to her then, with her eyes open. She had told herself it would be over soon enough; it was just a bit of excitement, a secret; something nobody would have expected of sensible, strait-laced Kitty, and that no one could take away.

She still remembered the first time he touched her, the moment they crossed that invisible, devastating line. He'd given her a lift back after the class, the air in the car fizzing and cracking with what was happening between them. He had pulled up a street away and cut the engine; they had sat quite still for a long moment, and then she had turned to look at him, the blood surging in her veins. And after that kiss she was for ever after a different woman – a different wife.

Yet where was the harm in it, really? None of her and Howard's friends knew Richard, and she'd known she would never blurt it out to him, whatever happened. It certainly wasn't about leaving him; in fact she didn't believe, then, that it was about Howard at all – though in the years that followed she would come to understand more about what had driven the choice she'd made. With Richard she could be irresponsible and inconsistent; she could have a sense of humour in a way she couldn't at home, because Howard co-opted all that territory and someone had to be the grown-up and that someone was always her.

As weeks and then months passed she'd found that her attraction to Richard only grew. She tried to dismiss it – she had fallen in love with Howard, after all, so she knew better than to trust her feelings. Not that they had been wrong, exactly; she had wanted Howard's irresponsibility and his sociable nature back then. But it took a long time to find out what people were really like, so what was going on with Richard was infatuation pure and simple. She barely knew him, not really; she only got to see his best side, so the magic didn't diminish; and more than that, she was free to invest him with all sorts of qualities, safe in the knowledge that she would never know him well enough to discover whether he had feet of clay.

But despite all her level-headedness it slowly came to feel as though their drinks in out-of-the-way pubs and snatched afternoons in hotels were becoming her 'real' life, while her marriage became a kind of anteroom, a place she slowly, imperceptibly, stopped inhabiting. And yet for months she continued to believe that she could do it; that she could somehow have both lives.

'Do you feel guilty?' he'd asked her once. They were in a dingy pub in Ruislip, sitting next to each other in a booth, rather than facing, so that he could put his hand on her thigh under the table.

'It's funny, I don't. I must be a terrible person. Anyway, I'm sure Howard has secrets of his own.'

'You think he's had affairs?'

'Of course he has. He's out drinking practically every night, for one thing, he comes in at all hours. Why wouldn't he?'

'Does it bother you?'

She frowned. 'I've given up that right, haven't I?' She looked away then, and Richard had turned her face back to his and kissed her, slowly, carefully, in a way that Howard never had.

It couldn't last, of course. One day she'd found out she was pregnant again. The baby was Howard's; she wasn't stupid enough to get caught out like that. She'd finished it with Richard then; she'd had to, although it had felt to her like the end of her real life; her true self, so newly discovered, put away again in a box out of sight.

For two weeks she had cried gaspingly, messily in the shower, and silently in bed while Howard slept. She'd planned to blame it on hormones, but Howard never even asked her if anything was wrong. And when Jenny was born the whole thing began to feel as though it belonged to a different life, so that with the passing of years it was almost as though she'd got away with it scot-free.

Almost, but not quite. Even at the affair's dizziest heights she'd known there would be a price to pay, and she was right: the bill had simply been deferred. The damage to her marriage turned out to be to its founding story: that of she and Howard and why they were together. It was the creation myth every couple produces, and she had written a new one with someone else, an act of heresy that made a lie of the first one and could never be undone. And ever since the affair, when she had needed to call on that story, to remind herself of the reasons why she was married to Howard – in the difficult months after Jenny was born, and later, when his drinking was at it worst – she had found that it was no longer there.

But she had stuck it out. They had given the kids a decent start in life; for the most part, Howard had turned out to be a good father to the two of them, loving and kind. Admittedly he irritated her, but that was just marriage, wasn't it? It wasn't all passion and gazing into each other's eyes, not for the long haul; she knew that. So why, twenty years on, was she thinking about Richard again?

Perhaps the doctor had unsettled her. After years of Howard's endless minor complaints she'd become a bit cavalier about her own health, and hadn't thought much about the appointment other than as a way of putting her fall in the field out of her mind. So when he'd said he was referring her to a neurologist it had come as a shock; back in the car she'd sat for several minutes staring ahead, her mind a blank. It had made her think of something Howard had said, when he retired: 'This is it, then. The last act of my life starts here.' She'd dismissed it; he had a melodramatic streak, he always had. But sitting motionless at the wheel, the keys swinging gently in the ignition, she'd experienced something similar: a sudden glimpse, perhaps, of the finishing line. And it had made her think about her life and about the choices she'd made.

The camera shop was in one of Connorville's retail parks; it was always hard to remember which block of units to pull into, and she kept an eye out for its logo on the big banks of roadside signs. There seemed to be more and more of them every day, and new estates springing up, named after the places the developers had destroyed: The Pasture, Tupp's Wood, The Millrace. Along with the empty new bypass and the huge, clapboard Church of Latter-Day Saints that squatted at one of the roundabouts you could have been in America – or anywhere else, in fact.

In the overheated shop with its air as dry as static Kitty did more than just replace the old camera, upgrading instead to a far better model than the one she had lost in the ditch. After all, what else were they supposed to do with their money but spend it? Howard had done well out of the business, and they had sold the Finchley house at the right time; they'd given Chris a deposit for his first flat, and would do the same for Jenny when she finally moved back to the UK for good, but other than that they could do what they liked, something about which she felt intermittently guilty, but for the most part enjoyed.

Kitty often thought about travelling, but deep down she knew that the *entente* between her and Howard would not survive such enforced intimacy. She would have liked to have gone somewhere by herself – the Norwegian fjords, perhaps, or Finland, somewhere wild and remote – but to ask for such a thing would have changed the landscape of their marriage irretrievably, and after a lifetime together that idea came with a sense of vertigo that might not have been proof of her feelings for Howard, but was real enough.

Outside the shop the breeze was tacking to the west, and as Kitty emerged with her plastic bags the first fat drops of rain were flung across the car park as though flicked from a brush. She drove back with the windscreen wipers on as the sky darkened and the wind picked up. By the time she got home the weather had set in.

15

Borage, self-heal, first wild clematis flowers
(old man's beard, traveller's joy)

All over the country the oilseed rape was in flower, turning fields into bright yellow squares and rectangles. Near Crowmere two farmers had planted some for biofuel and as a break crop, and as far away as Lodeshill the streets and back gardens were filled with its pungent aroma.

Some of the bees that were working the yellow fields came from farm hives, some were Crowmere bees, and some had travelled all the way from Bill Drew's back garden in Lodeshill.

'It's a bugger,' he told Jean after breakfast, looking at the hive with his hands on his hips. 'I do wish they wouldn't. You can't spin the honey out when they've been at the rape, I don't know why.'

'Well, you can hardly stop them from going, can you, love?' she said. 'Anyway, I like it. Makes the fields look pretty.'

'Never used to see it, though, did you? Rape. I don't know.'

'Things change, love. Even here.'

Walking to his first shift at Woodwater Farm Jack frowned at the brash yellow escapees that had sprung up by the side of the road. He liked to see wilding apples and damsons; why was this any different? Plants moved around all the time, and quite right too. Maybe it was just the name he didn't like.

He was looking forward to getting out into the fields. Nothing felt truer than a day's work out in the open air: the well-earned sense of tiredness, and the knowledge that you'd helped things grow, or survive, or be harvested. As he walked he wondered about the other pickers, what they'd be like. He hoped he wouldn't have to speak to them too much; these days he was unused to conversation, its hidden rules and subtleties, and mostly found it a strain.

When he got to Woodwater he could see from the gate that a few pickers were already out on the beds. He went to the pack house to find Joanne, the sky flat and white overhead, the air close and still.

'Morning, Jack,' she said, handing him an asparagus knife. 'Take three rows on the top field – you'll see which ones. Mihail over there will come after with a crate and pick up. Then when we've finished I'll want you in the pack house until about four. That OK?'

'Thanks.'

Leaving the yard Jack passed through a gate, then began walking uphill towards the asparagus beds. They looked, from a distance, completely bare: the field brown and gently humped as though from years of ridge and furrow.

Woodwater's sixteen acres of asparagus had originally been Mrs Gaster's idea: something to occupy her once their two boys started at school, and perhaps bring in a few quid. At first they'd just had one two-acre field which she'd cut more or less by herself, selling the bundles at the farm gate for a pound each. But since then the market had taken off; TV chefs had gone all-out for seasonal produce, and asparagus really flew the flag for that kind of thing. So they had converted the old foxhound kennels into a pack house, and while they still sold some locally most of it went to a wholesaler. Now, Nigel wanted to put in even more beds and maybe invest in some harvesting buggies, but Joanne was reluctant: what came into fashion could go out of fashion, she reasoned, and there was a risk in turning over more land to it: once you'd prepared the soil, bought in new crowns from Holland and hired the equipment to plant them it still took each bed a few years to come into production. 'It keeps us ticking over, Nige,' she'd say to him. 'Let's just be thankful for that.'

Jack reached the top bed and looked down its length. Even from fairly close it was hard, at first, to see the asparagus shoots. Once you got your eye in, though, the fierce green spears were everywhere. He slung the bag over one shoulder and bent to the first shoot, slicing it at ground level with the knife in his right hand while the other held the bag open for it, his eyes already moving ahead for the next stalk. As soon as he began his muscles remembered the movement and his feet the pace. It was the same with scything: once you had learned it your body would always know the motion. It was nothing to do with thinking; it was deeper than that.

The shoots were breaking ground with astonishing energy. You could almost see them growing on a warm day like this: pulling the goodness out of the soil and driving upwards into the light. Jack felt the sun warm on the back of his neck, felt his knees and back begin to complain. 'Ah, give over,' he grumbled to himself happily, and worked on.

Jamie had spent the morning tinkering with the trail bike. The rear suspension had gone, suddenly and with no warning; it was rideable, but only just, and probably not for long – not without a trip to the scrapyard for a new shock.

Then, when he arrived for his shift at Mytton Park, he was told he was being moved to a different hangar.

'How come?'

'Don't worry, you're not the only one,' said Megan, handing him his lanyard. 'Lee's going too. Not Dave, though.'

'Why?'

'They've already got a transport clerk. You'll get training, don't worry.'

'No, I mean, why are we being moved?'

'Just what happens. You work for the Park, not the client; they can put you in any shed they like. People are always being moved around. Just hasn't happened to you yet.'

Jamie felt uneasy; it was like the first day of school or something, a new building, new people. And he hadn't been expecting it, he'd just turned up for a normal shift. He wasn't ready for a big change.

'Is it because they lost a contract?'

'Yeah, but it'll probably pick up. You're on a catalogue company now, 14B. Come on, I'll show you.'

It was nice of Megan, Jamie thought as they left the site office and made their way around the outside of the huge, grey sheds, following coloured arrows set on short, neat posts by the walkways. He wondered what she was really like – when she was with her friends. He wondered what she thought of him. She probably thought he was thick, doing this job, and maybe she was right; she probably laughed at him when he wasn't around. At least she didn't call him Dicko, like the others did – although he couldn't remember her calling him Jamie, either. He wondered what his hair was doing; sometimes it got a dent all the way around from his bike helmet. He felt the nape of his neck surreptitiously as they walked.

'You coming out on Friday, then?' he asked.

'Yep. You?'

'Yeah. Who else is going?'

'Nick – d'you know Nick? From HR? And Andy. Lee, of course. Not sure who else.'

'What's the plan?'

'Not sure really. Few drinks in town, then maybe the Vault if anyone's up for it. Have you been before?'

Jamie considered lying, but there wasn't really any point. 'I haven't, I – it's not really my thing.'

'And what is your thing?' They were outside one of the hangars now, and she had stopped and turned to look at him, pushing her blonde hair away from her face with an easy, unself-conscious movement. This was clearly 14B.

Jamie felt himself flush. *Fuck's sake.* 'Oh, I like all sorts of things, you know, just . . .' It was ridiculous; the only thing he could think of was the car, and she wasn't going to be interested in that.

'Well, you might like the Vault, you never know. Anyway, this is you. Ask for Andy, he's the foreman. See you later –' and she was gone.

Inside, 14B turned out to be almost completely identical to his previous shed, which somehow made it more disorientating. The shelving was laid out in the same way, with the same wire-guided forklifts making the same noises; the toilets were the same, the office was in the same place, but it wasn't Dave in there, it was someone else. It was unnerving, like those dreams where you're somewhere familiar, but everything is slightly different.

As the foreman, Andy, took him through the stock-control system, Jamie's mind drifted back to Megan. Did he actually fancy her or was it just because everyone did? Either way, it was ludicrous to think she'd ever be interested in him. He'd only ever got off with four people, after all.

The girls at school – getting anywhere with them had involved a sort of subterfuge; the sense, almost, that you had to trick them into it. Though that was probably just with him; he probably wasn't doing it right. Maybe girls wanted it with everyone else; that was certainly how his friends made it sound. 'She was gagging for it,' they'd say after a party at someone's house, and everyone would laugh – Jamie too. Which were real, he'd often wonder: the girls he knew, reluctant and intimidating, or the ones his friends described?

At secondary school it had become clear that girls fancied Alex. It was odd, seeing as he mostly ignored them– but then, that was probably why. Even girls like Melanie Abbott and Ciara Williams – Jamie could see what they were like around Alex, how they softened and tried to impress. To them he was invisible, and he knew that if he let himself he could start hating them for it.

His friendship with Alex, by then, had begun to change. They were in different classes for a lot of stuff, and Alex had a new group of friends who Jamie didn't really know. He'd got a haircut, too, and didn't look like a farm boy any more; he'd begun to talk about becoming an architect or a surveyor, instead of a farmer, when he grew up. And yet, outside of school they were still close: they described things for each other in a way they'd never had to before, and for Jamie at least, the new distance between them made Alex both less familiar and somehow more interesting.

They still did their homework together after school, more often by then at Jamie's than at the farmhouse. His parents were used to Alex being over, and although they had never properly talked about what was wrong with his mum he'd always had the feeling that Alex knew and didn't mind. The dolls, for example: there they were in the lounge, lined up on the windowsill in their baby clothes. But Alex had never said anything, and he'd been grateful for that.

It had taken him far too long to realise that other families might not be perfect either, that it wasn't just his that was fucked up.

A couple of weeks before Alex had gone to live in Doncaster Jamie's dad had come into his room at bedtime and sat on the bed, and Jamie had put down his magazine, warily.

'Listen, son, I just wanted to ask you. Is Alex OK?'

'Yeah – why?'

'Just – I just wondered if things were all right for him at home, that's all. Alex's dad, he's – well. I was just wondering. Your mum too, of course.'

'I – I think so, he's not said anything, I've not noticed anything bad.'

'That's good, son. As long as things are OK, that's all that matters.'

And his dad had said goodnight, and left, switching off the bedroom light as he went; and Jamie had lain there, eyes wide in the dark, wondering why he suddenly felt so upset.

Bindweed was rampant in Mytton Park; it overran the far corners of the lorry parks, rioting along the fences when nobody was looking and carpeting unclaimed areas with heart-shaped leaves and white bells. The ground crew went round regularly with backpacks full of glyph and spray guns – like something

out of *Ghostbusters*, as Lee often said – but there was no eradi-
cating it, or the Japanese knotweed that sprang up in thickets
each year behind the cafe. 'Makes good pea-shooters, that,' said
Lee, watching them hack the hollow stems down once again.
'We used to love it when we was kids.'

On his break Jamie went to watch the koi carp in the lake.
They swam in lazy circles near the footbridge, overfed and com-
placent despite the scraggy heron that regularly stalked the
shallows. They were too big for him to take, and they knew it.

He wondered whether Alex had expected to see him at his
father's funeral; whether it looked as though he had stayed away
on purpose. Like everyone else in the village he'd assumed it
would be held at St James's. But it had been at the crematorium
in Connorville and he wasn't sure how that worked, whether
you had to be invited. And so he hadn't gone.

But there was more to it, too. The night Alex's parents split
up, all those years ago, he knew that he'd let Alex down. His
mum was bad; she hadn't washed for a few days and she was
saying some weird stuff. His dad was on a late shift so it was just
him and her, and he didn't know what to do except make tea
and change the channels on the telly when she got upset. So
when Alex texted him he'd said not to come over.

'PLEASE,' Alex had texted back. 'I know yr mum bad this
time of year & I dont care. Dads going mental.'

What time of year? But Jamie couldn't think about any of it
just then, he just couldn't. 'Cant 2night,' he'd replied, and
switched his phone off.

He'd bunked off school the next day, had nicked four of his dad's beers from the fridge and drunk them in the big oak in the Batch, his mind as blank as the sky overhead. He'd twisted the empty cans until they tore and hung the sheared halves on the branches around where he sat so that the sun bounced off them cruelly. Just after home-time he'd walked to the farmhouse, light-headed with hunger, his hands bleeding and sore. Mr Harland had opened the door, something about him, about his manner, making Jamie take an unsteady step back.

'Well, if it isn't young Dicko,' he'd said, his face disordered somehow. 'Now there's a fucking surprise. I've often wondered, do you not have a home of your own?'

Jamie felt the blood drain from his face. He'd never been called Dicko at Culverkeys – at least, not within his hearing. Perhaps they said it all the time behind his back.

'Oh, I do apologise,' said Philip, 'that was unfair. But anyway, you can't see him.'

'Why not?' Jamie managed.

'Because Alexander has *gone*, Dicko. They've all fucking gone.'

Jamie had just stared at him then until Philip had laughed and shut the door, and then he'd walked slowly to the copse where the goshawks nested. But when he arrived he'd found that someone – and surely it could only have been Alex? – had got there before him. The nest was on the ground, the two speckled eggs smashed and stamped on, the glutinous feathers amid the blood and broken shells more than he knew how to bear.

16

Brambles. Showers; wind from the south-east.

The next swap meet wasn't for nearly a month, and Howard didn't want to wait. He went online and posted a few messages, made some calls and arranged to meet a couple of other collectors at a restorer's workshop in Harrow.

'Why don't you get a hotel in London for the night, meet up with the old crowd?' Kitty had said, when he told her. 'And I'm sure Chris would love to see you.'

'Trying to get rid of me?' he'd replied.

'Oh, just get it out of your system.'

Howard wasn't sure exactly what she'd meant, but she was right: it was a lot of travelling to do in one day. He booked a Holiday Inn and gave Geoff, his old general manager, a ring. Hopefully Geoff would get a couple of the others out; they could have a few beers, go for a curry – maybe Camden or somewhere. It would be good for him.

He'd known Kitty wouldn't be interested in the radios themselves, but on the way back from Wales he'd made an anecdote of it in his head, how he'd been honest about the value of the three best sets and thrown the seller off the scent when it came to the rest.

'So you cheated him, effectively?' she'd said, when he got home.

'No ...' he'd replied, bridling. 'It's business. He wanted them out of the way.'

'But they were worth more than you paid him. His grandfather's old radios.'

'Not his grandfather's; they were old returns and repairs, they were sat in the back room of his grandfather's shop, collecting dust. I told him to take them to a car boot, but he couldn't be bothered. Look, Kitty, why am I the bad guy here?' he'd called after her retreating back. 'For God's sake!'

It was like that, now. Not arguments – or rarely – but irritation. She didn't think much of him, or that's how it felt. Sometimes he wondered how long it had been like that, and found he couldn't remember. Certainly when Jenny was still living with them things had been easier, and sometimes when he thought of their home in Finchley everything seemed so much lighter and ... easier, somehow. Perhaps it was as simple as there being other people in the house. Or maybe things really had worsened between them.

They had always had their own interests, though; they had never been the kind of couple who were always in one another's pockets. Kitty wasn't a pub person, not really, and she had quickly stopped wanting to come out with him in the evenings. That was OK, though; she had her own life: evening classes, drinks with women friends, that kind of thing. Years back she'd even talked for a bit about doing a degree, although he'd never been able to see the point of that. Now, though, painting was her thing. And they were in the countryside, where she'd always wanted to be. Life hadn't treated her too badly, when all was said and done. She didn't have a lot to complain about. Not that she did complain – not exactly. It was more the constant sense Howard had these days that everything he did irritated her. Childishly, he found himself acting up to it. And so it went on.

'So when are you off?' she asked when he eventually got up for breakfast on Wednesday. She'd clearly been up for quite a while; she had that busy, virtuous look, and was doing something with vegetables. 'I'm making soup for lunch, by the way. There'll be enough if you want some.'

'Thanks. After lunch.'

'Better get a move on, then,' she said, looking critically at him where he stood in the doorway in his dressing gown and boxers. And then, over the whine of the blender, 'You know, I think there's a tramp in the village. There's a man been seen behaving oddly, and there are empty beer bottles all over Ocket Wood, according to Christine Hawton. She walks her dogs there.'

'Ah . . . bottles plural?' Howard asked, ambling over to the worktop and putting the kettle on for coffee. The sound of the blender subsided, so that he found he had spoken almost in a shout.

'Apparently so. I mean, it's one thing if it's just some local kids, but we can't have someone actually living there. Especially if he's . . . not well.'

'Terrorising the gentle folk of Lodeshill,' said Howard, pouring hot water into his mug. After living in London there was something faintly ridiculous about the fear of crime out here in the sticks, and he'd sometimes read out the headlines from the local paper to Jenny over the phone, for comedy value: *Connorville woman's fears after statue stolen from front garden, Heartbreak for Crowmere dog owner*, that kind of thing. It wasn't as though he didn't believe there was crime in the country – kids were kids all over, and every area had its black sheep – but you could hardly compare it to the gang territories and organised crime of a big city, with its sink estates and areas of genuine deprivation.

It was strange, though: when he lived in Finchley he'd often joked about how middle class he'd become, especially to the drivers at work; it was a bit of a running joke, his holidays in Italy, shopping at Waitrose. But since moving to the countryside he'd found himself more than once talking about Finchley as though they'd lived in the bloody Bronx, exaggerating its dangers and confirming the locals' impression of the capital as somewhere where law and order had broken down. He was aware of the hypocrisy, but the fact was, half the people who lived in the countryside didn't know they were born, gossiping at church about some guy camping in the woods. Anyway, as for the empty bottles he had a queasy idea where they might have come from.

'Not having breakfast?' she called as he took his coffee into the living room.

'No, I'll just . . .' He picked up the sports pages, subsided into an armchair and let the sentence trail away. Kitty stood and looked at him through the kitchen doorway for a few moments before continuing with the soup.

It had rained hard during the night and the road surface remained dark where the hedgerows cast shade; where the May sun reached it, though, it steamed briefly and indiscernibly, and then paled to grey. Thrushes sang in the woods, trying out each note four times, five times, before moving on to something new.

In the fields around the village the new grass had pulled the rain straight up from the soil, making each blade stand up tall, but the leaves on the sycamores and horse chestnuts hung low with the accumulated weight of water, shaking fat drops down when the breeze came. And the breeze, even brisker higher up, moved the clouds on quickly, chasing their shadows across the fields. The sun, in between showers, was clear and warm.

Howard looked at it all through the windscreen of a cab on the way to the station. He'd decided to get the train down to London; petrol was expensive, and these days he drove as little as possible, anyway.

He sat in the front seat of the cab; he couldn't stand sitting in the back, and besides, he knew Charlie, the taxi driver; they'd had a pint together a couple of times in the Bricklayer's Arms, they were practically friends. He only ever used Charlie, although there was a computer cab company in Ardleton with flasher cars; and he always tipped.

Charlie had once been a tractor driver, hired out to drill wheat, plough, spread muck, whatever needed doing. He'd loved it, too; he once told Howard that he'd wanted nothing more since he was a little boy than to sit in the jouncing cab and look out across the fields all day. At first the taxi had just been a sideline to try and make up the shortfall; nowadays, though, it was all he did.

Still, Howard reasoned, he couldn't be far off claiming his pension; he probably only kept it up for a hobby. A way of getting out and meeting people, not getting stuck in the house; he could relate to that.

'Keep the change, Charlie,' he said when he got out at the station, slapping the roof of the cab twice before it pulled away.

The path she was looking for was only about a mile or so outside the village, but Kitty took the car; the weather forecast said showers after about four and she didn't want to have to walk all the way back if it started raining. She had consulted a map – it looked as though the easiest way to get to it was by parking up in one of the lay-bys and cutting across the fields. She had her walking boots on, and the camera, and a rain hat in her pocket just in case.

Not that it was entirely clear where the path might be, or whether it still existed. According to her local history book it was one of a network of tracks, formed by long habit, that had once run out of Crowmere – to the church, to Lodeshill, and this one to one of the outlying farms – but the farm associated with the Puck legend had either disappeared or changed its name, and none of the footpaths and bridleways marked on her OS map looked right. Still, she knew it had once run through Copping Wood and forded a small stream, so she reasoned that if she could find the stream it might be possible to spot where a path had once crossed it.

The big field next to the road was lumpy and uncultivated, and there were no cows in it; what little grass there was looked poor and weedy, and Kitty wondered if it was deliberately being left fallow. Here and there rooks stalked it, their brute grey beaks stabbing at the soil. They eyed her beadily and walked crabwise away as she approached.

Copping Wood turned out to be quite hard to penetrate. There were clumps of brambles at the field's edge, beyond which eglantine and honeysuckle, not yet in bloom, formed a dense barrier. Eventually, ducking and using her arms to protect her face, she simply pushed her way in.

Once under the canopy she found it was relatively easy to move between the trees. Much of the ground was carpeted with dog's mercury, but apart from a few stunted hollies the shade kept most other things down.

The wood seemed trackless, quite unlike Ocket Wood with

its well-trodden footpaths and dog bins. There were no trails on the ground leading her towards anything, nothing to say which was the best way to go. Here and there were fallen trees, rotting where they lay; low branches barred the route between trunks in most directions. It was trackless, like virgin jungle, and somehow disquieting. Kitty stood still and listened for a moment: nothing. It was as though even the birds had fled.

The stream had to be at the lowest point, so she decided just to try to move forward and down. It was slow going, and she frequently had to duck under branches or climb inelegantly over dead trees, clutching the new camera anxiously to her side. But after a few moments, there it was: a channel cut into the wood's floor, the suggestion of moving water. She had found the stream.

On the bank Kitty stood and looked down at it critically. Only a very few gleams of sluggish water caught the light, and there was nothing picturesque about it, nothing at all: no sunlit rills or fern-shadowed pools. It was a muddy channel in a dark wood, and it was becoming clear that the path wasn't going to make a good subject either – even if it still existed. Still, she had come this far.

Rain began to patter on the leaves overhead, although for now the forest floor remained sheltered and dry. Kitty turned right along the dark rivulet, wondering if she'd even be able to recognise a path crossing it, disused for all these years.

After a hundred yards or so it began to seem as though more sunlight was filtering down between the trees ahead, and Kitty wondered if she was about to emerge from the wood into the field beyond. The canopy overhead began to thin, and then, miraculously, the ground underfoot was transformed into a shallow pool, the tree trunks rising from it like pillars, moored to their own reflections. It could only have been a few inches deep but it lay there like mercury, incongruous, baffling. Kitty reached for the camera, unclipped the lens cap and framed a shot. Then froze.

On the other side of the little flood crouched a bearded man, looking directly at her through her viewfinder. Kitty's heart banged, and she lowered the camera. He was less than twenty yards away, but seemed impossibly remote.

Slowly, the man straightened, letting water fall from his cupped hands back into the pool. The ripples reached Kitty's boots, making her step back in a wash of panic; she hadn't realised that she had stepped into the shallows.

Her eyes were locked to his, but after a second he dropped his gaze. She realised she had expected him to crash away through the understorey as a deer will once startled; but he remained.

She groped for the reassurance of the nearest trunk. Her momentary panic had started to ebb, and she recognised him as the man she had seen on the road, although without his gaudy-looking pack this time. She took a breath, looked at him carefully. He didn't seem menacing, or even mad. He looked ill, though, or damaged in some way.

'Hello,' she called out. 'I've seen you in the village, haven't I? Lodeshill.'

He looked briefly at her, then away.

'Don't go. I just – what's your name?'

'I'm not – I'm just – I'm on my way somewhere.' He gestured vaguely. From high above them both, a thrush repeated its phrases.

'In here? Look, I don't mean you any harm. I just – I wondered if you needed anything. Are you – can I help, in any way?'

'No. I – I don't need anything.'

'Your name, then? I'm Kitty. I live in Lodeshill, you know, just up the road? I'm trying to paint, I've been looking for places, I don't suppose you know if –' Kitty could hear how it was coming out, and it was all wrong. What on earth was the matter with her?

Between them the water had resumed its glassy stillness. A plastic bottle hung, half submerged, at one of its margins, its cap very blue where the sun struck it.

'I'm sorry. Please don't go. To tell you the truth, I think I might be lost.' She gave a little laugh, then smiled apologetically, wondering if it was true.

'You're not lost,' the man said, with sudden directness. 'You're just not looking properly.' He turned and began to disappear between the trees.

'What do you mean?' said Kitty, hearing her voice become strange and shrill. She felt ridiculous somehow; something had gone wrong, something had been turned on her, when all she had wanted to do was offer help. It was like one of those nightmares when things slew out of your control, where reason is somehow not enough; something else is required, but you don't know what.

'Please!' she called; but he was gone.

17

Meadow foxtail: first inflorescence. Increasing heavy rain.

The shower that fell on Copping Wood that afternoon fell on Lodeshill, too, although it wasn't heavy enough to send the swallows back into their nests. It fell on Crowmere and Ardleton, and on Connorville's retail parks and roundabouts; at Mytton Park it pattered on the grey roofs and drove the smokers back indoors.

The rain formed part of a weather front that had slid in overnight to bisect the country west to east; below it skies were blue, and in London the afternoon wore on warm and humid, the sun flashing off office blocks and car windscreens, and the air, by the afternoon rush hour, humid and still.

Howard was in the Royal Oak in Camden waiting for Geoff and the others. He wasn't sure how many there'd be, which had made choosing a table a bit tricky; in the end he'd gone for one with four places, putting his jacket on the back of the seat oppo-site his own; they could always pinch a couple more stools if necessary.

The jacket had been a mistake, he felt now; not only was it too warm, but now he was back in town it looked wrong. It wasn't as though it was a wax jacket or anything, but something about it struck the wrong note. He'd bought it in Connorville; it had looked fine there.

He checked his phone again and took another swig of brown ale. They'd be here soon – if they left on time, that is. He won-dered if Geoff had mentioned to Chris that they were going for a few jars; he couldn't exactly have asked him not to. Not that he didn't want to see his son; they were going to meet at the depot in the morning to go over a few things, and Howard thought they could go for lunch together. It was just that it might be odd for Chris; he might feel caught between acting the boss and being Howard's son. It would probably be easier all round if he didn't come out tonight.

The afternoon had gone well; he'd sold the Hitachi, the Murphy's Pocket Portable and the Hastings table radio, all to the guy in Harrow, and another collector had shown interest in a couple of the 1960s ones, too, based on photos Howard had on his phone. He hadn't bought anything apart from a little lead solder, not this time; he didn't want to be lugging anything about. But there had been a real pleasure in being the one holding the cards: the one who had discovered the old shop – pretty much – and had made such a brilliant find. Collectors could be a funny bunch: so cliquey, so guarded about their secrets. Not that he really counted himself as one, of course.

Howard had nearly finished his drink and the pub was getting busier; he hoped they wouldn't be too much longer, as he didn't really want to abandon the table to go to the bar. It was Geoff he was mostly looking forward to seeing; they'd worked together for nigh on twenty years, and you didn't do that without getting to know someone really well. Though it had been a surprise a couple of months back when Geoff had phoned to say they weren't coming for the weekend because he and Anne had split up; he'd never said anything about problems at home, and Howard had always thought they were pretty solid as a couple: three grown-up kids, decent enough house, trips to Spain every year. But he wasn't one to pry, and anyway, other people's marriages were like foreign countries: you could never have any idea of the territory, not really. Take him and Kitty: Howard was pretty sure that nobody would suspect that they slept in separate rooms. All of which just went to show: appearances could be deceptive.

'Howard!' – there was Geoff now, grinning affably down at him. Howard stood up and shook his hand, unable to prevent himself looking past him for a moment. 'Geoff. Good to see you. The others not with you?'

'Just me, I'm afraid. You know what it's like. I see you're still on the Brown –' he took off his jacket and put it on the chair with Howard's – 'I'll be right back.' And he grinned at Howard and went to the bar.

Howard sat back down, feeling unaccountably and briefly foolish. He drained the last flat, warm mouthful of beer from his bottle and pushed it to the side of the table, picked a little at a bit of loose veneer with his thumbnail. Ah well. And at least he hadn't brought Chris out, that was the main thing. They could get on the beers, the two of them; have a bit of a laugh.

Geoff came back with the drinks and sat opposite. 'So how've you been?' he asked, clinking his pint glass on Howard's bottle before leaning in to it for a long pull.

'Cheers,' said Howard, grinning and taking a swig. 'Good, you know. Well. How about you? Hope that son of mine isn't being too much of a tyrant.'

Howard hadn't meant to bring Chris up so soon; they'd never really discussed the fact that he'd put him in charge of the business, and Geoff had found out at the same time as everyone else – a month before Howard retired. But he'd had a sudden fear that Geoff might start talking about Anne, or say he was lonely or something.

'Chris? No, he's ... I'd say he's settling in well. No complaints.'

'Good, good. And how's everyone else? What about that new ... Chantelle, is it?'

Geoff exhaled through pursed lips, shaking his head a little. 'Yep, Chantelle. She's something. She is something. Smart girl, too – doesn't take any shit off the drivers. They don't dare, you know?'

'Your type, is she?'

'Twenty years ago, maybe. You know she's having a drink with your son tonight? I'd say he could do a lot worse.'

'I did,' Howard lied, leaning back in his chair and looking out towards the bar; 'it's why I didn't ask Chris to come out tonight. Good luck to the lad, I say. You've got to get while the getting's good, and all that.'

'You're not wrong. Though it's never too late, you know. You wouldn't believe how many divorced women there are on the Internet, just looking to put it all behind them. Makes me wish I'd done this sooner.'

'I can imagine,' said Howard, trying to keep his expression neutral. From what he'd heard, Anne had thrown Geoff out of the house and it had been nearly a week before she'd even let him pick up clean shirts for work.

'So you're living in . . . what is it, Harlow now?' Howard tried to line up a couple more questions; he didn't really want to hear Geoff's dating anecdotes – not yet, not until they'd had a few more beers, anyway. He'd always liked Anne, for one thing, and while he and Geoff had been out drinking many times, previously he'd always been the boss, which was probably why the conversation hadn't ever got really personal. Now, though, they were equals. He eyed the level in Geoff's pint glass and wondered if it was too soon to get another round in.

The pub was really filling up now; the level of conversation around them rose, and as Geoff began to tell him about the flat he was renting, about his plans, the two of them gradually became hemmed in, the spare chairs carried off, other people's drinks left in sticky rings on the unused end of their table.

By half ten they were both fairly drunk, though Howard could feel himself battling against it. When he got up to go to the Gents he was careful to stand up cleanly and walk purposefully; before leaving the toilets he looked at himself briefly in the mirror and assumed a steady expression.

On the way back he stopped at the bar for another round. He wasn't sure why it had been necessary to start in on the shots, but it had been. And he was having a good time, wasn't he? It was good to be back in London, having a few drinks; it was all good. He felt like his old self, or something. Not quite, though; not the boss, not that old self. But more himself than in the countryside. Was that right?

It didn't matter, he could just enjoy it. Could do it more often, maybe. Maybe get more of the guys out next time, though. Shouldn't have left it to Geoff, he thought, fumbling in his pockets for the playing card they'd given him for his tab. There it was. Don't leave without getting the card back. Perhaps get Geoff to remind him.

He picked up the beers and shots and jostled his way carefully through the crowd. It was so familiar, having to do that. People so close in the city, all around. But distant, too. You could just have a few drinks. That pub in Lodeshill, it was on its arse. Try going in there and minding your own. Not a chance. Community, according to Kitty; nosy, more like.

'Nice one,' said Geoff as he sat down. 'Cheers.'

They tipped back the shots, Geoff with a comedy shake of the head, Howard with a grimace. Geoff seemed drunker than he had a few moments before; he was leaning back in his chair with an unfocused expression and one of his shirt buttons had come undone, revealing a sliver of white, hairy stomach. Better make these the last, Howard thought, get some food inside him. Should've signed the card off.

'Curry after this?' he said. 'On me. Might as well.'

'Could do. Or we could head into town.'

This was a surprise; as far as Howard was concerned they were already in town, though he guessed that Geoff was talking about the West End.

'Yep,' he replied, 'though I've got a hotel in Brent Cross to get back to.'

'Get a cab. It's not like you can't afford it.'

Howard looked up, but Geoff's expression was bland. 'Can't face Soho any more, not these days,' he said. 'Let's go to that Japanese place round the corner. You can't get a decent chicken katsu outside the M25.'

'Lost your edge,' said Geoff, taking a large swig of his pint. 'Happens.'

'What do you mean?'

'Oh, you know. Retire. Move out of London. It's all over.'

Howard bridled, despite himself. Geoff was obviously joking, but all the same. 'And you're living the high life in Harlow, I suppose?' he said.

'Temporary, I told you. Anyway, I come into town, I go out. Saw a band last week.'

'Oh yeah?' Again, Howard was piqued; bands were somehow his thing. 'Who'd you see?'

'Oh . . . at the Palace. Or whatever it's called now.' It was clear Geoff couldn't remember the band's name, but there was no sense in pushing the point; Howard knew he'd only have to admit he hadn't heard of them anyway. Still, he had a sudden fierce urge to go out, do something, anything. The fact was, he missed London. No point pretending. He fucking missed it.

'Who'd you go with?' he asked.

'Steve and Nikki from work and this girl I met off the Internet. I say girl, I mean woman. Thirty-eight, two kids. Box of frogs, you know. But fit.'

'Good night?'

'Yeah. She brought some coke out with her, cocaine. Bit like the old days, you know?'

Howard hadn't realised that Geoff had ever had 'old days', not like that. He'd always known him with Anne; when on earth was this period he'd been seeing bands and taking drugs, this period he now felt able at last to return to?

Perhaps it had only happened once, when Geoff was a teenager, or perhaps it had never happened at all. The image people had of themselves didn't always have much basis in fact; it was something you came up with in your teens, Howard believed, and which you then spent your life trying to stay true to – or maybe leave behind. Although perhaps some people weren't like that, perhaps they just

162

were who they were without worrying about it. Or perhaps their real selves came out when they were older, in their marriages and with their kids – like with Kitty. Who could say?

'Listen,' he said, 'I'm going to pay off my card. Then we'll eat. Then we'll go into town. OK?'

'Knew it,' Geoff said, finishing his pint and standing up. 'You can take the man out of London ...'

Howard grinned; Geoff was OK. His mate. He was glad he'd come out. 'Be right back. Keep an eye on my jacket.'

'Fucking tweed though. I ask you.'

'Camouflage, Geoffrey. I've got to blend in somehow. They still lynch outsiders in the sticks, you know.'

Halfway through the meal it was clear that Geoff wasn't going to make it to the West End. His eyes slid dozily around the room; each time Howard spoke it took him a long moment to pull his focus back.

'Not enough women here is the problem,' he said, quite loudly. Howard realised he was going to have to try and put him in a cab; he just hoped Geoff knew his new address off by heart.

Howard, by contrast, was feeling more and more sober. What had he been thinking, anyway? Soho was bad enough at the best of times; it would have been a disaster with Geoff. He'd have tried to chat up groups of twenty-somethings, or, worse, he'd have wanted go to some Godawful strip club, and Howard had a prudishness about such things that he knew was quite at odds with his rock-star past. Rock star! Jesus, who was he kidding?

Third-rate roadie, more like. Anyway, he would have hated it.

He asked for the bill and settled up. Geoff was becoming hard work now; mulish and unpredictable. He'd clearly worked out that Howard wasn't going with him to Soho any more, and what's more he could tell he was being managed.

'Fucking . . . lightweight,' he said. 'Knew you weren't up for it.'

Howard stood up and shrugged his jacket on. 'Sorry, Geoff. Another time.'

'Give us a hug, then. From the old boss. The boss that is no more. Father to the new boss, *plus ça change*, is it? – but I still stay the fucking same.' And he stood, knocking some cutlery from the table and holding out his arms.

Howard looked at him for a long moment. 'Come on. Home time.'

'What? Home time? Not for me, I'm free as a bird. I'm going into town, mate. You should come.'

Howard decided to make for the door and hope Geoff followed. There was a cab office nearby; he'd order two, and if Geoff wanted to tell his to go to the West End that was his affair.

The night air was cool on his face as he stepped out onto the pavement and lit up a cigarette. It could've been such a good night, it could've been so much fun. Briefly the picture he'd had of it returned, but he closed his eyes for a second and it was gone. He just had to cope with this last bit with Geoff, and then he could cab it back to the hotel. And hopefully when he arrived at the depot to see Chris in the morning Geoff wouldn't remember any of it. Or he wouldn't be in.

18

Speedwell, ragged robin, meadow saxifrage (rare).
One early foxglove.

There was a starling in Lodeshill that could do a perfect imitation of a car alarm being set; Jamie often listened out for it as he worked on the Corsa in the drive. A hundred years ago they had mimicked the ringing note of the blacksmith's hammer, and after the village smithy finally closed the sound had lived on for a little while, persisting like a ghost in the repertoires of one or two generations of birds. And then it had faded away.

Now, as Jamie reattached the air filter to the Corsa, he thought he heard the starling call, but it was the woman from Manor Lodge letting herself into her Audi. He straightened up, easing his back, and watched as she drove off.

For a long while he'd felt secretive about the Corsa; he hadn't wanted to show it to anyone until it was completely finished. The tarp, in his mind, had been like a chrysalis, and what came out would be transformed: a shining, perfect ride. But now the weather was nice he found himself itching to get it on the road and see what it could do. It wasn't finished yet, but he'd have to make the decision sometime; the fact was, he could keep improving it almost indefinitely. And in any case, the motorbike was on its last legs.

He'd considered taking it out on Friday, but then he wouldn't be able to have a drink, and he'd be left out while everyone was talking and laughing, and Megan might think he was always like that. No, it was better to wait a bit longer, get the sound system installed, too. Although not for too long; summer was the best time.

Having a car wasn't just about showing off. Ever since he could remember he'd needed to go away by himself sometimes, to be where nobody could find him: not his mum, or his dad; not even Alex. To not have to think about anyone else, or be answerable to anyone. When he was a kid he used to go up Babb Hill by himself for a bit, or climb the big oak in the Batch; now, having his own car was like always having that on tap.

When he was little he'd sometimes dreamed of running away and becoming an outlaw or something; just camping out by himself, nobody giving him a hard time. One schoolday when he was eight or nine he'd just walked to the station and taken the first train he saw. On the train he'd found a ticket under one of the seats and put it in the pocket of his school shorts: it was dated the day before, but it was better than nothing.

It was brilliant being on the train by himself. He could still remember looking out at the unfurling landscape and the rows of back gardens, and the moment when he spotted a boy with a school backpack, a boy who could have been him, emerging from an alleyway and looking up at the train. He'd found himself waving, and another boy sitting near him with his mother had laughed. He had turned from the window to smile back in delight, but when he looked he'd seen that the other boy's expression was cruel.

The town he got off at had until that day been a word he knew and nothing more. He didn't really know why he got off there and not somewhere else. He just did.

The barriers were open, which felt like a sign. The town straggled uphill along a shop-lined street: Superdrug, McDonald's, JD Sports. He walked all the way up the hill to where the shops began to give out: there was a dentist's there, a big, red-brick church with a square tower and the gates of a school. He could hear the children in the playground: it was morning break. Nobody in the world knew where he was; it was as though he had stepped outside of his life for a little while, like he was invisible, a ghost.

The town was different from Connorville, but the same as well; it wasn't another world, like he had pictured finding when he was on the train. He'd spent the morning just wandering around with his hands in his pockets, looking at the faces of the people going in and out of the shops: old people with shopping trollies, mums with prams. Did they have secrets? Were they happy, or worried, or afraid? Were they even real – as real as him, as Alex? It was impossible to know.

He'd sat on a bench outside the library to eat his packed lunch, and a tramp had come and looked at him for a while. Jamie had looked back at him, guardedly, and after a while the man had laughed and gone away.

At last Jamie slammed the bonnet shut and dragged the tarp back over the Corsa. He had been trying to fit the turbo all morning, and now his shoulders ached and he was in need of a shower before his shift started.

Working on the car quietened his thoughts. It was about problem solving: doing one thing and then the next. It made him believe in things changing.

Claire's VW Beetle was parked slightly haphazardly by the kerb when Kitty arrived at the studio. Kitty let herself in, calling out a hello.

When Claire and her second husband had divorced she'd used her half of the money from the sale of their house to buy a flat in Ardleton and take out a lease on a vacant shop nearby. Once a greengrocer's, it had since then been a cab office, a florist's and a nail bar; none had survived for more than a couple of years.

Claire had painted the inside white, had a skylight installed and hung her own work on two of the walls; Kitty, who paid her a good amount each month in rent, had suggested they each put a painting on an easel by the window in case of passing trade, but Claire wanted to make the most of the light. 'It's a studio, Kitty dear, not a gallery,' she'd said. 'We're here to work, not flog our wares.' It was all right for her, though; you could buy her cows and dogs across half the county. Sometimes Kitty wondered if she was jealous of Claire; she didn't want to paint the kinds of things Claire did, however popular they were, but she had to admit that while it was only a hobby, something she enjoyed doing for its own sake, she would love to sell a picture, to have a stranger want to look at it on their wall.

'In here!' Claire called out cheerily from the little galley kitchen. 'Fancy a tea?'

Kitty put her bags down and went to look at Claire's easel. 'Yes please. What are you working on?'

'Oh, that's just a sketch really. I'm doing a pack of Basset Vendéens, I met the breeder at the agricultural show last year. Lemon and ginger, or raspberry?'

'Oh – normal tea please. There's some there, I think. A pack of them – so they're hunting dogs, are they?'

'Yes, well, sort of. For hares, originally. Lovely little things. Most sell as pets now, I think.' She came out of the kitchen with the tea and handed Kitty a mug. 'How are you feeling?'

'I went to the doctor. They're referring me.' Kitty had already told Claire about the fall; she had responded with a story of a friend of hers – 'a bit younger than you, Kitty' – who had fallen in the street and later been diagnosed with multiple sclerosis. Kitty hadn't been able to work out, from the story, if the friend was still alive.

'Who are they referring you to?'

'A neurologist. Queen Elizabeth's.'

'A neurologist? Really?'

'I know.'

'Oh – not to worry,' Claire said, although she continued to frown. 'I'm sure they're just covering themselves. What did Howard say?'

'I haven't told him.'

'Oh, Kitty. Whyever not?'

'He'll just – I just want to find out myself. I'll tell him when I know.'

Claire folded her arms. 'Is that wise? Not to communicate like that?'

Kitty laughed. 'Oh, Claire – we don't communicate anyway. We haven't for years.'

'Really? And you're OK with that?'

Suddenly Kitty wanted to reel the conversation back; she felt far too exposed. Claire's views on relationships were very black and white, and there were things she didn't think she could bear to hear her say; not now. Yes, in an ideal world she'd find a way to tell Howard that she was scared, and he would really hear her. But they weren't in an ideal world.

She sighed. 'Anyway, the appointment's next week. Perhaps – would you come with me?'

'Of course I will, my dear. And afterwards we'll go for a large glass of wine and a proper chat, shall we? Really get to the bottom of things.'

'That would be lovely,' Kitty said, wondering what she had just done. 'But now I must get on and do some painting.'

'And how is all that coming along?'

'Oh – not brilliantly. I don't know. I feel stuck.'

'Still?' Claire put her head on one side. 'With all that countryside out there?'

'I know.' Kitty sighed.

'I wonder what it is that you're *not seeing*,' Claire said, narrowing her eyes. She could be like that sometimes; Kitty often thought she fancied herself as a bit of an amateur psychologist. 'You must be looking at things in the wrong way. Have you read *The Way of the Artist*? It's very good on observation versus inspiration. I'll bring you my copy tomorrow. You must promise to read it though, OK?'

But Kitty's mind was elsewhere. Who else had said that to her recently – about not looking properly? The image came to her of a silent pool in the woods, a plastic bottle bobbing slightly in the water. She set a sketch pad on her easel, found a pencil and, from memory, began to draw.

'Kitty dear, are you drawing litter?' Claire said a little later, coming to stand behind her easel. It was lunchtime; usually they walked up the road together and had a sandwich and a coffee or, sometimes, a glass of wine.

Kitty laughed. 'No. Well, yes, I suppose I am. Listen, I'm going to work through lunch – would you mind getting me some water? Any kind, just make sure it's in a plastic bottle?'

'Of course,' Claire said doubtfully. 'I can't believe you're really going to paint a plastic bottle, though. What next? Crisp packets and condoms?'

'It's the way the light catches it in the water. Think of it as an exercise,' Kitty said.

When Claire had gone she turned back to her sketch. It wasn't exactly pretty, Claire was right, and it might well be that she didn't take it any further. But she could feel an excitement building that she couldn't quite identify and didn't want to examine too closely in case it fled. Just something about focusing in. Something about detail, not vistas, and about it being *real*. A bottle floating over submerged grass. A scrap of dirty wool caught on barbed wire. A dank tangle of briars, the sunlight shafting in.

The others had finished work at five thirty, so when Jamie and Lee caught up with them after the evening shift they were already fairly drunk.

'*Dicko! Dicko! Dicko!*' chanted Nick as they pushed their way in among the crowd. It was packed and hot, the music thumping.

The Mytton Park lot were all standing at one end of the long steel bar. Jamie barely knew Nick; they'd chatted once or twice on a fag break, but they weren't exactly mates. 'All right, mate?' Nick shouted now, draining the last of pint and reaching behind Megan to shake Jamie's hand. Megan had a backless top on; she looked great – though she probably knew it. 'Yeah, not so bad,' replied Jamie. 'What you drinking?'

'You legend,' said Lee, overhearing. 'Mine's a pint.'

'Nick?'

'Same, mate.'

'Andy? What are you drinking?' He mimed a drinking motion at Andy, who was grasping Lee's arm and shouting into his ear. 'Megan?' He touched her arm hesitantly, aware of how cold his hand would feel to someone who had been in a packed bar for a while. 'Can I get you a drink?'

She stood on tiptoes to answer, her breath warm on the side of his face. 'Can I have a Bacardi and Coke, please?'

'Sure. Can I . . .?'

'Course,' – and she made way for him at the bar.

As he waited to be served, turned away from the rest of the group, he told himself that with a couple of drinks inside him it would start to seem fun. It was always like this at the beginning, especially if you arrived late: you came in off the street to a packed crowd of people all laughing and shouting together and it took a while before you felt like you were one of them. It was always annoying at first, how hot it was and how loud, but soon enough he'd be part of it all.

When it was his turn he ordered a tequila shot and knocked it back on the sly before passing the other drinks over his shoulder.

The bar closed at midnight, by which time Jamie was definitely drunk. But so was everyone else, and worse than him: Lee had nearly got into a fight, and one of the bouncers had come over. Megan had had to calm it all down.

Outside a gaggle of people had formed around the bar's entrance, smoking, laughing, phoning for cabs. There was a crowd around the cashpoint across the road, too, a different one: doleys in hoods and caps, a blonde woman in pyjama bottoms and slippers with a man's coat over the top, a dealer half the town knew. Looking over Jamie recognised a lad who'd been in the year above him at school – except now he had a tattoo on his neck and his eyes were sunken and blank. Benefits, Jamie remembered, were paid out at midnight.

He turned away. 'You coming to the Vault, then?' he asked, grinning down at Megan who was sparking up a fag. 'Should be fun.'

'Oh, I see, it's like that now, is it?' she smiled back and blew out smoke.

'Yeah, it is. Come on.' And he started walking off, hands jammed in his pockets.

'Jamie!' she called, as though telling him off – but not really. It was lovely. 'You don't even know which way!'

Jamie laughed, spun on his heel, jogged back. 'I wasn't really. I wouldn't . . . we've got to wait for the others, haven't we?'

'We have got to do that, yes.' She only had a cardigan over her top, and she had her arms crossed, her shoulders hunched. What if he put his arms round her, just friendly, just to keep her warm? He pictured it: not anything sexy, just holding her against him for a moment, her letting him, maybe leaning in to his chest. Lee could have pulled it off, definitely; he wouldn't even have thought twice. But what if he tried and she pushed him away and things went weird?

'Want my jacket?' he asked instead.

'Ooh, d'you mind? You're such a gent.'

But just as he was taking it off she called out a name, dropped her cigarette and clattered across the street to embrace a girl in a red dress and heels, the group around the other girl looking over non-committally as Lee, Andy and Nick joined Jamie on the pavement.

'Who's Tits talking to?' said Andy.

'Tits?'

'Megan.'

'Oh. Don't know – friends of hers,' replied Jamie, grinding out her abandoned fag butt with his shoe and shrugging his jacket back on. He could feel himself turning red. 'She just went.'

'Oh Christ,' said Lee. 'Not that lot.'

'Why?'

'Been out with them before. Fucking ... young farmers or whatever.'

'Don't look it.'

'Honestly, mate. Unbelievable.'

Andy started saying something filthy about pigs, but stopped when he saw Megan coming back over. 'Ready, lads?' she said. 'That lot are going too – might as well all go together. Come on, Jamie!' and she put her arm through his and led him back over the road to be introduced.

Four in the morning and Jamie was stumbling along the Boundway towards Lodeshill. The horizon jumped up and down as he walked, and when a car roared past he leaned too far into the hedge and nearly fell.

Where the fuck was his jacket, anyway? No idea. And where were the others, why had they left him? Or had he left them?

He remembered being in the club: the flashing lights, the backs of people's heads as they danced. Elbows, people jostling him. But it was OK, he didn't mind. Then they were at the bar. Shots, they did shots. Something green. Whose idea was that? He fumbled in his trouser pockets for his wallet: thank God. And his keys. OK. But then what? He'd talked to Megan a lot: oh fuck, what had he said, had he told her anything, had he made an idiot of himself? And then Lee, shouting into his ear over the bass whumping out of the speakers – something about females in general, then about Megan, something nasty. Calling her 'Tits' again. The buzzing pain in his eardrum as Lee yelled, making him flinch.

Perhaps Lee had his jacket, or had he left it in the club? He couldn't remember leaving, the last thing he could think of was being on the dancefloor. Oh fuck, that was a point: he'd *danced*. Not actually with Megan, but they'd all danced. But if everyone had that must be OK. None of them were looking anyway. And that other lot, they were all right, weren't they? Why didn't Lee like them? He'd ripped the piss out of them all night, copying them behind their backs. Funny though.

There was a sour taste in his mouth. Fuck, he'd thrown up! He remembered it now, crouched on the floor of the cubicle. Just a little flash: seeing the vomit streaking the side of the toilet bowl, how it had made him retch again. What else? He remembered having a piss, and – *Jesus* – snorting something off the corner of a credit card. What was that? It had stung his nose; he still couldn't breathe out of one nostril now. Bloody Nick that was, where'd he get it? Good fun though – wasn't it? They were his mates, all his mates. Just wished he knew what the fuck had happened to them all; how had he lost them? Why was he stumbling home like this, by himself?

He wasn't far from the Lodeshill turn-off when he saw it: something on the carriageway ahead, something he couldn't yet make out in the dim, pre-dawn light. The straight road pointed to it like an arrow, and as he drew closer, growing more sober with every step, it moved from the realm of the dreamlike to the disbelieved to the real.

For the most part the deer looked unmarked, although there was a black puddle spreading from somewhere underneath it and Jamie could smell blood and fear on the night air. He knelt down near it, its big eye rolling whitely at him in panic. 'Oh shit, oh shit,' he found himself whispering, and then, 'It's OK, it's OK.'

He took a breath and laid one hand on its warm flank, gently. Its front legs kicked and a low noise came from it like the pure spirit of pain and fear itself. He stumbled back, then walked off a little way, looking up and down the road, but there was nothing coming; the fields on either side were dark and silent, and above him the Milky Way slashed the sky as though in echo of the road beneath. There was nobody to help.

He became conscious of wanting to be the kind of person

who could just act, who was effective, adult, unmoved. Wasn't it in these crises that you found out if you were a man? '*Fuck – fuck –*' he heard himself mutter, over and over.

He fumbled his shirt off, the night air constricting his nipples and raising the fine hair on his arms. The shirt would smell of him, which wasn't ideal, but he had no choice.

An owl shrieked from the dark wood to his right as he knelt, no longer drunk at all, by the twitching deer and dropped the warm fabric gently over its head. Immediately its legs became still, although its ribs still heaved in and out. The shirt's hem was already soaking up blood, but it hardly mattered: it wasn't as though he was ever going to wear it again.

The pool beneath the deer's flank grew and spread like slow, black oil, and he tried to keep clear of it, rocking back on his heels as he thought through what he had to do next. It was a roe buck, and probably strong. Its back legs didn't seem to be working, but the front ones were, with their lethal slotted hooves – and who knew what agonies it would drive itself to once it understood what he was going to do.

Jamie stood up again and looked down at the hooded deer. His heart thumped under the fine, bare skin of his chest as the knowledge came to him that he had to kill it now. Briefly he looked up at the sky: the black fading to blue, dawn gathering somewhere behind the treeline in the east.

He stood astride the deer, facing its head. He crouched down, using one knee to hold its front legs still, and hoped the stricken back legs wouldn't move too much. He held his shaking hands above the white shirt for a moment, as though in benediction, and at last wrapped the warm fabric tight around its muzzle and squeezed his shaking hands where the hot breath came and went – and came and went – and then, as the big deer heaved and bellowed and weakly tried to run, did not come again.

19

Yarrow, dropwort, common spotted orchid.

It was the middle of May and the first really warm weekend of the year. The breeze, when there was any, was light and came from the south-west, and almost the entire country was bathed in sunshine. The rookeries were busy, blossom was turning the hedgerows creamy-white and the song thrushes nesting in the lilac beside Manor Lodge's front drive were onto their second brood.

Once Kitty had left for morning service Howard went downstairs and put the first Burning Rubber album on loud. It was the one the band had been touring when he first started roadying for them, and he knew it inside out: every word, every chord, every riff. The feelings it brought back were so strong: it was like a time machine, a portal back into another self. He didn't play it too often any more; it was – not painful, exactly, but somehow acute.

He'd agreed to meet Kitty outside the church in an hour for the annual Rogation walk. 'Sounds happy-clappy,' he'd said when she'd explained what it was. 'Walking and praying? Bit New Age for you, I'd have thought.'

'No, Howard, it goes back centuries,' she'd said. 'Don't you remember, I went last year? You walk the boundary of the parish, a bit like claiming your territory. It used to be really important, before proper maps. Everyone goes, practically the whole village.'

'And there's praying?'

'Only once or twice – it's more about the local landmarks, and the crops, and just . . . well, getting to know each other. And then afterwards everyone goes to the pub.'

'What, the Green Man?'

'Yes, they're doing a ploughman's. Howard, I'd really like you to come. You've barely met anyone in the village, and last year I said you weren't well. If you don't come again people will think you're unfriendly.'

And so he'd agreed, although he wasn't actually feeling too friendly. But why was that? He considered himself an affable enough guy, but it was true, he hardly knew most of the people in Lodeshill – certainly not enough to dislike them. So why was he so unwilling to make the effort?

Perhaps it was just because it was a churchy thing, he thought. But if he was honest with himself he knew it wasn't just that; it was about not being *one of them*. But was that because he didn't want to be, or because he didn't think they'd let him?

He sighed and went up to the radio room, leaving the music on downstairs. The Philco People's Set he'd picked up in Wales had turned out to be even better than he'd expected: the Deluxe version, and not in bad nick. It wasn't working, though, and he needed to get at the circuits; he'd checked the power supply yesterday, but that had seemed OK. Thing was, given its provenance it could have been sent back to the shop because of a manufacturing defect; there was no real way of telling. He'd have to take it apart and start from scratch.

Kitty's key in the door made him jump. 'Howard?' she called up the stairs. 'Rogation. Have you forgotten?' The music stopped abruptly.

Shit, he thought. He'd been supposed to meet her outside church, and he wasn't even ready. 'Sorry,' he called out. 'Just coming.'

Downstairs, he fetched his walking boots and began putting them on. 'Is it warm out?' he asked. 'Too warm for a jacket?'

'Far too warm,' Kitty replied. 'Oh, do come on. The others are all waiting.'

But when they got to the church there was a further delay while a couple of children and someone's dog were fetched. Kitty stood and gossiped with Christine Hawton while Howard smiled vaguely into the middle distance. Eventually, after a few words from the vicar, in dog collar, short-sleeved shirt and walking trousers, they set out.

Twenty-two: Howard had counted. It was hardly the whole village, though most of them were probably too old to make it, he supposed.

'It's Howard, isn't it?' Bill Drew had appeared alongside him; Kitty was still talking to Christine, who was alternately listening to her and chiding her cocker spaniel for pulling on the lead. 'Bill Drew,' he continued, sticking out his hand. 'We've met once or twice. It's good to see you here.'

'Thanks, yes,' said Howard. 'Thought I'd come along. I was ill last year, or I would have made it.'

'Of course. Such a lovely tradition, especially for newcomers. A great way to be welcomed into the parish.'

The word 'parish' had unstable connotations for Howard; was it a religious thing, or just a countryside thing? They hadn't had them in Finchley, or not that he remembered. He hoped it wasn't like being welcomed into the family of God or something.

'Thanks – though I'm not religious, I should say.'

'Oh, few people are these days, it seems, or if they are they say they're "spiritual", which is something different, I suppose. It's quite all right, anyway – beating the bounds is more a village event than anything.'

The vicar had led off down the road past Hill View, and was about to turn into Ocket Wood. 'Beating the bounds?' asked Howard.

'Yes, at Rogationtide. They used to beat the boundary stones with sticks – and beat the village's little boys, sometimes. It was a way of drumming the landmarks into the next generation so that they'd know if there were any landgrabs by neighbouring parishes.'

Howard looked around doubtfully; there were a couple of under-tens and some reluctant-looking teenagers at the back. 'I don't think that would go down too well these days.'

'No, quite. Anyway, how are you enjoying life in the country? You've been here, what, a year now, it must be.'

'Oh – wonderful. We love it here.'

'You were in London before, I believe? Must have been a bit of a shock to the system at first.'

'We've settled in OK. How about yourself, have you always lived here?'

'Here and hereabouts. My wife Jean, over there – have you met her? – she's originally from the Welsh Valleys. We met at a dance in Ardleton when I was doing national service. But we've lived in Lodeshill for a long time now, a long time.'

Howard wondered what that must be like: never to have lived in a city, always to have been marooned somewhere inconsequential. Never even to have moved around the country very much. It was hard to imagine.

Before he could say anything in reply, the vicar, out in front, turned to them and held up his hand.

'This is the first place where we pause,' he said, as the small group came to a halt around him. 'Here, behind me, is one of the parish's oldest trees, an ash stool believed to be at least six hundred years old. I'll read a short lesson, and then we'll give thanks for our local woods, their beauty and benison.'

Oh God, thought Howard, remembering his piss puddling at the base of the ancient tree. *Benison.* Why did they have to use language like that? It was offputting. He glanced over at Kitty as she listened to the vicar read from the Bible; she was hunting for something in her handbag and didn't look particularly reverential, which was something.

At least the God bit was brief; in a couple of minutes they had moved on, emerging from Ocket Wood to follow the line of a ditch along a field. Howard found himself almost tripping over the cocker spaniel and then, as Christine apologised, he was drawn into conversation with her.

Jamie was walking with his dad and George Jefferies, who was on good form, lucid and cheerful. It was the first Rogation walk he'd been on in years. His mother had nagged him into it, but once he'd got out of the house he found it helped to distract him from the uneasiness he still had about Friday night.

He'd missed his shift at the bakery the day before, had phoned in sick. His hangover had kept him in bed most of the day; that and an obscure but inescapable feeling of shame. The thought of how uncomfortable the bike would be to ride until he replaced the rear shock hadn't helped.

To distract himself he began counting off the birds he could hear: song thrush, skylark, jackdaw, wren. There was so much birdsong at this time of year, although according to his grandfather the fields were almost silent compared to when he was a boy. But then, didn't everyone think things was better when they were young? And besides, the old man had been slowly going deaf for years.

The group turned into what he and Alex had always called 'treasure field' because of the potsherds and jug handles it gave up each time it was ploughed. Jamie tried to remember its real name – Wood Rean? New Rean? – but found he could not. When they were little he and Alex had spent whole afternoons there, fossicking around in the mud. His mother would go spare at his trouser knees when he got home, but on one of the windowsills at the farmhouse was arrayed the treasure they had found: fragments of pot, glass beads, a couple of cloudy marbles, hobnails, a triangle of willow-pattern plate. Alex had wanted to look it all up on the Internet, but Jamie hadn't been bothered about that, he'd just liked finding things and thinking about who had touched them last, and how they had been lost. As they walked he wondered what had become of it all since he'd last been there; whether, without Alex to stop him, Mr Harland had thrown it all away.

The vicar stopped halfway along the field margin. 'This is the first of the parish boundary stones we'll come to. There are nearly forty around the village that we know of, but you'll be pleased to hear we're only going to stop at a few.'

Although he hadn't been this way in a few years Jamie knew the stone, with its inscribed 'L', so well he didn't even have to look to see where it nestled in the hedge. Still, going round with everyone else like this made the woods and fields feel shared; defused, somehow, rather than dense with his own, complicated web of significance.

'Bill Drew has been making a map of them, so if you've got any on your property, do please let him know.' Bill held up his hand to show who he was, and the group moved on, the children laughing and calling at the back and Christine Hawton's cocker spaniel running out ahead. Five rooks flew lazily overhead, their black wings working the air like oars.

Kitty watched the dog nose the ground and half listened to Christine, who was no longer chatting to Howard and had fallen into step with Jean Drew behind her.

'Poor George saw him in his garden,' said Jean. 'Bold as brass, he was.'

'Do you think he's a gypsy?' said Christine.

'No, I think he's a tramp of some kind.'

'A tramp? Out here, in the countryside? You'd think if you were homeless you'd go into Connorville, at least. What is there for a tramp here? Unless he's after something.'

'Well, I don't see what we can do. Report him to the police?'

'Well, why not? It was trespass, at the very least. George's garden, that's private property.'

'He's probably long gone by now, though,' Kitty intervened, looking round and letting them catch up with her. 'Don't you think? That was last weekend, and I don't think anyone's seen him since.'

Jean looked doubtful. 'Any sign of him in Ocket Wood, Christine? You'd know, you walk the dog there every day, don't you?'

'No, I don't think so. Maybe Kitty's right.'

'It's the kids I worry about,' said Jean. 'You can't be too careful these days.'

'And now, at the top of the rise you'll see our Gospel oak,' said the vicar, out in front, turning and pointing to a stag-headed tree in the centre of a large field. Kitty recognised it as the one she had been intending to paint; it seemed an age ago now.

'We'll stop there and give thanks for the crops. This oak and the one just a little further on – can you see? – they used to be part of a hedge that was probably planted during the Inclosures, but as you can see the rest of it was lost when the fields were enlarged, along with the footpath from Lodeshill to Crowmere. We'll trace the old line of it, though. Just be careful not to damage the young, er – the corn, I think.'

'Oats,' muttered Jamie.

Behind them, Kitty looked out across the field. It was an impressive enough tree, standing by itself like that, but she could see now that any painting she had made of it would have been utterly generic. She thought of the sketch that she had started the day before, on a small 10x10″ canvas: an old gate rotting into long grass. Already it was coming to life in her mind, and more than that, it felt like her own.

The warm weather suited the asparagus, and at Woodwater they had begun harvesting twice daily. Some of the other pickers grumbled about being out on the beds all day, but Jack preferred it to working in the pack house; loading the grader, packing and labelling the asparagus made it feel to him like a product rather than food – and him like a cog.

For the most part the other pickers spoke Romanian to one another, though a couple of them made the effort with Jack. He didn't mind not chatting, though; it allowed him to avoid awkward questions, like where he slept at night.

At the end of the row he straightened up. The bundles of cut asparagus were in neat piles for Mihail to collect; as soon as the others finished their beds it would be time to move to the next field. Sweat was beading on his forehead; he went and sat in the shadow of the hedge, where he'd left a bottle of water, and drank. Cider would have been better, sour and cloudy and refreshing, but he hadn't been offered cider on a farm for a decade.

The field sloped away in front of him, brown and gently ridged, until it met the blue spring sky. At one time there had been a line of elms at the far end, but they had died thirty years before, the carcasses finally falling in the high winds of '87. Jack fumbled in his pocket for an acorn and pressed it into the bank, a sudden flock of goldfinches dipping and chirruping briefly around him before moving on.

As he watched them fly off Jack's eye was drawn to a movement, and he saw that there was a line of people on the other side of the hedge, their heads showing briefly above the hawthorn blossom as they walked. It was quite a big group, perhaps twenty or so; they passed along the margin of the far field and then turned in through the gate towards the asparagus beds. He saw a couple of the other pickers, nearly at the end of their rows, straighten up and look over.

The group began to toil up the far side of the field beside the beds. Instinctively, Jack shrank back into the hedge, glad of his khaki combats and dark T-shirt. As they drew level he saw that it was led by a man in a dog collar. Of course, he thought. Rogationtide: they were walking the old parish boundary.

Mihail had gone over to talk to them, and he could see the vicar explaining, gesturing with his arm over the fields to where the tower of St James's could just be seen between trees. The other pickers had all finished their rows by now; Jack watched as Mihail shook the vicar's hand and, when the group moved off, he picked up his crate and began to collect the bundles from the final two beds.

On the way back to the village Howard let himself fall behind. The only person who wasn't deep in conversation with someone else was the lad who owned the muscle car, and he certainly didn't want to talk to him. He wondered why the boy was even on the walk; he didn't look like the churchy type. Though of course, he reflected, looking at Kitty, you never could tell.

All in all it had been OK though; quite nice, even. A bit of a stroll around some places he hadn't been to before; a look at the farms, which you wouldn't normally trespass on. And that had been asparagus! He'd never realised. Actual people picking it, too, rather than machines. Probably it was cheaper that way.

He thought about his night out in London. It was nagging at

him, he couldn't quite make sense out of it; he didn't know whether to put it down as a good time or not. OK, so it had been a bit awkward at the end, but it had still been good to see Geoff, hadn't it? Though there'd been an edge to a couple of things he'd said – Howard struggled to remember exactly what, now, but the sense remained.

And there was more than that. Yes, he missed London; but he'd known that before he went down. That was natural; he'd lived there nearly all his adult life. But there had been a moment, in the Royal Oak, when he'd found himself imagining – what? That he could return there? Kitty would never go with him, he knew that. But he'd thought it anyway, just for a second. Christ.

It didn't mean anything, though. You could think about all sorts of things; it didn't mean you wanted them to happen. And look at Geoff: he had no desire to be like that, a middle-aged man making a fool of himself. No, what he needed to do was come to terms with the fact that things had changed: really embrace it, instead of trying to keep one foot in a life that was past. Grow up, as Kitty might have said.

He looked at the people walking in front of him: the two old men, the vicar, the husbands and wives, the children. Decent people; villagers – whatever that meant these days. He was never going to start going to church or anything, he was never going to sit on the bloody parish council. But perhaps belonging was as simple as deciding to. He quickened his pace to catch up.

2 0

Common nettle, purslane, dandelion; tormentil (high ground).
A lesser stag beetle emerging.

Despite having been up until the small hours the night before, James Albert Hirons woke around dawn. Sometimes these days he found himself confused first thing, and had to lie very still until the world assembled itself around him. But not today. His old bones ached, but for now his mind felt clear.

He had gone to get a bit of fish the evening before. He'd arrived at the shop but they'd talked gibberish at him, said they didn't sell fish, only newspapers and magazines and sweets. He'd turned to Edith, but she wasn't there. After a while he'd remembered; the shame of it had caught him under the ribs. In the end a complete stranger had walked him home, like he was some kind of basket case. 'No,' he muttered to himself now, closing his eyes for a moment. 'No.'

He got out of bed, slowly, and went to sit on the cold porcelain for a piss. The bathroom smelled damp except on the very hottest days, and the grout between the old pink tiles was black. He tried, of course he did. But it was hard. And some things – like the bloody mat in there, the towelling grey and flat – they didn't matter anyway. Not any more.

He hawked and spat into the bowl, pulled the chain, then washed his face in cold water. His hands trembled for a moment as he held the threadbare yellow towel to his face. Gillian had told him once that the council sent a woman round to wash poor old George Jefferies. It didn't bear thinking about; he knew he couldn't have borne it in George's place. No, he wouldn't let it come to that.

'It's better than being in a home, Dad,' Gillian had told him, daft as ever. 'Home? Don't call them that,' he'd said.

The sun poured in through the nets and he could hear a blackbird singing from somewhere nearby. Spring was almost over, he thought, pulling on his trousers and lifting the braces over his bony shoulders; the last he'd ever see. It was enough to make you weep. Children noticed the trees coming into leaf, but for most people what divided up the year was Christmas and trips abroad and school bloody holidays. God's green acre: it was what he'd dreamed about when he'd been in Singapore, but apart from the loony bloody eco-warriors nobody these days gave two hoots about what was going on outside.

Except the farmers, of course, he thought, taking the stairs down very slowly and putting the kettle on; they noticed. And he did, even now. A little part of him still thought of himself as a farmhand; always had, despite all those years making kettles and bloody washer-dryers.

It had been hard to understand at first: rationing still on, the farmers told to grow more, but less and less farm work to be had. But then, he hadn't made it back until '46, and then there'd been the sanatorium; it had been a couple of years before he'd got his strength back, by which time he was at the back of the queue. Perhaps Edith was right, and it had been for the best; yet the conviction still lingered that, but for the war, and Edith, he'd have had a different life.

Once he'd found an old iron coulter from a plough when he was out dipping with his grandson in the lake near the big house in Lodeshill. Even covered in rust he could tell how worn and notched it was, how well used. He'd tried to explain to the lad how it worked, but it was clear he hadn't really caught on. He'd thrown it back, of course, like everything else; though once or twice since then he'd wondered how old it might have been. There were things that, until his own lifetime, had hardly changed for centuries. Most had now been swept away.

He drank his tea black, rinsed the cup carefully and put it away; then he looked around the kitchen and whispered a last goodbye to Edith.

It was time. Before he left he took his Pacific Star with its once-bright ribbon from the trouser pocket where it had lived for over half a century, passed his right thumb from habit over its familiar contours and placed it gently on the hall table. Then he pushed his feet into the boots he kept half laced to save bending, shrugged on his worsted jacket and walked out into the heavenly morning.

After he had gone a breeze crept in at the open door and fluttered the pages of the *Racing Post*, obscuring and then revealing the medal, its royal cypher worn smooth by the old man's anxious hands.

The outline of Babb Hill was part of the architecture of Jamie's self, like knowing which lintels he needed to duck his head under, or the way he wrote his name. He didn't have to look for it on the horizon; he always knew which direction it was in, and its differing silhouettes from all sides: how the summit looked wreathed in cloud, the way the sun fell on its slopes and the cloud-shadows chased over it. He knew where the badgers dug into it, and the texture of the earth they brought out from its interior; he knew the weak-tea colour of the water in the clay pits. These things were so obvious that had he thought about it it would have seemed impossible that people in the very same county could live with only a vague image of Babb Hill in their minds. And although he dreamed so often of escape, the idea that all this knowledge would leave him – that one day these places might be to him a memory and nothing more – was not something he could easily conceive of.

He'd woken early, like his grandfather, and had decided to

climb the hill before breakfast. He took a short, steep route up to the summit, avoiding any dog walkers and early joggers who might be on the main track. Beneath the trees the damp ground was thickly clothed with the limp leaves of bluebells and wild garlic, dying back; the dew quickly soaked into his trainers, making his feet feel cold, but he knew that on the east-facing side the morning sun would be warm. As he climbed a wood-pecker drummed once and was silent, and from somewhere deep in the trees a woodpigeon murmured complacently to itself.

On warm nights there were often couples in the long grass on Babb Hill. Jamie had seen it a few times: pairs of pale knees and buttocks moving; cries that made his skin prickle and flush. Up at the trig point there were sometimes telescopes pointing skywards; it was a good place to look for meteors or read the map of stars above – the same stars, he often reminded himself, that had watched over the men who made their fort there thou-sands of years before. The fort was gone, but the hill itself was the same, and the shapes of the land around it. He wondered why it seemed so hard to believe.

Now, though, the summit was deserted, and he was glad of it. He sat down with his back to the toposcope and looked out at the landscape below. The copse where the goshawks had nested was hidden in a fold of trees, but further away he could see the spire of St James's marking Lodeshill's position between the four farms, and the Boundway scoring a straight line past the village. Somewhere along it was the deer he'd killed – unless someone had taken it away for the pot by now, as his granddad had told him to. Further out was the dull stain of Connorville and the glittering motorway, and then the bluish rumour of hills. Buzzards mewed from the invisible staircases of the thermals overhead.

Around him grasshoppers, having stilled themselves at his approach, restarted their tiny saws, and a magpie paced speculatively towards him where he sat with his arms loosely linked around his knees. The sun was warm on his face, and he could almost believe himself to be a child again, up here on a May morning with nothing to do for the rest of the day but inhabit this place in which he had been born as an animal does, unthinkingly and with something that was not love, but had something of love's depth and simplicity.

He looked at the valley below, the line of the water table made visible on its distant slopes by the old farms and hamlets built along the spring line. Somewhere down there was Mytton Park, its blank sheds humming inside with activity, the reed beds in the artificial lake filtering out the shit from the staff toilets. It still troubled him, why Lee and Megan and the others had abandoned him at the Vault. Had he embarrassed himself – or them? He couldn't remember. In a few hours, when he got to work, he'd find out.

Breakfast first, though, and then some time on the Corsa. The sound system was wired in now, though he hadn't had a chance to test it out properly yet; not on the driveway, his mum would have gone spare. He'd take it out for that, turn it up, really feel the bass vibrate.

This morning's job was to fit a set of underglow LEDs that

would make it look as though the car was floating on a pillow of blue light. He'd seen them in an auto magazine, and they were pretty cheap. When they'd come in the post his mum had said he was like one of those birds off the TV decorating a nest and hoping that a female would come; the way she'd said it was like a joke, but with a trace of mockery in it he couldn't quite put his finger on. He'd told her that was just stupid; it wasn't anything to do with girls.

Jamie began to descend again, clouds gathering behind him to the south-west. A breeze picked up, shivering the young oak leaves as though the flanks of Babb Hill were sighing.

'Bricewold,' Jack said out loud. It had finally come back to him, what this place reminded him of.

It had been a bad night. Dreams had troubled him so that the boundary between waking and sleeping was uncertain, and he'd felt himself surrounded, part of some vast and shadowy throng. Finally he had cried out, waking himself with a great effort. There had been nobody there.

When it began to grow light he had sat up and found that he was bone-tired, his lower back stiff, and so he had decided not to go to Woodwater today. Instead, he was in the grounds of the big Manor House in Lodeshill, picking his way through the low box maze towards the tennis court. There was no car in the drive, and no movement from inside; he'd checked. He wondered who the owners were: Russians? accountants? rock stars? A world away, no doubt, from the family who had passed it down through the generations and to whom the villagers of Lodeshill had for centuries tipped their hats. He pictured the long-gone carriage house, pictured the hounds massing at the gate.

It was the tennis court that had made him think of Bricewold, a deserted village owned by the MoD where he'd spent a bitter winter many years ago. He had filed in, with a couple of dozen others, to its little church for a special Christmas service, and in the darkness afterwards he had simply slipped away. Someone at Twyford Down had put him on to it; soldiers still trained there, but not very often, and you could camp in the empty houses. He'd walked there, on the off chance; he was sick of protesters, their bickering and politics, and he had a sore on his leg that wouldn't heal.

That the army owned the valley in which Bricewold stood was immediately clear: notices informed him of the danger to his life, and in one field an old tank was rusting away, a buzzard heraldic on the gun turret, a freezing wind off Salisbury Plain ruffling the dappled feathers of its breast.

The village itself was startling, a site from which meaning had become fugitive. Apart from the modern road, thick with clods of mud from caterpillar tracks, only the path to the church, open twice a year, bore any signs of use. The pub, smithy and schoolhouse were still identifiable, but nearly everything else was gone, replaced by ugly breeze-block cubes knocked up specifically for training. The land around the buildings was humped and grassy and mute.

He'd chosen a small, square house with the legend '18F3' on one wall. Like the others it had no windows, but it was safe enough to light a fire inside and he clearly wasn't the first to do so. With nothing in there, no hearth or fixtures or plaster on the walls, it was a strange simulacrum of a home, one made to practise death in.

Now and then, flocks of migratory fieldfares blew in to strip the blood-red berries from the hawthorns, but other than that little moved in the settlement. Yet there had been times, during those two months, when Jack had been sure he wasn't the only one moving through Bricewold's blank and silent spaces; though whether others like him were living there, or it was locals from nearby villages, or ghosts, he couldn't have said. Sometimes the past was right up close against his skin, sometimes he could not have said with certainty what was real. Perhaps he was mad, after all, like some of the lot at Twyford Down had said.

One day in January he'd climbed over a breeze-block wall to explore Bricewold Court. It had been beautiful country house once, that much was clear; but now it had the same MoD-issue tin roof as the rest of the village, and its two dozen tall windows were boarded up. He had tried for an hour to get in, picturing a rich interior hung with dust sheets and cobwebs, a frozen monument to a world that had passed. But he couldn't get the shutters off, and it was probably empty inside anyway, just dim light and echoes and dust.

There hadn't been much left of the grounds except a few ruined outhouses and an avenue of limes, their branches black against the winter sky. But then he had discovered the rectangle of an old tennis court, cracked and weedy but recognisable still. And for a moment then Jack had seen the women in their white skirts and blouses, the wooden racquets in their ash presses and the jug of lemonade with its neat lace cover hung with cowrie shells. Where were those shells now? he wondered. Where were the racquets? The tennis players themselves, he knew, must be long underground.

The brash, red-clay tennis court at the Manor House in Lodeshill looked like a recent addition. Jack sat by the net post for a moment, feeling the sun on his face and bringing his thoughts back to the present moment. Last year a butterfly had been fooled into laying its eggs on the net's green mesh, and here and there they remained, a whitish crust like hundreds of tiny barnacles. Jack wondered if the caterpillars, with nothing to eat, had survived for long.

The morning sun fell on the back of the lovely old house with its mullioned windows, turning it golden, and after a while Jack got up and climbed the steps onto the terrace. A carved stone balustrade ran around it, and against the house wall there was a cracked stone trough from which wisteria grew. A set of teak garden furniture had been neatly folded up, and Jack wondered where the owners were, and how often they were even there.

Approaching one of the narrow windows he cupped his hands around his face and peered into the room inside.

★　　★　　★

Up in the radio room Howard looked up from the Philco and saw the homeless man the village was up in arms about trying to break into the Manor House. Or was he? Certainly he had no business being there, but you'd be a fool to risk setting off the alarms in a property like that. Still, perhaps he was unhinged, like Christine Hawton had said. He had a brief image of himself telling Kitty, urbanely, 'It's OK, I spoke to him. He's harmless.'

Howard jogged downstairs and out of the back door, but by the time he'd pushed through the conifer belt that separated their garden from the Manor House's the man on the terrace had disappeared.

2 1

Red campion, windflowers, broom. Commas and one brimstone.
Ground elder. Hot and humid.

It was the first time Jamie really hadn't wanted to go to work, though there was something familiar about the feeling. To put his helmet on after his shift at the bakery, to walk the half-knack-ered bike off the drive and gun it into life was to clench his teeth and push through a tangle of something dark. All the way to Mytton Park he maintained a high pitch of thoughts in his head, song lyrics from the radio, repeated phrases that made little sense. He even spoke out loud once or twice. What he was drowning out he couldn't have said.

The bike wasn't legal on the motorway, even for the five hundred yards to the site turn-off, so instead he wheeled it over a concrete footbridge that gave him a vertiginous feeling crossing water never did. Halfway across he peered down at the cars and lorries speeding below with a shiver that was almost an impulse to jump, or if not an impulse the shadow of an impulse, the ghost of a feeling about what it would be to be flung – falling – mid-air. And then he brought his eyes back to the narrow strip of macadam under his feet and carried on.

Far above the little bridge three gulls sculled with leisurely wingbeats; further up again an A320 headed for Spain, its contrail unfurling slowly behind it in the high, thin air.

Megan wasn't in the site office when he arrived, and he collected his lanyard from someone else. Unthinkingly he walked to his old hangar, not realising his mistake until he saw Dave the transport clerk swing round on his chair, page 3 spread out on the desk before him, and greet him with surprise.

'All right, Dicko, you back with us?'

'Oh – no. Wrong shed. I'm an idiot. Sorry, mate.' Jamie turned to go.

Dave laughed. 'You'll forget your head one day, lad. Eh, you OK?'

'Yeah, not so bad. How's things?'

'Quiet. Where're you? Catalogues?'

'Yeah. It's OK.'

'Heard you were out on Friday night.'

'Yeah – why?'

'Good night?'

'It was OK.'

'That Lee – he behave himself?'

Jamie tried to think. 'He got a bit lairy once, but it was OK. Why, what've you heard?'

'Nothing. Just … I don't like that Lee, I don't mind you knowing. Or that lot he hangs about with. You're a good lad, Dicko. You remember that.'

Over at 14B a shout went up when he entered the shed. '*Dicko! Dicko! Dicko!*'

Lee strolled over, his hard hat on back to front, palm outstretched flat. It took Jamie a moment to register that he was supposed to slap it in greeting.

'All right, Lee,' he said, smiling and putting his palm out in return.

'The man himself. You good?'

'Not so bad.'

'Good weekend?'

'Yeah, it was OK. You?'

'Hungover, were you?'

Already it seemed odd to Jamie that he had felt so uneasy on the way in. Maybe they were proper mates now, him and Lee; maybe it was OK. 'Yeah, I was a bit,' he replied, and grinned down at his shoes.

'You legend. Get home OK?'

'I walked. Wasn't so bad.'

'You fucking walked? No way! Should have got a cab, mate.'

The hangar echoed with the drone of the forklifts and

indistinct shouts from the men directing the movements of pallets and boxes. Jamie shrugged on a hi-vis vest and followed Lee to one of the conveyors.

'Is that how you lot got home?' he asked.

Lee's eyes drifted to the other end of the warehouse. 'Yeah . . . I mean, we weren't too far behind you. We didn't hang around that long after all that, you didn't miss a lot. Well, not too much.'

'After all what?'

Lee looked at him in surprise. 'What, you can't remember?'

Jamie's heart thumped. 'Course, I – I –'

'Bouncer caught you with Nick's speed, mate. You got chucked out. Still, could've been worse. Police could've come.'

Howard was in two minds about the tramp he'd seen at the Manor House. He considered phoning Kitty at the studio, but he could picture the way the conversation would go. She had a soft spot for people who were a bit different, and more than that, she was contrary.

'So you can't see the man now,' she would respond, deadpan. 'And he's not actually broken in. So nothing, essentially, has happened.' He decided to mention it when she got home instead, but when he got back upstairs he found he was too keyed up to concentrate on the Philco.

'Who do you bloody tell?' he muttered to himself, going downstairs again and pocketing his keys. No point dialling 999. Perhaps he'd just take a turn round the village, see if anyone was about. The vicar or somebody.

It was afternoon and there were no cars moving at all in the village. Howard stood at the lychgate and stared at the church, but there was no reason for anyone to be in there and he felt shy about trying the door.

He walked up Hill View and back without seeing anyone, then took the road out to the nearest farm – though of course it was standing empty right now, and as soon as he remembered it he turned back. God, it was like a ghost town. He tried to picture himself just knocking at a random door, and failed.

The Green Man was probably the best option; it wouldn't be open, but somebody would surely be in there. Yet when he knocked on the side door by the kitchen nobody answered. 'Sod it,' he muttered to himself, and went back to the house. At least he'd tried.

Later on he backed the Audi out of the drive and headed to Connorville. Jenny would be arriving at the weekend and there was something he wanted to buy – although perhaps it was a stupid idea. They probably wouldn't have it anyway, he thought, and that would be the end of it.

It would be so lovely to have her back – and Chris too. He pictured himself, a father again, smiling expansively at them all over dinner; pictured Kitty putting her hand over his and smiling back. God, like a bloody advert. He must be getting daft.

In Connorville he parked in the multi-storey and strolled around the main shopping centre. It was quiet in there: women with pushchairs queuing for the glass lift, old men with plastic bags. The air felt dry and full of static.

After two circuits he had to concede that there was nowhere that sold CDs; it was all online now, he supposed. Checking the time on his parking slip he headed out to try the pedestrianised central area.

Eventually he found a charity shop specialising in books and music at the dingy end of a precinct.

'Do you have any Simon and Garfunkel?' he asked at the counter. He felt, for some odd reason, exposed.

'It's alphabetical,' the woman at the till replied. 'Try under S.'

Howard felt himself flush as he turned away. For God's sake, it wasn't actually obvious; not in a charity shop. It might have been by genre. There was no need to be rude.

But he forgot his irritation when he found, on the shelf, the CD version of the exact same tape Jenny used to make him play in the car when she was small: *20 Greatest Hits*. Even its cover was familiar, and he smiled to see it again now, turning it over in his hands to read the song titles on the back.

Where the tape had originally come from he could no longer recall; certainly not from him, as his music collection was almost exclusively rock. But there had been a long period – years, it felt like now – when Jenny had demanded this one tape in the car, over and over and over. He had hated it at first, but the songs had somehow got under his skin until they were both belting them out and grinning at each other across the gearstick.

Chris, being older, had deemed it embarrassing, and when Kitty was in the car they usually listened to Radio 4. It wasn't a secret, but they'd both tacitly understood – even Jenny, at only what, ten? – that Simon & Garfunkel were theirs, and nobody else's.

At the till Howard was effusively friendly to the woman and felt that by this he had regained both the moral high ground and, obscurely, the upper hand. When he got back in the car, he put the CD on and sat with his eyes closed for the first three songs, tapping the wheel, whispering the lyrics to himself and smiling. He drove back fast with his window down, the restless spring air thundering past and bringing with it into the car the ambiguous scent of May blossom.

Kitty had started another painting; there was a press of them in her head, all the little things that had not seemed fit subjects for a picture before but now spoke to her powerfully and mysteri-ously of what the place she lived in was actually like. She felt for the first time as though she had something to say, something particular to her, rather than the reaching-out for second-hand transcendence that had characterised her previous work. She almost couldn't bear to look at her other paintings now, they seemed so timid and imitative: bluebells in a wood, distant hills, a ruined abbey. For goodness' sake, she thought when she looked at them now; what on earth had been wrong with her? The picture she was working on was of the brutal footing of a pylon, the way it was anchored in cow shit and dandelions. It couldn't have been more different.

At the studio hours passed without her noticing them, a stiff back, or Claire's departure, often the only way she'd realise how long she'd spent at the easel. On the days she didn't go in she took the camera out and walked the fields, alert for things that declared themselves to be real, to be particular, rather than the kind of idealised pastoral vision that, she now saw, had been obscuring the actual countryside around her. And stronger than ever was the sense that with these paintings she could communicate something true and have it heard; that she could, somehow, connect.

Less than a week, now, until the appointment with the neurologist: it came back to her as soon as she stood up and took her brushes to the studio's little kitchen to wash them ready for the next day. And tomorrow it would be a day closer, she thought, watching the colours unspool in the sink. With the tap on, she pressed her thumbnail against the base of each brush to release the pigment trapped at the root of the bristles; Claire had once told her not to, but then Claire was funny about her brushes. You could always buy more.

Kitty locked the studio and got into her car. Sometimes she wished she really could believe in God; if something bad happened you could tell yourself it was all part of a plan. But most of all, it would be comforting, now, to say a prayer and think that someone was listening.

Though it wasn't as if she didn't believe in anything at all. She believed in the church: not as an organisation, but in St James's itself, and parish churches like it: somewhere a village had brought its fears and hopes for centuries, that had marked its births and marriages, and buried its dead, for time out of mind.

The idea that that could be lost – *was* being lost – seemed unthinkable.

Yet rationality could be very lonely, she thought, starting the engine. The little folded prayers on the board at the back of the church; the ancient entreaties written on lead and cast into Roman wells. What else could you do, when all was said and done? How else, really, could you ask for help?

'There you are,' said Howard when she got in. 'Fancy a drink? I'm having one.'

'I do, actually,' she replied, taking off her coat. 'I'll have a glass of wine, please. How was your day?'

'Good,' Howard called out from the pantry. 'You? Painting going well?'

'It is. I've started a new series.'

'Oh yes?' said Howard. He handed her a glass of wine, picked up the sports section and subsided back into his chair. 'That Puck fellow?'

'No – it's sort of – well, it's a bit more complex than that.'

'Oh yes,' said Howard again, turning a page.

She looked at him for a moment. 'It doesn't matter. You know, I think I'll have a bath.'

'Righto.'

When she came back downstairs Howard was still reading the paper. 'I'm going to start dinner,' she said.

After a while he drifted in to the kitchen.

'I meant to say. I saw that homeless guy.'

'Which homeless guy?'

'The one that's been hanging around the village.'

Once, a few months after she had had ended her affair with Richard, someone had casually mentioned his name in conversation. The mismatch between her inner reaction and her offhand response was similarly acute now, and she wondered why on earth she felt so protective of him.

'Oh yes? Where?'

'He was at the back of the Manor House, peering in at the windows. I kept an eye on him – he wasn't actually trying to break in, otherwise I'd have called the police.'

'Surely there's no need for that. He's not doing any harm. Did anyone else see him?'

'I don't know – I don't think so, there was nobody about. Why?'

'I just . . . people can be funny about anyone who's a bit different, you know? I don't like to think of someone like him being locked up. It's not right.'

'He should go into Connorville. They'll have a homeless shelter there.'

'What if he doesn't want to go into a shelter? What if he just wants to live outdoors?'

'Well, that's all very well, but I can't see the locals tolerating it. Think of the gypsies – they've not exactly been made welcome round here. The vicar was telling me about it on that Rogation thing.'

'Yes, but that's completely different. And anyway, he's not a gypsy.'

'Well, what the hell is he, then?'

'I don't *know*, Howard. Look, why don't you go and pour me another glass of wine?'

Howard raised an eyebrow but said nothing, retrieving the bottle from beside his chair and bringing it into the kitchen.

'After dinner shall we sit down and go through what we need for the weekend?' he asked as he topped up her glass.

'You mean for the kids? I've been to the butcher and ordered a shoulder of lamb, and we can go to the supermarket on Friday. Why, what else were you thinking of?'

'Well, vodka for Jenny. And I thought I might buy her some wellingtons in case we all go for a walk. She won't be bringing any proper outdoor things, you know what she's like.'

'She can wear mine – we're the same size.'

'And we'll need to get the spare room ready, and on Friday I'll wash my sheets and make up the sofa bed for Chris.'

The fact that they would share a bed for the weekend flickered and crackled between them for a moment. 'Of course,' Kitty replied shortly. 'Howard, I –'

'I just want it to be nice. A nice weekend.'

'I know. I do too.'

'And for them to have somewhere to come. You know: home. I mean, I know it's not their home, but I want the kids to feel welcome.'

'They *do*, Howard. But they've got their own lives now.' She cut the florets neatly off a head of broccoli and put them in a saucepan to boil.

'I know that.'

'Do you?' Kitty replied, suddenly irritated, suddenly wanting to resist, for some reason, the rosy picture he was painting of the coming weekend. 'Well, you need to actually accept it, Howard. The kids may visit, and it's lovely when they do, but it's just us now.'

22

Mallow, pineapple weed, goosegrass ('cleavers'?).
Weather set fair. Swifts, swallows, house martins.

Spring was at its most fervid and riotous. The grass was lush and high, the cows sleek and giving good milk, and the narrow lanes around Lodeshill were hemmed with goosegrass and umbellifers. They stroked the sides of cars when they pulled over to pass each other, whispering along their hot flanks and striating the dust accumulated there from faraway city streets and motorways.

Ahead beckoned the summer, with its as-yet-unreckonable weather. *Please God*, muttered the farmers, checking and rechecking the long-term forecast. *Not like last year.*

There was still no word on what was to happen to Culverkeys, and as spring drove on it felt as though the village was held back, waiting. All day the swallows swung around the empty farmhouse, looping up to the eaves like stitches pulled tight; but in the evenings no light shone out from the windows into the silent yard where a century ago a steam-driven thresher had roared and clanked and where, before that, long-dead men had beaten the grain free from the husks with wood and leather flails. Now, with every night that passed, the shrieks of tawny owls pressed closer and closer around the dark barns.

It wasn't much discussed in the Green Man any more – there was no point speculating, they all knew the possible outcomes – but it lay somewhere behind the farmers' conversations, although an outsider wouldn't have been able to tell. The other thing they talked about of an evening was Jack.

'That Talling chap – you know, Kitty's other half, who moved into the Graingers' old place – he saw him snooping round the Manor House the other day,' said Jim the landlord, resting his meaty forearms on the bar. He'd heard it from Jean Drew.

'Did he call the police?' asked Harry Maddock, one boot on the bar rail, his Jack Russell asleep and twitching by his feet.

'No point. Anyway, there'd've been hell to pay from his wife, I reckon. From what Jean said.'

'How'd you mean?' – that was Charlie the cabbie, nursing a pint at his table. Apart from the three of them, the pub was empty.

'Well, just that she didn't want Jean telling anyone. She thinks he wants help, not the police involved.'

'He wants moving on, is what he wants. Before someone does it for him. And anyway, she's told the wrong person if she wanted it kept quiet.'

'Well, there is that,' said Harry, with a grin. 'I'll ask at the farms. Maybe they'll know something.'

'Funny you should say that,' said Jim. 'Nigel Gaster's got an older chap on the asparagus; he said something about him the other night, about how he hadn't turned up for a shift. But I got the impression it was a regular – someone who came every year. And I'm sure he wouldn't take anyone on who was, you know . . . deranged.'

'Thought pickers was all Eastern Europeans these days?' said Charlie.

'And students,' said Harry, with a nod to Jim. The nod was because of Jim's girlfriend, although she'd never shown the slightest interest in studying, even when she'd been at school – which wasn't that long ago. 'Where is she, anyway? In town with her mates tonight?'

Jim began unloading the glass washer. 'No, that's Fridays. The Vault, it's called. I'm not going to stop her, am I?'

'Never been tempted?'

'I'm too old for all that.'

'Not too old for everything, though, eh?' Harry winked at Charlie, who grinned down at his pint. It was a complex mixture of envy and ridicule, and Jim understood it perfectly.

'Speaking of kids, what's the story with your trainee?' Jim asked Harry. 'He quit, has he?'

'Didn't even have the decency to tell me,' replied Harry. 'No word for three days – I had to stop round at his parents' house.'

'And what happened?'

'Doesn't want to get up early, doesn't want to work at night. He's got a job in a computer-game shop in Connorville. A shop. I ask you.'

'They don't want to be outdoors these days, I saw it with my two,' said Charlie. 'They want to be inside, in an office or whatever. Why? It was good enough for me, more than good enough. I'd still be driving a tractor now if there was the work, not sat in a bloody taxi ferrying people around like a chauffeur.'

'What I want to know is this,' said Harry, standing back from the bar and folding his arms. 'Who's going to be left on the land in thirty, forty years?'

'Never mind that,' said Jim, hanging up the last tankard and slamming the glass washer shut. 'What about your assistant? Who the hell are you going to train up now?'

The night was soft and clear and brief; it seemed as though the village blackbirds had barely stopped singing before the dawn shift took over and chorused the next day in.

Jack was halfway up to the top field when Joanne Gaster hurried up behind him.

'Jack – sorry –' she said, touching his arm. As he turned he knew instantly what she was about to say.

'We – we don't need you today, Jack.'

He looked at her, a feeling of despair coming over him. It wasn't the fact that he'd missed a day; they must have found out that he'd skipped probation. Somehow, his past had followed him north. There was no point asking Joanne how she'd found out; she'd only stutter something about the asparagus slowing, or having enough pickers, when they both knew that wasn't true.

'Not tomorrow either?' he asked, just to be sure.

'I'm sorry.' She had flushed bright red, but to her credit she didn't look away. 'If there was anything I could do . . .'

'It's all right.'

He turned and began walking back the way he'd come, wondering if the other pickers knew, and whether they were watching. He felt ashamed, although there was no reason for it. He wondered if there was anywhere left for him to go.

At the pack house he handed Joanne his asparagus knife.

'I should give you this.'

For a second she looked as though she was going to tell him to keep it – as what? Some kind of compensation? – but she took it, her forefinger absent-mindedly tracing the back of its curved blade.

'Jack, look. Before you go . . .'

'It's OK.'

'A cup of tea. Please.'

And so he followed her out of the morning sun into the bungalow's kitchen, where an old collie in a basket thumped its tail in greeting and then settled back to sleep. Jack pulled out a chair and sat at the table with its bright vinyl cloth, clasping his hands in his lap, as Joanne busied herself with the kettle.

'Milk and sugar?'

'Please.'

She brought the mugs over and sat down across from him, shifting a pile of laundry from the chair first.

'Will you be all right?'

'Course.'

'Where will you go?'

'Oh . . . I'll find something,' he said, looking down at his mug. 'Or perhaps I'll move on. I suppose the other farms here won't have me either.'

'You don't seem to have too much luck round here any more, Jack.'

'You know about Culverkeys, then?'

'No – did something happen? Is that why you've not been back for so long?'

Now it was Jack's turn to flush. 'No, that was – well, we had an argument. It wasn't my fault. Philip Harland, he –'

'I never liked him. I know you shouldn't speak ill of the dead, but . . .' Suddenly she was confidential, keen to take his side. Guilt, Jack supposed.

'He tried to cheat me. My wages. I was helping with the milking – a couple of years ago now. At the end of the first week he held it over, said they weren't paying weekly any more – but he hadn't told me that when he took me on. And then at the end of the month it wasn't all there.'

She shook her head. 'I know they had money trouble over at Culverkeys, but that's no excuse. How much was it short?'

'I don't know. I can't remember.'

'What did you do?'

'I told him he'd made a mistake, but he wouldn't have it. I – I don't cheat people, ever. But he said I was lying.'

'Between you and me, Jack, I'm not sorry he's gone,' said Joanne. 'He'd borrowed money off us for some cock and bull story – well, off of Nigel, I didn't find out 'til after – and he never paid us back; and we weren't the only ones. Given everything . . . well. The only surprise was it took him that long to do it.'

Jack felt everything go still. 'Do you mean he – did Philip kill himself?'

'Thought you knew. Awful, when you think about it. That poor boy, and his little sister.'

'His – weren't there two sons?'

'No, one of each. They live with their mother in Doncaster now, best place for them. And the farm's been put up for sale, so it doesn't look like they'll be back.'

Jack wanted her to stop, wanted to get up and escape into the sunshine and spring air, but at the same time he had to know the rest – and Joanne was clearly enjoying having an audience.

'It was Nigel who went over and found him,' she continued. 'He'd taken rat bait, you know, up in his son's room. Nigel said the kitchen table was covered in unpaid bills, final demands, letters from the bank, from Tesco, DEFRA, you name it.'

Rat bait. Jack felt sick. 'And Philip had – how long had he . . .?'

'Oh, not long, they said, a day or so. It was the sound of the cows, you see – they hadn't been milked. I'll never forget it to my dying day.'

In Lodeshill the front gardens were bright with aubretia and forget-me-nots, and woodpigeons clattered in rage or lust in the yew beside the church. As the day warmed, clouds of greenflies rose, and swifts screamed high across the blue skies overhead. Half a mile north a tractor and harrow moved across the slope of a distant field, attended by two bounding dogs; the clank and hum of the engine and the occasional shout of the driver drifted into the village, as he warned the animals away at each turn.

Jamie was in the middle of his shift at Mytton Park when the foreman came to tell him there was a phone call for him. He set the box he was carrying down, took his mobile out of his pocket and looked at it blankly. There were three missed calls.

'In the office, Dicko,' said Andy, strolling off.

Jamie pocketed his phone and made for the glass-walled office in the corner of the shed. The grey receiver lay on its side on a slew of stock-control sheets, its cord in tight, overwound curls. He picked it up, gingerly.

'Hello?'

'It's me. I've been trying to call your mobile.'

'Mum? What's the matter?'

'It's your granddad. He's gone missing.'

Howard and Kitty took the Audi to the big supermarket in Connorville and brought it back laden with food and booze.

Opening the boot on the drive, Howard noticed how hot the bodywork was.

'First real day of summer!' he remarked, passing an orange bag to Kitty and taking two himself. From Hill View came the insistent sound of a door knocker; Harry Maddock was banging on the Dixons' door, but it didn't look as though anybody was in. 'Jamie?' they could hear him call through the letter box. 'You in there? I've got a proposal for you.'

'It's not summer yet, it's only May,' Kitty said, from the porch.

'May's summer, isn't it? Anyway, looks like it'll be nice for the weekend.'

'No need for those wellies, then.'

'They were only a tenner. They can live in the shed, it hardly matters. She'll wear them next time.'

Kitty let herself in the front door and set her plastic bag down in the hall; Howard passed her, taking his two bags into the pantry.

'Let's get these unpacked, then I thought I might make up Jenny's bed,' she said over her shoulder as she went back to the car. 'You can hoover.'

'All right.' Howard fetched another two bags from the boot as the gamekeeper's buggy reversed out of Hill View and drove away.

'Are those two booze as well?' Kitty asked, indicating the bags he was carrying. Howard was aware how heavy they looked, and had purposefully taken them himself. 'How much are you planning to drink?'

'Not for me, Kitty, the kids,' Howard shouted from the pantry. 'And you saw them in the bloody trolley.'

'There's no need to swear, Howard. For goodness' sake.'

'Well, I'm sorry, Kitty, but you can be an awful prig sometimes.'

Kitty turned to him, her face flushed. 'A ... *prig*. I can be a prig, can I? Thank you, Howard. Thank you for that.'

'Well, I hardly bloody drink any more. You know that. But you never let an opportunity go by to remind me of my past sins.'

'Hardly drink? That's a good one. You can barely go a day without one.'

'Is that a fact?'

'It is, yes.'

'And why should that bother you, exactly?'

'Oh, I couldn't care less what you do, actually. I'm just setting you straight, when you say that you hardly drink. At least get your facts right.'

Howard's heart was thumping. They stood and looked at one another across the kitchen worktop, both shocked at what had erupted so suddenly.

Howard passed a hand across his face. The kids would be with them tomorrow; he'd arranged to pick Jenny up from the airport at the crack of dawn. They couldn't afford this; not today. If they ever could.

'Look, Kitty. I don't want to argue. Not now.'

'Do you think I do?'

'Well, it seems like it, actually. Whatever's got into you?'

'Nothing has got into me, Howard. Just . . . oh, just go and do the bloody hoovering, will you? I'll unpack the rest of these.'

Howard hesitated, his face clouded.

'*Go on!* For God's sake.'

When he had gone she leaned on the counter and wept.

Jamie took the bike straight onto the motorway, gunning it into the slow lane amid the belching lorries and turning off at the first junction. Fuck not being allowed. And fuck work, too: Megan had wanted him to go and see HR, fill out some form about not completing his shift. Let them sack him. He didn't care. He'd slung his lanyard on the desk and walked out.

'Dicko! Don't be an idiot!' she'd called after him.

Dicko. 'Stupid fucking bitch,' he'd whispered under his breath as he jogged away.

At his grandfather's house Jamie parked the bike on the drive and hung his helmet on the handlebar. The front door was open; his mum was in the kitchen on the phone, a blue school tabard on over her T-shirt and leggings. It was odd to see her there.

'I've asked,' she was saying. 'They say he never came in this morning . . . I know, but the front door was stood wide open.'

She mouthed at Jamie, 'Your dad.' He nodded, and went to look around the house.

Upstairs the bedroom and bathroom seemed absolutely normal, the bed made, the faded old bathmat draped neatly on the side of the bath. Jamie wandered into the smallest of the spare rooms. Crowded with old furniture and boxes now, it was almost impossible to picture his mother sleeping in it as a little girl. And yet, when he stood at the window, the view down into the back garden was the same one she must have looked at all through her childhood: the apple tree a little bigger now, the shed a bit shabbier, but in most respects the same.

He came back down the stairs just as his mother was getting off the phone.

'Your dad's on his way,' she said. Her voice was clipped, but her face looked grey.

'Are you sure he's not just at the shop, Mum?'

'I've been – they said he's not been in today.'

'But – he always goes, he goes every morning.'

'I *know*, Jamie. But – something bad's happened, I can feel it.'

'What do you mean?' Jamie knew he was being obtuse, but he couldn't help himself; he didn't want any of this to be happening.

'He knows there's something wrong with him, Jamie, but he won't bloody admit it. It's selfish, is what it is. Just like when I was a little girl: everyone having to worry about him all the time, everyone having to dance around him, but is he grateful? No. Now tell me this. Who's going to have to spoon-feed him if he goes gaga? Who's going to have to take him in? Because it won't be any of your uncles, I can tell you that.'

'But you said it was just old age! Look, Mum, I reckon he's just gone for a walk.'

'You know what he's like about routines, Jamie. He's been like it as long as I can remember. He doesn't just … go off somewhere on a whim.'

'Maybe it wasn't a whim, maybe he's gone to visit someone.'

'*Who?* He hasn't got any proper friends in Ardleton – who's he going to suddenly pop in on? Anyway, he knew I was coming over, I was going to take him to the doctor's. I reminded him the other day.'

Jamie's dad appeared at the open front door, still in his work overalls. 'You've checked the house?' he said as he came in. 'Nothing out of the ordinary?'

'No,' said Jamie's mother, her hands jammed into the front pocket of her tabard. Jamie shook his head.

'Let's not panic yet,' he said. 'Gill, I'd give you a hug, but –' and he gestured at his clothes.

'Should we call the police?' she said.

'Not just yet. Let's have a proper look for him first. Silly bugger's probably not far away. Son, why don't you hop in the car and have a quick drive around town? Take your mum with you – you can look on both sides of the road that way. I'll head out across country in case he's gone for a walk or something. OK?'

Culverkeys farmhouse had an unmistakable atmosphere of abandonment, and Jack could see that it was empty from quite some distance off; there was a kind of blankness to it that told him that nobody had passed through the yard or any of the outbuildings for some time. He'd known the animals would all be gone, and hadn't expected to find anyone there, but still, to see it so utterly silent was a shock. It seemed impossible, as though so many centuries of productivity, so many hopes, should leave an echo; as though a working farm could not so quickly die.

And yet it had. He leaned on the farm gate, idly twisting a maythorn switch into a rough circle and wondering why he had come. He could have been miles away by now.

He had been the last of the hired hands to quit. He had left Philip alone on the farm – abandoned him to his eventual suicide. Of course, he wasn't to know what would happen; but nonetheless it weighed heavily on him. He should have seen the man was in trouble, should have thought about the reason his wages were short. He hadn't even bothered to ask; he'd just assumed that Harland was a crook. It was a failure of imagination, of compassion, and Jack condemned himself for it utterly.

He'd half expected that local kids might have broken into the farmhouse already, claiming the empty rooms with little fires or tagging the walls with cans of auto spray. But it was clear even from the gate that the house was untouched, and he was glad of it.

He knew he had to go inside, though he couldn't have said why. It was far too late to atone for anything now. At the back of the house he broke a pane on the kitchen window with his elbow, reached in and unlatched the casement. It was the first time in his life that he had ever broken into a building.

In the kitchen he stood for a moment with his eyes shut, braced for whatever the house had to tell him about what had happened there – but nothing came. 'I'm sorry,' he whispered, uselessly, into its motionless and unechoing air.

Back at the gate Jack stopped and took a last look at the farm-house, as though it could still tell him something. But it remained mute, and he knew that he was running out of time.

He wondered how bad it was – whether they had called the police, whether they were actually going to try and have him arrested. Not Joanne Gaster, perhaps, but one of the village busybodies. He pictured it: a police van, a custody desk, his full name, his prison record; then a duty solicitor who would barely look at him, a police cell. He would be in the system again. A vision of his last stretch inside broke over him like a wave: a vast cage for men, loud and strip-lit, the air fetid. *Just to be able to go where I like*, he thought. *Just to live how I see fit. I don't do any harm.* He felt his guts contract and a sob heave its way up his throat. 'I can't,' he said.

He knew what it meant: that his time with people was over now. No more farm jobs, fieldwork or pot-washing; no more winters in borrowed vans or bunkhouses. No more shops; no more money. He would disappear into the woods and fields – for good this time.

Standing by the gate, his eyes squeezed shut, he began to whisper to himself an old song; and as he sang he imagined that the wood of the gate grew warm under his hands, and that near the latch there appeared an impossible, brand-new shoot:

I dream of a mask that hangs from a tree
(All along, down along, out along lee)
I dream of a road that runs to the sea
(All along, down along, out along lee)

When the song was over Jack stood for a moment with his eyes closed, feeling the precious spring twilight press close around him; and then, shouldering his pack, he took an old field path towards Copping Wood as somewhere in the dim distance a faint siren sounded and grew, hastening his steps. He would sleep in the wood for one more night, and at dawn he would be gone: a shadow moving quietly along a hedgeline like something half remembered, and vanishing like a dream.

23

Elderflowers, bittercress, dog roses. Dead nuthatch
chick on a bridleway. Sunny and warm.

Both cars were on the drive at Manor Lodge, Kitty's tucked in at the side of the house, the Audi reversed in ready for the trip to the airport in the morning. Looking down at them from her bedroom window as dusk fell, Kitty knew that Howard wanted to go and pick Jenny up by himself – and given the row earlier perhaps she should let him have his way. It would take an hour to get to the airport and she could already picture how claustrophobic the car might seem at dawn, the two of them barely speaking and hardly anyone else on the road. It was all so painful, so very painful, she thought: the gap between how things were and how they should be. And impossible to bridge.

She and Howard had avoided each other carefully for most of

the afternoon, Howard hoovering downstairs while she got her daughter's room ready. Because she'd already been at university when they moved to Lodeshill Jenny's room had the provisional feeling of territory which had never been fully claimed. She had slept there in the holidays, and her old clothes and books were there, but she had never really made it hers in the way that her Finchley bedroom had been. Because she had gone straight into the internship in Hong Kong her things remained there, and would do, Kitty supposed, until she came back to the UK for good and got a place of her own. She had tried to persuade Howard that they should at least box it all up and put it into the attic, but he wouldn't hear of it.

'But that way we'll have a proper spare room,' she'd said, 'not just the sofa bed downstairs.'

'The sofa bed's fine. Just leave Jenny's room as it is,' he'd replied tersely. It was one of the conversations they had without looking at one another.

Perhaps she should go to the airport after all, Kitty thought, so that the two of them wouldn't already be locked into some kind of conspiracy by the time they got home. It would mean making the sofa bed up for Chris tonight, though; if she did go with Howard they would need to leave the house before dawn.

Sighing, she went down to the study and began to strip the sheets. They smelled familiar, human; Howard didn't change them as often as she changed hers. She could hear him in the living room, flicking through the channels on the television; most likely he was having a drink, she thought.

There had been a long period after Jenny's birth when his drinking had got really bad: every lunchtime, every evening, and more or less all day at weekends. He'd grown paunchy and pallid, the whites of his eyes like dirty laundry; when questioned he began to lie about it, lies that hurt her because they were so transparent, because they showed her so little respect.

She'd tried talking to him about it, but it went nowhere and made her want to scream. She'd written him a letter in the end, telling him that if he didn't cut down she would leave and take the kids with her. She left it on the kitchen table one evening and then lay in bed, eyes wide, until he let himself in at one in the morning; then, when he eventually came carefully to bed, she'd pretended to be asleep. To give him his due, he had taken it on board – more or less. But you couldn't just magic up trust again just like that.

Yet Kitty knew she was far from blameless. At the time she had been distant, getting over her affair with Richard; he was still present to her, still real, and the daily act of keeping him secret meant that part of her had to be shut off from Howard. And far from being the easy second baby that everyone promised, Jenny had been nervy, demanding: she wouldn't sleep, and cried easily; she seemed to want something from Kitty that Kitty wasn't able to provide. Later, as a teenager, she had stopped asking Kitty for anything, had become resentful and scornful of her – though, thank goodness, that phase passed once she had left home, and they got on well enough now. But Chris had somehow always been so much easier to love.

'Oh, are you doing that now?' asked Howard, wandering in from the living room.

'Yes, you'll need to sleep upstairs tonight,' she said shortly. 'We won't have time in the morning.'

'You're coming to the airport, then?'

'Yes, I think so. Is that OK?'

'Of course, of course.'

'Here, put these on, will you?' she said, handing him the bed-linen. 'Fifty degrees.'

She fetched clean bedclothes and began to make up the sofa bed. After a few minutes Howard came back in and picked up his bedside book and reading glasses to take upstairs.

'There are your shoes under the bed,' she called after him. 'You'd better take those, too – not that we're fooling anyone,' she added, under her breath. But Howard stopped on the stairs, and came back down.

'Kitty. What is it? Aren't you happy the kids are coming?'

'Of course I am.'

He looked at her for a while; she ignored him, but kept on tucking a pillow neatly into a new case.

'Look, perhaps it's better if I stay down here tonight after all. I'll get up and fetch Jenny and you can make the bed up for Chris while I'm gone.'

'No, it's perfectly all right. I've nearly finished now.'

'I just want it to be a nice weekend, Kitty, that's all. For the kids.'

Without warning Kitty found herself shot through with rage

and trembling with what felt as though it could, in a heartbeat, become something close to violence.

'*Damn you*, Howard,' she said, her voice shaking. 'You're not the only one! Why is it that *I'm* always the one spoiling things, why am *I* the one who's being difficult, the bloody – what was it – *prig*? We all know you want it to be a nice weekend, Howard, but sometimes life's a bit more complicated, sometimes you can't just magic up a nice time just like that – especially if you don't take any blasted responsibility for it, just whinge all the time when it looks like it might not happen!'

'Christ, Kitty, what's the matter with you?' Howard had taken a step back, his eyes wide. Kitty found herself trembling; she picked up one of the lumpy pillows, raising it to shoulder height, only to fling it back down again on the bed with all her strength.

'I've had enough! I've bloody well had enough, Howard! You don't *listen*, you just bumble around in your own blameless little world, with your pictures of yourself in your head – first it was mister rock star, then mister life-and-bloody-soul, for *years* when I was stuck at home with the kids, then you were father of the sodding decade with your daddy's little girl and now – what is it now? Country ruddy squire, with your tweed jacket, or do you still think you're too good for life in the sticks? I don't think you even know yourself, do you?'

They looked straight at one another, Kitty horrified but somehow exhilarated by what she had said. She let out a long breath and turned back, shaking, to the stripped mattress with its sad marks.

'Oh for God's sake, Howard,' she said, suddenly exhausted. 'You're a joke.'

All over the village the birds were roosting for the night. The jackdaws returned to their chimneypot nests and the swallows to the eaves, and the hedgerows lining the quiet lanes were full of chaffinches. On the Connerville roundabout the rookery in the poplars was filling up with black silhouettes, their gabble quietening as the light faded. In Lodeshill two little owls in an ash tree by the Green Man awoke and began to preen and shake out their feathers, and a roding woodcock circled the edge of the Batch on blunt wings.

In the village's back gardens songbirds were brooding warm eggs; here and there, in hedges, half-feathered chicks huddled in nests, their wide gapes closed for the night. Slowly the sun faded in the west, and the moon rose low and bright. It was a windless night, still and peaceful and warm, and the woods and fields were dark.

Four miles away, in Ardleton, all the lights were on in James Hirons' house where Jamie and his parents were anxiously awaiting the arrival of the police. His mother sat at the kitchen table, her heavy forearms resting on the patterned yellow Formica, her face drawn. She had cried earlier, when they had first got back from searching, but now she seemed scoured out. Jamie's father sat in the old man's usual chair, covering her hand with his own.

'Put the kettle on, will you, son?' he said. 'No doubt they'll be here soon.'

Jamie filled the kettle at the coughing cold tap and switched it on. 'Is anyone hungry?' he asked.

'I couldn't eat. Not here,' said his mother.

'You should have something, love. We all should.'

'I can't.'

'You got a pizza number, son?'

'Might do. Hold on.' Jamie got out his phone and began to scroll. 'Doesn't look like it – but there'll be beans or something I can make.' He looked in the bread bin, but it was empty and scrupulously free of crumbs. 'No bread. Hang on –' and he began to open the cupboards. There was nothing there. 'There isn't anything here – they're just – there's no food. Nothing.'

'Well, you can nip to the shop, eh?'

'No, I mean, there's nothing at all. Nothing.' And he was right: each cupboard, as he opened it, revealed only clean, bare shelves.

'Oh my God.' Jamie's mother stumbled up and wrenched open the fridge, but its humming light illuminated only its own arctic interior. Jamie stood on the bin pedal and looked in: only a couple of used tea bags huddled at the bottom.

'I don't understand,' Jamie said.

They were still looking at one another as the squad car pulled up outside, its blue revolving light passing across each of their faces. Without speaking, Jamie's dad got up and went to let the police in.

★　　★　　★

Kitty sat at the dining table with two bowls of rapidly cooling linguine and a glass of wine. She'd gone up and knocked on the door of the radio room, but there had been no response.

She knew she'd behaved appallingly and knew, too, that she would have to say she was sorry. But beyond the territory of this particular argument there lurked a wider landscape, one for which they both had equal responsibility. Whatever their marriage was, they had created it between them: they had colluded in all of its weaknesses, had allowed elisions and half-truths to pass for truth, had failed to ask the right questions, or to listen kindly to the replies; they had set up unspoken rules that were now barely visible, but under which they both chafed. Tonight she might have acted as the catalyst, but they had both brought this about.

She could apologise, and Howard would doubtless accept her apology so that the weekend with the children would pass off all right; and afterwards there would be another degree of distance between them, a further wariness. Or she could own what she had said to him, and try to explain why.

'You must tell Howard about your appointment, you *must*,' Claire had said earlier, on the phone, and perhaps she was right. Yet to tell him her fears now would be a way of getting herself off the hook; and as uncomfortable as it was, she felt stirring in her a grain of courage, a determination to live in the bleak light of her pronouncement, because although parts of it had been cruel and unnecessary, parts of it had been true, too.

She gave up on the linguine and drank some wine, letting her mind drift from habit to her three new pictures and wondering why she drew such strength from them. It didn't matter that nobody except Claire had seen them yet; the feeling of having created them was like saying her own name out loud, and she used the image of them to comfort herself now. Even Claire thought they were good, or as close to good as she'd allow herself to admit.

'I must say, I think you've really got something there, Kitty,' she'd said, lingering behind her easel. 'Whether you'd actually want a picture of litter, or a cowpat, on your wall is a different matter, but who knows? They're certainly unique.'

Kitty was just about to get up and take the supper things through to the kitchen when she heard Howard's tread on the stair. She picked up her fork and busied herself with her pasta.

He came in and sat down, but pushed his bowl away.

'Do you want to talk to me, Kitty?' he asked.

It was a far braver start than she would have given him credit for. She looked at him in surprise and found that his face was hurt, but open. She put down her fork and clasped her hands in her lap under the table.

'I'm sorry, Howard. I shouldn't have said that. You're not a joke.'

'No. You shouldn't.'

'I didn't mean it. Well, I –'

'You did, Kitty. You've not thought much of me for a long time.'

She picked up her fork, wound some pasta around it, then put it down again. 'There's so much we've never said. Isn't there?'

'Do you want to say it now?'

'Partly, I suppose. But – the children . . .'

'Sod the children.'

'Howard!'

'I mean it. I'm sick of it, Kitty. I'm sick of the way things are with us. It's not too late for you to make a new start, you know – if that's what you want. But we can't go on like this, picking away at one another. It's no good.'

Kitty felt her face go stiff with shock. 'Is that – is that what you want? To make a new start?'

Howard shrugged. 'Do you?'

'I – I haven't thought –'

'Oh come on, Kitty, of course you have. Don't tell me you haven't considered it. You say I never listen, but I'm not a total fool. You wanted a new life away from London for so long, and now you're here, and the only thing that doesn't fit is me. Isn't that right?'

'But – there's a difference between thinking about it, and – and –'

'It's not so big a difference, in the end. It's doable, Kitty. If that's what we decide.'

'And what would you do? Go back to London?'

'I don't know. Probably. I miss it; it's lovely here, but I don't belong.'

Kitty could barely believe they were talking like this. Where had he found the courage? Howard, who was usually so bluff, so . . . hard to reach?

'Look, Howard, can we — we don't have to decide now, do we? I mean, the kids are coming, and —'

'And that's another thing, Kitty. "Daddy's little girl".'

'I know. I'm sorry.'

'I love Jenny, of course I do. But I love Chris, too.'

'I know.'

'Do you? And it's not as if you don't have your favourite, too. Well, perhaps not favourite, but . . .'

'Chris was an easier baby, that's all.'

'That's not all, Kitty.'

'I love Jenny, Howard, you know that.'

'Things were difficult for a long while, though.'

'That's just what happens with girls and their mothers. We're close now.'

'Well, she needed me then, she needed one of us behind her. It was important.'

'It felt to me like you were taking sides.'

'There aren't any sides, Kitty. You should know that.'

'That's easy for you to say. Let's not forget what else was going on around that time.'

Howard exhaled, sat back. 'I know, Kitty, I was drinking a lot. And we've never been able to move on from that, have we?'

'I don't think you have any idea how bad it was — how bad *you* were.'

'I've got a pretty good idea.'

'No, I don't think you have. I was doing everything, Howard: looking after the house, the kids, the cooking, taking them to school. Oh, you did the odd thing here and there, when I asked you, but I took all the responsibility, I had to be the grown-up, every single day, for *years*. And I couldn't even talk to you – you were pissed half the time, and at work the rest. I felt as though I was completely on my own.'

'I'm sorry.'

'So you've said, a thousand times.'

'And I've meant it, Kitty. Why is it never enough?'

'Because ... I needed you *then*, and you weren't there. How can you make it up to me *now*?'

Kitty was aware that her hold on the moral high ground was tenuous, but the fact of her unfaithfulness seemed somehow irrelevant; after all, she had ended the affair with Richard, she had done the right thing – despite how unhappy it had made her. And it would never detract from how awful Howard had been.

'And what about now, Kitty? Do you need me now?' he asked.

They held one another's gaze for a long moment; then Kitty let out a breath and turned away. Did she? She hadn't thought so, but perhaps she was wrong.

'Howard, I –'

'Actually, don't say it. Let's – let's leave this for now. Have a think, eh?'

Kitty nodded, slowly. 'All right.'

He reached over and touched her arm where she sat: lightly, hesitantly. 'Come on. I'll pour you another, shall I?'

And she nodded again and handed him her glass. 'Please.'

24

Stitchwort, cow parsley, wood sorrel (oxalis). Maybugs.
Nightjars churring on Babb Hill. No breeze.

Jamie was at the bungalow, picking up some things for his
mother. The police had said that they would send out a team,
and that someone should remain at his grandfather's house in
case he came back.

'Any signs of dementia?' the officer had asked; the other one
was upstairs, and they could hear him pacing around the empty
rooms.

'He's – he's been a bit confused recently,' his mum had said.
'Just once or twice. Who people are, that kind of thing.'

'He's been sad too, Mum,' Jamie had chipped in. The officer
had turned to look at him.

'What kind of sad?'

'Just . . . I don't know. Quiet.'

'Are you close to Mr Hirons?'

Jamie had shrugged. 'I suppose so.'

'Thick as thieves, them two,' his mother had said. 'Go on, ask him what my father's like. He's the expert.'

Jamie had turned away from her then. Staring out of the window, he'd listened to but had not been part of the rest of the conversation, which was about sniffer dogs, about helicopters, about night-time temperatures. It was insane, it wasn't real. It was fucking unbelievable.

'Try not to worry too much,' the officer had told them at the door. 'Elderly people do sometimes wander, and we usually get them back safe and well.'

After they'd left his mum had properly fallen apart, her hands clenching and unclenching in her lap as she cried, tears and snot coursing down her mottled face and into the creases at her neck. His dad had steered him into the hallway and asked him to go home and pick up some things, said he'd sit with her and calm her down. Jamie had gone outside without speaking, but his dad had followed him out and put an awkward hand on his shoulder as he'd lifted his helmet from the bike's handlebar. He'd turned, his shoulders up; his face had felt fixed, somehow, and he couldn't quite meet his father's eyes. It wasn't anger, though, because who was there to be angry with?

'She doesn't mean it, son,' his dad had said. 'She just wants to be close to him, like you are. But he won't let her.'

'Well, maybe this is her chance,' he'd found himself replying.

'If he really is sick in the head like she says, if he needs looking after. Has she ever thought of that?'

Back at home he fetched his rucksack from his bedroom and went around filling it with the things his father had asked for, flinching inwardly a little as he chose some grey, faded underwear from his mother's bedside drawers. He wondered for a second if he should take her one of the dolls, but he couldn't bring himself to pick any of them up.

Racing the bike back to Ardleton through the dim, narrow lanes, he tried to think what else he could do. Fuck what the police had said about waiting: he'd head out and start looking. None of them knew the countryside around there anything like as well as he did, or the places his grandfather might go. And witnessing his mother's grief and fear all night was beyond him.

Half an hour later he headed back out on foot, this time into the fields, leaving his mother whey-faced at the kitchen table with Mrs Dudeney from the corner shop. His dad had gone out again to search the surrounding streets with some of the neighbours, including Mr Dudeney and the couple who lived next door; they planned to go house-to-house, asking people to look in their sheds. Jamie knew somehow that it was a waste of time.

The spring night was still, the air smelling faintly of cow parsley and dung. Warm currents rose from the fields and stirred the leaves of the trees, and little rustles spoke of the hidden lives of voles and rabbits. From somewhere off to Jamie's left a tawny owl asked a shrill question of the night.

He was glad, now, of all the times he'd spent with Harry Maddock; he felt at home in the dark landscape, he moved quietly and didn't startle easily. More importantly, he had a sense of what should be there and what shouldn't; he felt he would spot a lost or injured man more easily than the police would – although that could be wishful thinking, he knew.

After an hour or so he ran into a police search team on the outskirts of Copping Wood; one of their dogs had alerted there, they told him, but they had quartered the wood and found nothing. 'Probably a poacher,' Jamie said. He watched as they moved on, their high-powered torches criss-crossing the fields; Jamie had only his eyes and ears, but there was a moon, and more than that he wondered whether it might be more important to come to his granddad gently, calmly, than with torches and dogs. He called his name now and again, but softly, and tried to keep the desperation from his voice.

Harry would have been useful now, he thought. He didn't have his number any more, but he wasn't that far from Lodeshill so he decided to head across-country to the Green Man and get Harry and whoever else was in to come out and help him look. He wished he'd thought of it before.

The village, when he got there, was still quiet. Clearly the police didn't think the old man could have made it out this far; they hadn't been knocking on doors from the looks of things, and there were no flashing lights that Jamie could see. The church was dark, the houses lit but silent, as though nothing at all had happened. It made the fact that his granddad was out there somewhere in the dark seem even more surreal.

As he opened the door of the Green Man and stepped into its warm, beery smell he realised how tired he was, how much he would have liked to just sit, for an hour, with a pint. The lure of normality was so strong for a moment that he almost gave in; it was Jim, ringing the bell and shouting 'Time!', who refocused his mind.

'Where's Harry, Jim?' he asked, his hands urgently tapping the bar.

'He's not been in, lad. Did he not catch up with you earlier? Think he had a bit of an offer for you.'

'Can you call him? I need him. I need everyone –' and Jamie looked round at the tables and snugs. There were only half a dozen in.

'What's the matter, lad?'

But Jamie was addressing the whole bar. 'Everyone, my grand-dad's gone missing. You all know him: James Hirons. He was born here, in the village. Now he's disappeared, and I need you to help me find him.'

The cow parsley along the field margin was ghostly in the deepening dusk, and Jamie followed it to where a couple of planks wrapped in chicken wire made a rough ford over a stream. The bank was churned up where the cows had until recently come to drink, and he stepped carefully, noting almost without thinking the dog's mercury dying back under the trees and the last shrivelled curl of a bluebell in the moonlight. The sound of running water as he crossed was faint, but deeply familiar.

The narrow footpath on the other side was little used and edged by stinging nettles; he was glad of the thick denim of his jeans. From the uppermost wire of the fence a row of dark shapes was suspended above the nettles' dim leaves: two dozen moles, each one caught by its nose on a twist of barbed wire, their bodies desiccated, their spade-like paws spread in mute supplication to the stars. At the end of the line hung two longer shapes: mink, Jamie guessed, given the stream nearby. It wasn't Harry's work; Philip must have had the mole-catcher in before he died. He stood for a moment by the pitiful fencework gibbet, listening, then called out 'Granddad?' – but there was no reply.

After he had been to the pub Jamie had gone home briefly to pick up a jacket and torch. Coming back out of the house he'd seen Jim knocking on doors at the top of Hill View; he wondered now how many people would come out to help look. Bill had gone home to see if he could get Harry Maddock on the phone; 'That's who we need, lad,' he'd said. 'Harry'll find him, don't worry.'

Howard and Kitty lay next to one another in the dark listening to the voices fade away outside. Their doorbell had rung a little while before, but by unspoken agreement neither of them had got up to answer it.

'What do you think it is?' Kitty had whispered after a few moments.

'I really don't know. Probably someone's lost their dog. It can't be that important or they'd have rung again.'

'They must know we're in.'

'Yes, but we're in bed, for goodness' sake. It's nearly one in the morning.'

Kitty was silent for a while.

'Do you think it's an emergency?'

'Like what?'

'I don't know.'

'I'm sure we'll hear all about it tomorrow,' said Howard, turning over. 'I'm going to try and sleep, Kitty. I have to get up in a few hours.'

There had been some delicacy about bedtime; Howard had fiddled about downstairs for a while, waiting, she knew, until she was safely in her nightdress and in bed. She'd kept her eyes fixed on her book as he came in and got into bed beside her. The tact on both sides, after so many years together, was almost too much to bear.

And then someone at the door, so late at night. Somehow, strangely, it had made her feel as though they were a couple again – though why that should be so she couldn't have said.

She could see, now, that there had been more to her decision not to tell Howard about her doctor's appointment than fear that he'd fail her; keeping it a secret had been a kind of punishment, too. He was right: it was no good. And with this new honesty she dared to asked herself: could she really bear to be without him now – for ever? And if not, didn't he have a right to know there was a chance that she was ill?

'Howard,' she whispered. 'There's something I want to tell you.'

By his utter motionlessness she knew he was listening, could tell, in fact, that his eyes were wide open.

'What?'

'Howard, I should have told you before. I –'

'Kitty, please –' He rolled back over towards her. She could feel the mattress shift beneath her as he moved, knew that he was being careful that their bodies did not accidentally touch, and somehow it was that rather than anything else that finally made her start to cry.

'Something – happened . . .'

'Kitty, please don't tell me. Please.' His voice was strained, as though the muscles of his throat were not working properly.

She felt herself go very still, felt the rising sobs stifle in her chest.

'No, Howard, I –'

'*For God's sake*, Kitty, it was such a long time ago. I can't – please, whoever he was, whatever you did, it doesn't matter any more.'

25

Poppies, deadly nightshade ('dwale' here?),
goat's beard seed-heads. Tawny owls calling, calling.

In Connorville that night a farmer's son was punched to the ground outside a bar for reasons none of his friends could afterwards recall. His head struck a green electricity box a glancing blow as he fell; although he didn't lose consciousness he was taken to Queen Elizabeth's as a precaution, where his speech suddenly became slurred. He died of a cerebral haemorrhage at two in the morning, as the ambulance crew smoked outside and waited for their next callout. By 2 a.m. the blood and hair on the electricity box was tacky and dark. It would not be washed away by rain for another nine days.

All night, lorries thundered along the motorway's bright seam and cars circled Connorville's roundabouts under flat, orange light. Further out, though, the Boundway was silent, a straight line between sleeping fields. At around 3.30 the sky in the east began to lighten, but almost imperceptibly. It was still night, but dawn would not be long now.

Out in the dark landscape Jamie stood just inside the gate at Culverkeys and watched as two cats shot from the barn into the moon-shadows at the back of the house. There had always been farm cats on Culverkeys and he wondered if anyone had thought to feed them after Philip had died, and how long it had taken them to give up on humans and go back to nature.

In front of him stood the farmhouse, silent and empty. It had the strange quality of a dream: the way it both was, and wasn't, Alex's home, the house he had half lived in himself until six years ago and that had been nearly as familiar to him as his own. Looking at it now it seemed stupid to think that his grandfather could be inside, but he knew he couldn't leave without being sure.

The front door was locked, of course, but Jamie rattled the iron latch anyway, just in case. The sound of it rang out like a challenge across the yard, making his heart kick in his chest. As it faded away, Jamie saw that there on the dining-room window ledge was all their old treasure: the muddy potsherds and beads, the marbles and coins and bits of rusted iron. Even in the dark he could see how commonplace it was, how pitiful; and yet Alex's father had left it there all this time. He picked up a fragment of plate for the way the moon gleamed off its pale glaze and considered putting it in his pocket; but after a moment laid it carefully back on the sill.

At the back of the house he found that the kitchen window was broken, and he stood still for a long while, looking at the missing pane. His grandfather had worked on the farm when he was Jamie's age; maybe he'd wanted to come and see it before it was sold – or maybe his mum was right and he had got confused and thought that he was a young man again.

Jamie opened the casement and climbed awkwardly into the kitchen, his breath coming shallow and fast. Once inside he reached for the torch in his back pocket and switched it on. How many times had he eaten his tea in this room? Hundreds, must be. The kitchen table and chairs were gone, and the room itself seemed bigger – but smaller too somehow. Perhaps it was because it was so empty and still. He couldn't remember ever being in Alex's house by himself before.

'Granddad?' he called out tentatively – but the word returned flatly to his ears, as though the house itself had rejected it.

At the doorway into the hall his left hand felt automatically for the light switch, but of course it produced only a click. Looking back at the half-open kitchen window, though, he could see the sky was a very deep blue rather than black, and from somewhere outside came the distant but unmistakable notes of a song thrush.

Jamie turned back to the dreamlike rooms. The torch beam illuminated things abstractly, out of context: a section of skirting board and a corner of peeling wallpaper, a newel post casting a swinging shadow into the hallway behind. It made the dark seem darker, made being there again, after all this time, feel even stranger, like trying to see down, past your familiar reflection, into black and unfathomable water.

The dining room was completely empty, the oval table and chairs sold, even the old piano that nobody ever played gone. He had sometimes sat in here to do his homework with Alex, less often as they had got older and Alex was allowed a computer in his room. Jamie tried to picture the family sitting down in here to eat together, perhaps when visitors came, but found he could not.

There was so much he hadn't known about the Harlands. He'd felt like one of them for most of his childhood, but he hadn't been, not really. When the family broke apart he'd realised that.

Upstairs all the doors were closed apart from Alex's, which stood ajar. There on the landing, in the dark, Jamie felt a sudden hysteria rising, an urge to shout, or laugh. His arm, when he reached out to touch the cold door handle, felt weak. Yet how familiar was the shape of the metalwork under his fingers, subtly different from the handles at home; how well his muscles recalled the door's precise weight and resistance as it swung open to let him in.

He stepped into Alex's room and raised the torch beam. The bed was gone but there was the wardrobe, the pine desk and swivel chair with the broken seat. In the corner was a cache of empty bottles: mostly vodka, some miniatures and wine. On the walls faded posters remained in silent testament to the boy Jamie had known six years before: an obsolete pop star, a blue Ford Mustang GT, Ronaldo celebrating a goal.

And below them, Blu-tacked to the wall beside where the head of the bed had been, were a dozen or so photos that Jamie was certain had not been there before. He crossed the room, adjusting the torch to a gentler beam, and crouched to look.

The Harland family smiled out at him in miniature from the wall. There was Alex's mother holding a baby; Alex and Laura in the kitchen with a bottle-fed calf; Mr and Mrs Harland, young and tanned and looking not much older than Jamie was now, on a beach somewhere; and older, in party hats at Christmas. There was Alex, a toddler, on his father's lap on the tractor, the dead man's arms around the little boy a lost artefact from another time. Jamie recognised himself in one, holding the stock bull with Alex; they could only have been seven or eight, and his eyes filled with sudden, stupid tears for everything that had been lost.

He blinked them away. There he was again, even younger, at a picnic he couldn't remember; he took the photo off the wall, stood up so he could examine it more closely. He and Alex, just toddlers, were on a bright rug eating what looked like sausage rolls; their mothers were behind them, Jamie's dad half cut off to the right, his hand resting on his mother's shoulder.

But it was his mum who Jamie couldn't stop looking at. She was slim and laughing in a light summer dress and sunglasses, she looked like a totally different person. And she was heart-breakingly, unmistakably pregnant.

He caught the rat's movement from the corner of his eye. The hatch in the corner of Alex's room that let into the eaves was ajar, and it flashed in there, his lunging torch beam trailing hopelessly behind. 'Jesus *Christ*,' he said, his palms slick with sudden sweat.

Sitting against the bedroom wall, the photo in his lap, Jamie tried to get his head around what it meant. He felt blank inside, somehow; he knew he should be feeling something momentous, but it wouldn't come. Alex was still gone, he was still an only child, his mother was still the way she was – nothing had actually changed. And he felt like he'd always known she'd lost a baby, anyway; it fitted, it made sense. He just wished someone had told him – Alex, maybe, or his grandfather. He deserved that.

He would speak to his parents about it, ask what had happened. He would show them the photo so they could explain. He tried to think what voice he'd use, and how he'd start. It was OK for him to ask, surely; he'd nearly had a sister or a brother, after all. Maybe they could tell him which it had been and what had happened, maybe even tell him its name – if it'd had one. None of this would be easy, but he knew inside that it was the right thing to do.

His mum would get upset, and that would be bad. But she was an adult, wasn't she? And she had his dad to look after her. No, even if it made them angry he would ask what he needed to, he would make them say what had happened out loud.

And then, once that was done, he'd tell them he was moving out, and that Granddad could have his room. He didn't yet know where he'd go – maybe someone at work's floor for the time being – but he'd be all right. It was what had to happen now.

But all that was for the future, once his grandfather had been found, once things were back to normal. He checked his phone again, just in case, but there were no missed calls. He'd search the barns and the outbuildings; after that, he wasn't sure.

At the bedroom door he turned back to bolt the hatch. There wasn't that much harm a rat could do in an empty house, but still, they were dirty, his granddad had always said. He hated rats, for some reason, the only living thing Jamie knew of that he truly couldn't abide. Once, one had run down the towpath when they were out dipping at the canal, its fur wet and spiky, its muscular tail held stiffly out behind. The old man had hurled the big disc magnet at it, though of course he'd been far too slow. That's when he'd told Jamie about the rat-catcher who came round to all the farms twice a year with his terrier and sack of ferrets, of the vast hauls of vermin from the barns and stackyard. And – something Jamie had always remembered with horror – he had described how, in summer, the men would cut the fields from the outside in, so that the last stand of wheat, or hay, was full of frightened animals facing their death – not just rats but rabbits, even hares – while the grinning farmhands with their guns and dogs waited for them to bolt.

Fuck. That was it. Suddenly Jamie knew where his grandfather was. He clattered back down the stairs, the photo in his back pocket, pitched himself through the kitchen window and out of the yard, not bothering even to latch the gate behind him. He knew, with absolute and perfect clarity, where he was going. But first, he needed to get the car.

26

A bad night broken by dreams of the sea.
The morning warm and cloudless. Lad's love,
wayfaring tree, hawthorn blossom almost over.
Just after dawn I heard a cuckoo again.

It was just after three when Howard finally gave up on sleep. There had been voices from the road a few times, a distant siren, but it was too warm a night to shut the window – and in any case, it wasn't really the noise that was keeping him awake.

Kitty lay on her back, her face towards the window, the sheet and the old silk counterpane her mother had left her tangled around her legs. The room was dim, but Howard could see her white nightdress and the pale, familiar shape of her face. He sat on the edge of the bed for a long while.

Downstairs, he made himself a strong coffee and poured

another into a Thermos for the car. Before leaving the house he fetched the Simon & Garfunkel CD he had bought, then went quietly back upstairs to the radio room for some batteries and the Dansette Gem. The Audi barely seemed to make a sound as he eased it slowly off the drive and headed out of Lodeshill.

The little car park on the flank of Babb Hill was deserted. Howard took the radio and the Thermos from the passenger seat, locked the car and began to climb. It was a warm night with hardly any breeze, although above him the new leaves at the tops of the trees whispered slightly to one another in the dark. The track to the summit was well used and fairly smooth underfoot, and once his eyes adjusted Howard found he could see the way ahead well enough.

It was only the second or third time he'd ever been to the top. The first was when they came to view Manor Lodge; the estate agent had mentioned it, had told them they could see nine counties, and so after they had been round the house they had come up Babb Hill to see. They hadn't talked about the house in the car, not until they'd got up here. They had looked out at the view as they spoke.

He'd been able to tell, of course, how much she liked it. He'd known that she was holding back – not just in front of the estate agent but in front of him, too, because she knew he didn't really want to move, not deep down, and that too much enthusiasm, now she was getting her way, would be ungracious, and would leave him no room to come on board. Oh, they may not have been close, exactly; they may not have thrashed everything out in words like some couples did, but how well they knew one another.

And yet, sitting up on Babb Hill in the dark, he wondered if it might have been better to have told the truth that day, to have said that he wasn't sure and that he couldn't quite picture himself living in a place like Lodeshill. Except that was just it: he hadn't been sure. It might have been fine, so there hadn't seemed any point – not when Kitty wanted it so much. In the end, he'd let her sureness stand in for both of them; but it had not proved enough to carry them all the way.

Up on the hill's broad and treeless back Howard made for the toposcope where he sat gingerly on its low concrete plinth. It seemed less dark up there than it had done down in the car park, as though, with so much sky in every direction, the summit could gather in all the available light. Much of the landscape before him was indistinct and unrecognisable, Lodeshill's church spire lost in black trees, but he could see the lights of the distant motorway and Connorville like a twinkling constellation beyond.

An hour or so before he had to set off for the airport. He unscrewed the top of the Thermos and poured himself some coffee, hot and black and sweet. At the back of his mind, like a body in a sack, was the row with Kitty, and what was to happen next. But he didn't want to look at it just yet.

Among the stars a light moved steadily; a plane coming in. Howard tried to work out which way the airport was and which direction Jenny's flight would arrive from, but gave up. Maybe it would be better to be honest with her when she arrived, and with Chris: just tell them they were having some problems. The kids were adults now, it's not like their childhoods were at stake.

All those years of not arguing in front of them. Had it really been for their good? He'd thought so at the time, but looking back it wasn't as though he and Kitty had had it out properly when they weren't around. They had just tacitly agreed to leave some things be; things that were too damaging, potentially, to discuss. His drinking, for one thing. Her affair.

Howard closed his eyes and leaned his head back against the concrete pillar. His back ached and the ground felt cold through his cords.

It was so quiet up here, so still. He pictured people sleeping, below him, in their thousands: safely tucked up in bed, sunk in their ordinary lives. Families in groups, like little planetary systems, bound to one another for life. He thought about Jenny and Chris, being pulled back even now by the gravity of his and Kitty's marriage. They were still a family; they always would be, whatever happened. Wouldn't they?

He took another sip of coffee, then reached for the Dansette. The radio felt comforting in his hands; it was the way the knob clicked on and the dial glowed, the way it immediately began to whine and babble softly, surrounding him with familiar noise. It reeled his thoughts back in.

Slowly he began to scan through the frequencies, adjusting the dial minutely, listening, waiting, listening again. Pops and crackles, garbled speech, snatches of music, and between it all the otherworldly heterodyne wails. The Dansette wasn't a shortwave set, but Radio Moscow, or whatever it was called these days, was supposed to bounce off the big mast somehow and piggyback in on medium wave and even TV signals, so it could be anywhere on the dial – if the rumour about it was even true.

He gave it half an hour, the black sky around him becoming deep blue, the stars slowly fading in the east. He'd no idea, really, why he wanted to pick up the signal; it was probably a myth anyway. But to have heard it would have been . . . what? A little victory; a moment of connection. But there was nothing that sounded like it could be from Russia, nothing at all; just the usual chatter and interference he knew so well.

It was nearly time to go and collect Jenny. He wondered if Kitty was awake yet, and whether she'd be angry that he had left without her. He pictured her moving around in the rooms of the house by herself; pictured her living there, alone and unobserved, for good. If this was it, if he were to move out, she'd be a separate human being once again, with her own plans and thoughts and desires. It made him feel utterly desolate.

And what of him, who would he be without Kitty? He tried to see himself as others doubtless would, without her making up a part of him, or making up for parts of him, perhaps: just a sad retiree in a crappy flat somewhere with a load of old radios and cirrhosis of the liver, most likely. After all, he was nearly a pensioner; it was surely all downhill from here.

The fact was, he couldn't imagine life without her, not after all this time. They had their problems, he knew that. They had got into some bad habits – not talking about things probably being one of them. But no marriage was perfect. He didn't always understand her, but he loved her, and surely that was all that mattered?

Even when he was drinking he'd never slept around: not once, not even after that awful evening when he'd seen her getting out of another man's car, had understood instantly the eloquence of her expression as he'd driven away; not even when they'd finally stopped touching each other. He just hadn't wanted anyone else.

Howard clicked the radio off and let the hill's silence rush back. After a few moments he got up, stiffly, picked the radio up and began making his way down to the waiting Audi. He'd meet Jenny off her flight and they could listen to his Simon & Garfunkel CD in the car on the way back. And then, as soon as Jenny had settled in, he'd take Kitty up to the radio room, close the door and ask her if she wanted to talk.

Four thirty on a May morning: a long, straight road between fields. Jack was on the Boundway as dawn gathered in the east and the air around him filled slowly with song: blackbirds; thrushes; wren after wren.

He walked on the verge with his usual loping stride. *Just to be by myself*, he thought. *Just to live out the rest of my days as I see fit. I don't mean anyone any harm, God knows.*

Crows began to call from the woods and spinneys, and beyond the hawthorn hedges that flanked the Roman road the still-dim fields were dotted with early rabbits. The daisies on the verge were closed, the thick grass heavy with dew and clotted with fallen may blossom. It stuck to Jack's boots like confetti as he walked.

Raising his eyes from his feet Jack saw there was something on the carriageway fifty yards or so away. He stopped and peered ahead. In the low dawn light, looking east, it was hard to see exactly what it was; a struck deer? A feed sack? Whatever it was, it was motionless.

Jack stood and listened carefully. Apart from the waking birds and the distant hum of the motorway there was nothing; no traffic approaching from either direction, no voices, no human sounds. He took a few paces forward and stopped again, keeping his eyes on the shape on the road. It didn't move.

A few more paces and it resolved itself into the shape of an old man, his white hair thin on his liver-spotted and undefended head. He was sitting on the road, facing away from Jack, and he wore an old worsted jacket. Trailing behind him, from one pocket, was what looked like a washing line. Jack approached to the very end of it and stopped.

'Are you all right?'

There was no response. Jack wondered how the man's old bones could stand it, sitting on the cold road surface like that.

He tried again, louder. 'Are you all right?'

Still nothing. Jack shifted his boots on the tarmac; coughed; waited. Then he walked around the still shape to crouch down facing him, swinging his pack down to the road beside him.

The man's eyes were open, but he was looking past Jack. His hands rested awkwardly and uselessly in his lap.

'Is it here?' he asked, shifting his milky eyes at last to Jack. 'I've been waiting ever so long.'

Jack felt his hands. They were icy cold. 'Is what here? What's your name?'

'I need to get back for Edith, she'll be worried. I always get this bus. I don't know where it's got to.'

Jack closed his eyes for a moment. 'How long have you been here, Mr . . .?'

'Hirons. James Albert Hirons. Where's Edith, do you know?'

Jack tried to think. If only he had a mobile phone.

'Where have you come from, Mr Hirons? From home?'

'Home? Where's that?'

'That's what I'm asking you. Where do you live? Do you live in Lodeshill?'

'I was born in Lodeshill. 1919.'

Jack stood up and scanned the road in each direction, then crouched down again and took the old man's chill hands in each of his. There were no bruises or abrasions on them, at least; it didn't look as though he had fallen. He tried to think. He'd have to stand him up, see if he could walk. At least get him off the carriageway.

'Are you injured anywhere, Mr Hirons? Does anything hurt?'

'Hurt?'

'Have you got any aches and pains?'

'Oh no.'

'Good. Do you think you can stand up for me, if I help you?'

'Stand up? Course I can, lad. Here, give us your hand. Old bones.'

Jack reached his arms around the old man's ribs and hauled him gently up. He weighed nothing; it was like embracing a bird.

'Don't fuss,' the old man scolded; but he held on to Jack tightly as they shuffled slowly to the side of the road.

'Can you stand? Are you OK there for a moment? Look –' and Jack guided his hand to a hawthorn branch in the hedge. 'Let me just get my pack.'

The old man smiled. 'Did you ever collect that deer, lad?'

Jack shrugged his pack onto his shoulders and adjusted the straps. Then he gently took the old man's hand from the hawthorn and slipped an arm around his shoulder. Together they began, very slowly, to walk back the way Jack had come. Towards Lodeshill.

'What deer was that?'

'You know, on the road. Not far off here, was it?'

If he could just get him home he could hand him over to his wife. Then he could get back on his way; then he could disappear.

'No, not far off.'

'Hundreds of deer in Ocket Wood, always was. We used to go in there, you know, when we were courting.'

'When was that?'

'Oh, after the war, lad. Edith was only a girl before the war, you know; six years younger than me, she was. But it made men and women of us all …' His voice tailed off for a moment.

'Anyway, she – well,' he chuckled, recollecting himself. 'You wouldn't credit it. Not that she was one of those good-time girls, you understand.'

'Course not.'

'She said we should get married straight away, rent a little house near her mother, but I wanted to do it properly. I worked hard and I saved it up: four hundred and fifty pounds, that house, have I ever told you that? It was a lot of money in those days.'

Lodeshill was only a mile or so away. Jack wondered if the old man would be able to find his house all right, and if he should take him all the way to the door. Whether he could risk being seen. He had the sense of something having been decided, although he couldn't have said what.

'I used to think about all this in Changi, you know,' the old man continued, gesturing weakly. 'The fields, the birdsong. Whether the may was out. If it was haying weather.'

'Changi? Is that ... was that a prison camp?'

'Singapore. I was just a boy, really. Twenty-three. I had a great friend there, Stan. Chorley lad, he was. They took him away one day, to build a railway, they said. I never saw him again.'

Stan. Oddly, Jack felt his eyes fill with tears.

'I used to imagine I was ploughing the Batch, you know? With a team. Lovely animals, Suffolks. Up and down. I'd do it over and over, all in my mind. Getting a straight furrow, steering round that big oak. Kept me sane.'

'You were a farmer, before the war?'

'A farmhand, lad. I've told you that.'

267

'And when you got home did you ever do it?'

'What, plough the Batch? No. When I got back there was no call for horses any more. Anyhow, Edith was proud of me going into manufacturing, bettering myself. When I was made foreman she cooked me a steak dinner and she made sure all the neighbours knew.'

'But you missed it.'

'Now and again. Never told Edith.'

'Why not?'

'She'd've had no truck with foolish notions, she had the children to bring up. Anyhow, you can't turn back the clock.'

'That's true enough.'

'I had to put food on the table, lad. I just had to get on with it. Oh, it's all different now – kids come out of school wanting what they call a career these days, but we were just glad to have honest work.'

'And did you ever see anyone again from when you were in Singapore? From the war?'

'No.'

'Did you talk to anyone about it?'

'No.'

'Why not?'

'What was there to talk about, lad? It was all in the past. Best forgotten.'

'And did you? Forget, I mean?'

'Oh, you never forget something like Changi. Not really.'

They walked in silence for a while, Jack keeping his arm

lightly around James Hirons' back to save his pride. He thought about the old man's life: a unique landscape of memories, parts of it sunlit and open, parts shadowy and unvisited, all of which would soon be – was being – lost.

'I'd like to see it one more time, though. Before I go.'

'The field you ploughed?'

'The Batch.'

'Is that where you were going?'

'Going?'

'Just now. Is that why you came out?'

'No, I was – I've been –' and he patted his jacket pockets and then turned to Jack, a look of sudden distress on his face. 'Who are you, anyway? What's this all about?'

'I'm just going to get you home, Mr Hirons, that's all. To your wife. Edith, was it?'

'I'm not bloody doolally, you know. Not yet.' He shook off Jack's arm, drew himself up a little taller. Jack glimpsed, for a moment, the man he had once been.

'I know you're not.'

'Well, why are you talking about my wife, then?' the old man asked. 'Edith isn't at home. She's dead.'

When Kitty awoke it was still dark, but she knew without turning over that the bed beside her was empty. With a sick lurch she remembered their argument; remembered, too, that the children were coming today. She got up and drew the curtain aside: yes, the Audi was gone.

'Please, just … let it be OK,' she said, sitting back down on the edge of the bed with her eyes closed and her nails digging into her palms.

She thought about what Howard knew and didn't know, and about the person he thought she was: passionless and critical; a painter of whimsy; a religious convert. She was none of those things, not really. She was someone entirely different, someone he had never really seen.

She wondered who had told him about the affair, and how much he knew. Dear God, all those years and he hadn't said anything; decades of ordinary family life, when she'd thought she was the only one with secrets. Poor Howard. No wonder he drank.

But they would have to talk about it now, wouldn't they? 'Please,' she whispered again, her head bowed over her knees, her hands cold and clenched. The kids would both be with them in only a few hours.

There was no point going back to bed; she wouldn't sleep. She got up and put on trousers and a shirt and went downstairs. In the kitchen she switched the kettle on, but as the water slowly heated and its rumble increased the house grew close around her and she knew it wasn't where she wanted to be. Before it boiled she had picked up her keys and pulled the front door to behind her, the young swallows in the eaves above her shifting uneasily in their mud cups.

The church was cool and empty, its roof timbers with their carved bosses lost in shadow, the air it held within it very still.

She sat down in one of the back pews. It was a moment of comfort, that was all, a way to step outside the confines of her life for a few minutes. To try to see the way ahead.

'Please God, help me,' she whispered under her breath. It was all she could manage for now.

If only she knew what she wanted; if only she could tell. Other people seemed to be able to: look at Claire. She'd known when both her marriages were over – at least that was the way she told it. But perhaps all anyone could do was make a blind choice and then justify it to themselves afterwards. Maybe there was never any real way to be certain what was right – or what the future held.

Including for her. She kept telling herself she was imagining it, but once or twice recently she'd felt briefly dizzy, as if she were floating.

'You'll need Howard on side if the news isn't good,' Claire had said to her on the phone. 'Kitty dear, don't leave telling him for too long.'

But it wasn't that simple. There were two conversations they needed to have, she saw now: one about the past, and one about the future. And her appointment didn't come into either; it shouldn't, she owed Howard that much. If their marriage was over, if he wanted to go back to London, she would give him that chance – without any illness of hers hanging over him. After all, if something happened to Howard she wasn't sure she could face nursing him for the rest of her life.

No; if there was anything wrong – which she still couldn't

really believe – then she would cope with it alone. It would be her penance for the choices she'd made.

Around the corner on Hill View Jamie was pulling the tarp off the Corsa. It wasn't far, but he'd need the car to bring his grandfather back – if, please fucking God, he was right.

The engine roared into life. Jamie felt it in his body, the blood surging around his veins. He'd dreamed about this moment many times, but not like this. Those images, so long treasured, were of no use to him now.

He backed out of the drive and dug his mobile from his pocket.

'Dad? It's me.' He transferred the phone to his other hand and put his seat belt on, changing quickly up through the gears as he left the village behind. 'I know where Granddad is. I think he's gone to the Batch – will you tell Mum? On Culverkeys. Tell her I'm taking the Corsa. I'm on my way there now.'

Then he threw the phone onto the passenger seat beside him, turned onto the Boundway in the rising dawn light and accelerated down the long, straight road between its sleeping fields, driving forwards, as we all do, towards the known and the unknown, and into everything that was to come.

EPILOGUE

It was mid-morning when they finally cleared the two cars from the carriageway, though you, having outlived your usefulness as a witness, were allowed to leave well before that. It was turning into beautiful day: the sky was an untroubled blue overhead, the spring air warm, with a light breeze. A cuckoo spoke its own name from a spinney nearby.

Through all the passing centuries I have loved that sound.

One of the police officers bagged up the stray phone and CDs lost from the cars, and someone else swept up the glass and the fragments of sheared metal from the road, though the tyre marks remained to mark the place. A handful of coins were left, too, spilled from who knew which vehicle; for someone to have collected them all up, one by one, had probably felt wrong. They'll work their way down into the earth in time.

The smell of cut grass hung over the scene for a little while after everyone left. The wheels of the smaller car had torn up the verge when it swerved to avoid the Audi turning onto the Boundway from Babb Hill – or so you'd guessed when you first arrived. The stout hawthorn hedge had flipped the Corsa with its brash paint job onto its roof.

That hedge was laid by a local man between the wars – though this is not something you know.

I can see it all from where I am. You're still shaking as you get back into your car, execute a slow three-point turn and drive away from the flashing lights and fluorescent jackets, back the way you came. You join the motorway, but you only stay on until the service station; then you park up in the half-empty car park, and although it's still early you take out your mobile phone and call the people you love.

I can tell you've never been involved in anything like this before, never understood how a hideous new reality can yaw out from the everyday without warning, swallowing the future whole. 'One fatality,' you'd heard one of the policemen say as you left.

You'd hesitated; for a moment you wanted to turn back and ask who: the young lad in the upside-down Corsa, veiled in blood? The middle-aged man in the Audi, utterly still? Or the ragged man on the tarmac, his body twisted and crushed? You took my hand for a moment as I lay there, and your simple act of kindness almost pulled me back. I am so grateful for that.

But you didn't go back and ask. It wasn't your story, and who could blame you for wanting it to be over now?

After you finish talking on the phone you see that you have blood on your hands and on the cuffs of your jumper, and you get out of your car and walk slowly to the strip-lit toilets in the service station where your face is white in the mirror, your eyes wide. Someone else's blood on you: for the first time, you look faint.

You have a coffee in the food hall because suddenly it's worse and you don't want to get back in the car. It's still early, and not all the little shops they have in there are open yet, but some of the other tables have people sitting at them: a few solitary men; an old couple; a woman with two small children, one of whom is crying hopelessly and repetitively. You feel so far away from it all, as though you are in another world. Briefly, you picture starting up a conversation, although they're all total strangers, just in order to say it out loud and make it real and make them part of it too: I came across a terrible car accident an hour ago and I think one of the people in it died.

You don't do that. You finish your coffee and you go to the toilets again and try once more to wash my blood from your clothes, and then you walk back to your car. You switch on that satellite thing you have and get it to work out a new route; then you put on the car radio for company and find the local news. There is no mention of any road accident yet, just something about an agricultural show and something about a housing development and something about a missing pensioner turning up safe and well in a village church somewhere. Because not everything is ending, although it can feel like that sometimes.

From where I am I can see, as at last you drive away, that the tyres of your car are stuck here and there with fragments of glass, and that there are tiny, bruised hawthorn petals in the treads.

It is the last thing I see before I let go.

ACKNOWLEDGEMENTS

Thank you…

…to my agent, Jenny Hewson, and my editor, Alexa von Hirschberg, both of whom helped shape this novel; and to my copyeditor, Katherine Fry, who showed me that it's possible to love semi-colons too much.

…to Kathy Belden in Bloomsbury's New York office, whose support has meant a great deal; and to all the brilliant team at Bloomsbury UK.

…to Lucie Murtagh, whose lovely illustrations brought Jack's notebooks to life; and to David Mann for giving the book its beautiful cover.

…to the continuously inspiring Pete Rogers. You know the score.

…to the wise women: Julia Tracey (juliatracey-counselling. co.uk) and Martha Crawford (www.subtextconsultation.com).

…to Peter Francis and Stephen Moss, who took the time to read and comment on this manuscript.

…to Jeff Barratt and the Caught By The River massive: see you at the bar!

…to Jo and Tom Ridge, for lending me a slice of village life.

…to Steve Harris of On The Air Vintage Technology.

...to Twitter, and all the helpful souls who sail in her: in particular Fiona Baker, Pete Ledbury, Andrew Pimbley, Tim Reid, Gail Robertson, Alan Simpson, Karl Wareham, Gaz Weetman and John Wilson.

And thank you to Ant and Scout, who are home.

A NOTE ON THE TYPE

The text of this book is set in Bembo. This type was first used in 1495 by the Venetian printer Aldus Manutius for Cardinal Bembo's *De Aetna*, and was cut for Manutius by Francesco Griffo. It was one of the types used by Claude Garamond (1480–1561) as a model for his Romain de L'Université, and so it was the forerunner of what became standard European type for the following two centuries. Its modern form follows the original types and was designed for Monotype in 1929.